THIN DISGUISE

For Rebecca, Rachel and Savannah Beal

THIN DISGUISE

To Anita

By Lynnette Baughman

[signature]

Top Publications, Ltd. Co.
Dallas, Texas

Acknowledgment

Thomas P. Valenta, Supervisory Park Ranger, Lake Mead National Recreation Area;
Staff and volunteers at the Alan Bible Visitors Center, Lake Mead NRA;
Computer graphics experts Chris Lindberg and Lynn Phipps;
Los Alamos Public Library;
EMS Chief Jerome M. Finn, Los Alamos Fire Department;
Readers, Bill Crabb, Connie Soderberg and Rosemary Benton
Karen Landers of Top Publications
John McHale (photographer)
And my most trusted critics and stalwart supporters–
Bill Baughman, Sonje Beal and Erika DeSantis.

Thin Disguise

A Top Publications Paperback

First Edition

ALL RIGHTS RESERVED

Copyright 2001

Lynnette Baughman

ISBN#: 1-929976-07-0
Library of Congress # 2001-131590

Cover photo used by permission of the Stardust Resort Hotel and Casino

The characters and events in this novel are fictional and created out of the imagination of the author. Certain real locations and institutions are mentioned, but the characters and events depicted are entirely fictitious.

Printed in the United States of America

Chapter 1

"I'm not worried about getting a job." I set one suitcase down and worked a cramp out of my right elbow. "My only restrictions are I won't do anything immoral, illegal, or on roller skates."

Candace made an unattractive snorting noise to show her disapproval. Clearly, my daughter felt two ways about my move to Las Vegas. On the one hand, she didn't like the idea. On the other hand, she hated it.

We stood in the breezeway entrance to her apartment complex, facing a wall of mailboxes, fewer than half of them marked with names. Many people in Las Vegas, I knew, valued obscurity. Candace patted both pockets of her linen jacket, then set the grocery bag gently between her feet and opened her saddlebag-sized purse. Without looking, she jammed her arm in up to her elbow and dug around, then jerked out a key ring with a purple tennis ball attached.

"I work 20-odd hours a day already," she said as she unlocked the mailbox marked 301. Above the number, printed on a label, was "MASON, FARRELL," the last names of Candace and her roommate, Letitia.

"When do you sleep?" I smiled and added, "Hmm?" to soften what she would take as an argumentative tone. I always felt like there were three people present when I was with Candace. There was Candace, 25 and gorgeous, and me, exactly twice her age and no dog either, and an imaginary umpire, ready to call "In" or "Out" or "Foul" each time I opened my mouth. Much of the time in our mother-daughter relationship, as in tennis, love meant nothing.

"The point is," she sighed in the exasperated tone I'd come to dread, "I don't have time to help you look for a job." She tucked the mail under her arm.

The imaginary umpire slapped a hand over my open mouth before I said, "*I* didn't have time to help *you* look for a job three years ago, but I typed your résumé and applications until my cuticles cracked anyway." Instead I lifted my purse strap over my head and hoisted my two suitcases.

As I followed her up the metal stairway, I noticed again how great she looked. Saying so was extremely tricky, however. Candace always looked for subtext in compliments, as if "You look great" really meant, "So, you finally lost weight." In the same way, I had to be careful not to comment on my weight, as she'd take it as a comment on hers. And heaven forbid I should ever slip and call her Candy as I had until she entered kindergarten and announced she would no longer tolerate that nickname.

In the apartment I set my suitcases end to end against the living room wall to get them out of the way. Candace placed the plastic grocery bag in the small sink, deftly slid the egg carton into the refrigerator, and took out a gallon jar of tea. She retrieved glasses from the drainer by the sink and poured tea in both, then returned the jar to the refrigerator.

"Well," she said, clinking her glass against mine as she handed me a drink, "here's to your. . ." She cleared her throat as if her next words were stuck in it, "uh, to your 'new life' in Vegas."

I smiled and silently asked the invisible line umpire, "Aren't you going to call that?" It was clearly a dig at me, implying that, well, hadn't I started a "new life" enough times already? And when – if ever – would I get it right?

I swallowed my pride along with my tea. "Good, thanks."

To say I was starting a new life was much truer than

Candace knew. I was still reeling from the words Dr. Bostwick spoke to me two weeks before in Las Cruces, New Mexico, my home for five years. I had been prepared for the worst, praying only that I'd die quickly, that the cancer would not make me linger in unspeakable pain. I'd written letters to my three children, made a list of who would get my few valuables. In the spirit of a final, magnanimous gesture, I thought back over my three marriages and asked myself if, being totally honest, I should admit any mistakes I had made that led to the three divorces. I asked, I really did, but the best I could do – being totally honest – was say, Hell, no! My mistake was to marry three jerks.

So, I was again Olivia Wright, after being married to three Mr. Wrongs who gave me the last names, chronologically, of Willsen, Mason and Vale. My whole name read like a listing in the yellow pages under Attorneys, Personal Injury.

Since I'd first sat in Dr. Bostwick's office, referred by my general practitioner, I had felt like a rubber ball tied to a paddle. A paddle studded with tough tacks. I had suffered fear of pain, denial, anger, and regret, and I'd experienced peace. Furthermore, I'd gone through each stage about five times in the period of ten days, ratcheting my anxiety to a higher plane each time. Then I sat in Dr. Bostwick's office for another appointment, making mental notes of all I saw and heard, thinking I might write it all down when I got home. I would describe the color of the walls, the framed posters of national parks on the walls of the waiting room. I would remark on the large photo on Bostwick's desk of his blindingly blond children, and the outdated copy of *Better Homes and Gardens* I'd leafed through to pass the time. I would describe – poignantly – how my eyes had filled with tears and dripped on the magazine as I thought of the redwood deck I would never need to waterseal.

Then Bostwick opened the door to his office and gave his nurse a medication order for little Bobby and an admonition to interrupt him immediately if Dr. Pacer returned his call, and added that he'd like tuna fish for lunch, on whole wheat, but no chips today. Oh well, I thought, trying to be charitable, but grinding my teeth in annoyance at his nonchalance. Even if my days were dwindling down to a precious few, life must go on for him. I'm not his only patient.

Bostwick half-fell into his maroon leather chair, tired, he said, after a long night at the hospital. Then he sat forward and slapped his hand flat against the mahogany desk. I jerked my legs in reflex and banged my right knee on the underside of the desk's wide overhang.

"The results are back from your second CT scan and the MRI," he said, with what struck me at that moment as unseemly cheer. Perhaps exhaustion was affecting him, I thought, the way someone might laugh during a funeral, an inappropriate but uncontrollable response to deep grief. Bostwick smiled broadly, and I met his gaze with a calm, dignified, but wan, smile of my own. I was still recording details of the meeting to transcribe later, perhaps by candlelight, sometime long after midnight, when coyotes howled at the moon and scorpions skittered across the still-warm desert sand. My daughters might want to publish my journal after my death. My bravery and dignity might even soften the heart of my son, Cable, who was a clone of his egotistical father. *Yes, I will pour my heart out on the pages.*

"You're going to be fine!" Bostwick boomed.

I banished the coyotes and candlelight with a blink of my eyes. "What?"

"The diagnosis of liver cancer was wrong! That's why we got a second opinion. You're fine! You'll probably outlive all of us!" He grinned like he'd just been granted a patent on oxygen.

"The diagnosis was wrong?" I asked. "Wrong? I don't have cancer of the liver? Or the pancreas?"

"Or of anything else!" His grin broadened, if such a thing were possible. He owned the patent on oxygen, and he'd just been told the royalty payments would be retroactive to the Civil War.

I didn't have cancer. I was fine. I was going to live, probably a long, long time. My wan smile faded; Bostwick was grinning enough for both of us. I felt color rise from my neck to my cheeks. I thought of two or three things to say, things worth writing in a journal, but my rampaging emotions got the best of me.

"Well, shit!" was all I said.

Instead of striding outside and throwing a hat in the air like a young Mary Tyler Moore, I plodded to my car. I stopped at the front of my nine-year-old Volkswagen Cabriolet – a car I would now outlive, for heaven's sake! – and watched the parking meter tick below its horizon and send up the orange Expired flag.

"Expired? Ha! Not hardly." I dropped a dime in the slot just to watch the flag drop and time begin ticking again for the little black arrow.

Then I started thinking, *If I'm going to live a long time, I might as well have more fun.* And that's when I decided to give notice at my job, pack up, and move to Las Vegas, Nevada. And I did, arriving the morning of April 11.

It was a vicious twist of irony when, on that very afternoon – just six hours after my arrival at Candace's apartment – I found myself in the mansion of movie star Margot Farr, huddled in a fetal position under her bed, looking at the gleaming barrel of a snub-nosed revolver. Huddling, hyperventilating – and praying Dr. Bostwick was right about my projected longevity.

Chapter 2

"Letitia's asleep." Candace sorted the mail into two piles as she drank her iced tea. "She's in the back bedroom." From the volume of her announcement, I surmised her roommate was a sound sleeper.

"Where does she dance?"

"Jubilee, at Bally's Grand. She'll get up pretty soon and go work out at Sinbad's. Same place I go. Great equipment." Her cell phone rang. "Hello? No, I'm at my apartment. My mom got here." She waggled her fingers in the air at me. "Kenneth says, 'Hi.'"

I waved at the phone and drifted into the compact living room, which opened to the kitchen across a breakfast bar. Pulling back a corner of the heavy drape that spanned the far wall, I looked out on the mini-balcony. Two folded lawn chairs had fallen across a hibachi and a bag of charcoal. Without unlocking the glass door and stepping onto the balcony, I could see a small section of the apartment complex's swimming pool, as essential in Las Vegas as a reliable deodorant. It was only April 11, not yet noon, and the temperature was 92 degrees already. I'd been here before when the temperature hit 117. In the shade, as they say.

"It's on my way, more or less." Candace continued her conversation with Kenneth. "I can fit the candelabra in my car. I'll see you around 11:00 at the country club. *Bueno*, 'bye." She darted into the bathroom for a few minutes, then to her bedroom. "You can put your suitcases in here," she called, then bumped into me in the hall as I hefted one bag and started toward her room.

"Sorry, I've got to go. We're putting on a party at a producer's house this afternoon, then we've got a Polynesian party tonight after a film premiere. I'll be home to change around 6:00." She took her purse off the kitchen counter and opened the door to leave. "Oh, I almost forgot. There's an extra key to the apartment in the butter compartment of the refrigerator." Then she was gone.

I'd met Kenneth, Candace's partner at Royale Catering, during my trip to Las Vegas the summer before. He was tall, but neither dark nor handsome. His trunk and limbs seemed assembled by random choice in a Mr. Potato Head game, his arms long and gangly and the legs short by comparison with his torso, where all his height was gained. I imagined his parents saw him shoot up in height and go through a clumsy stage of mismatched body parts, and thought forward happily (though futilely) to college basketball recruiters calling for their son. Luckily for them all, Kenneth's driving ambition developed not for sports but for business. And his awkward physique, as it turned out, was perfect for pulling himself up by the bootstraps. He worked on Vegas time, available 24 hours, seven days a week, and money grew in his pockets.

During my visit the previous summer, I'd helped out on an hour's notice with a banquet catered by Royale. A virus had cut a wide swath in Kenneth's service staff, and since I could wait tables in my sleep, anywhere from a truck stop to a penthouse suite, I pitched in.

"If you ever – *ever!* – need a job," Kenneth had said in gratitude, "call me! Call me *collect!*" Fortunately, Candace had not heard Kenneth's offer. She'd probably choke at the thought of my competing on her turf.

I shook the wrinkles out of my clothes and searched for a few unused hangers. I felt certain I could get a job in

Vegas, and I wouldn't need to ask Kenneth, or Candace, for any help. I'd compiled six different résumés, each emphasizing a different skill and targeted to widely different jobs. I'd had so many jobs in 38 years – babysitting being the first and worst – I knew I could find something. I had a sense of adventure about the whole thing. Contemplating my tragic, though erroneous, early death certificate had given my life-view a certain piquancy.

I hadn't had a chance to tell Candace before she blew out of the apartment, but I actually had a good job prospect lined up before I arrived in Vegas. Assistant Publicity Director at the Stardust Hotel and Casino was up for grabs, and I had a 2:30 interview on my pocket calendar.

*****

I allowed extra time to park and find personnel in the big complex. My instructions said I should go to the personnel office first and fill out paperwork. The director of publicity would send for me when he was ready for the interview. Inside the office was a bulletin board of job openings: change person, keno writer, wait person. Along the side were index cards noting cars for sale, free puppies and apartments-to-share. The office had all the ambience of a Greyhound bus station, including the pervasive odor of stale cigarette smoke.

I tried not to stare at the young receptionist's hair, although, in my experience at least, if a person deliberately colors her hair magenta, she probably *wants* to be stared at. I gave her my name and took the clipboard and application to a black vinyl chair against the wall. Over my head a poster proclaimed "Put safety first, make safety last."

A woman in a mauve raw silk suit and matching shoes stepped in from the hall and surveyed the room. I guessed her to be in her early fifties. She had a way of standing, a photographic pose, and a kind of challenge in her dark brown eyes that said she either had money or connections – or delusions of same.

"I'm Alicia Cormer," she said to the receptionist, who looked only half as bored by Alicia as she'd been by me. "Mr. Marker, that is, Paul Marker, asked me to complete some paperwork for the publicity position."

From the back she could have passed for much younger. Her blond hair was sleek and fluffy, like the old "Beautiful hair, Breck" ads. She sat two seats down from me and examined the cheap ballpoint pen the receptionist had provided. Wrinkling her nose in distaste, she slipped it into the top of the clipboard, then reached into a side pocket of her soft leather purse for another pen. The ebony and gold writing utensil looked like it belonged in her hand with its long sculptured nails, polished in mauve to match her suit.

Without good reason, I felt frumpy next to Alicia Cormer. My gray suit and aqua scarf were every bit as fashionable as her suit; they fit me just as well. At five-six and 130 pounds I was as well proportioned as she, and I looked younger than my age, 50, by at least five years. At *least* five years! The primary difference between Alicia Cormer and me, I guess, was *presentation*. She entered the room expecting to be noticed, while I preferred to remain in the background. My ability to blend in was always an advantage in jobs I'd held at police departments in three states. That was one of my six specialized résumés – criminal investigations work.

I looked over at the skin on her neck and upped my guess of her age to late fifties. To be perfectly honest, though, I've always had it in for blondes. I've been known to say, "Blondes don't really have more fun. It just takes less to amuse them."

I tucked my natural brunette hair behind my right ear and checked the backing on that earring. "Are you applying for the assistant publicity director position?"

"No, I got the job." She answered without a glance in my direction. Her voice had the raspy quality of a long-time smoker. "I'm just doing the necessary paperwork, after the fact." She lightly tapped the end of her pen on her right temple as if it would jog her brain to recall some silly data required on the form.

"Excuse me, do you mean the position as assistant publicity director? It's been filled?"

She gave me the once over, her brown eyes missing nothing. The closer I looked at her skin, the more years I added to her age, or to her time in the harsh Vegas sun. "Yes," she said with a girlish giggle. "I just came from Paul Marker's office. I start on Monday. I'll be working with Colin Marker."

Paul Marker, I knew, was the president and general manager, and his son, Colin, was head of publicity and heir apparent to the chief executive's office.

"I didn't realize they planned to fill it so quickly. I just got to town and I thought I'd be interviewed this afternoon. Maybe I misunderstood."

"Well, they wanted me for the job before they even advertised, but I didn't think I could rearrange my life. However, doors have a way of opening, and so here I am."

Doors have a way of closing, too, it occurred to me. *And this one just slammed on my foot!* "It sounds like you know the inside workings in Las Vegas," I purred, not above flattery when it might help me.

"Oh, yes. I've been in entertainment for years in Los Angeles and here. You say you just moved here?"

"Yes, just got here today. Say, if it wouldn't be too much of an imposition, I wonder if you'd look at my résumé and suggest where else I could apply?" *Ask for nothing, get nothing*, I told myself. Alicia hesitated, but I had the résumé that emphasized my writing experience on the seat beside me, so I held it out.

She looked at her watch. "I need to finish this and... Oh, I have a few minutes." She took the résumé and I looked away.

"This is very good." She sounded surprised; I uncharitably added another three years to her age. "Of course, these magazines won't make anyone around here genuflect. Most of the people in this business can't read a photo caption without moving their lips. I see you've got radio and TV copy experience, too, and ghostwriting. Very good. Hmm... that gives me an idea."

I watched her pull her wallet from her purse and flip through an impressive address book with her shapely nails.

"Margot Farr is a dear friend of mine," Alicia said, pausing dramatically as if I'd need time to let such a stunning announcement sink in. She found a blank page for notes at the back of her address book and tore it out.

"Margot has decided to write her memoirs, and she needs a discreet ghostwriter. I presume these other people you've ghosted for would give you a reference?"

"Absolutely."

"Margot is very upset about the unauthorized biography Philly Mitchell is writing. That woman has less shame than a common streetwalker. Makes her living by cutting throats."

She scribbled an address on the small piece of paper and handed it to me. "Margot asked me to help her with her book, and she would have paid well, but I need something with benefits. Diamonds may be a girl's best friend, but after age forty, a woman needs a 401K plan, don't you know? Why don't you go see her? She's expecting me at three-thirty or so. I'll call and tell her you're coming."

I slid the pen back in the top of my clipboard and studied the address on the slip of paper. *This sounds like the kind of adventure I'm looking for.* I beamed at my surprise benefactor. "Thank you, Alicia. I'll go see Margot Farr today."

*****

White, pink and red oleanders bordered the entrance to El Camino Real, the Royal Road. Bougainvillea cascaded over the top of the stucco walls that kept the riff-raff (like me, presumably) out of the compound of million-dollar homes. A guard "shack" was flanked by tire rippers on both sides, both sets folded into the ground like the claws on a kindly cat. Red tile topped the stucco of the shack in keeping with the California mission style of the homes beyond the gate, and a profusion of red geraniums draped its front, below the reflective window.

I pulled up to the side of the guard post, prepared to state my name and wait while a guard called Ms. Farr. The red metal arm was already up when I stopped.

"Hello?" I called out my window. The door to the guard post stood open, but no one appeared.

I put my Volkswagen in Park and pulled up the hand brake. "Hello?" I said again as I stepped out of the car and looked inside the five-foot square building. Empty.

I walked to the metal arm and scanned the area. Seeing no guard, I got back in the car, checked the address Alicia Cormer had written for me, and drove into the compound.

I hadn't encountered so many varieties of flowering plants and trees since I last visited an arboretum. I counted six kinds of palm trees alone in the extravagantly landscaped yards. An alien set down in that lush setting would never guess water was a scarce commodity, and that outside the stucco walls lay acres of sand and tumbleweed, land as desiccated as a mummy on the moon.

Number Three Manzanillo had a five-car garage that angled back on the corner lot so one could enter by either of two concrete driveways. All the garage doors were closed, and a silver BMW was parked on the concrete apron in front of door number two. A third driveway, constructed of brick in the exact shade of red as the tiled roof, circled up and under a Spanish-style *porte cochere*. A grandee could alight from his carriage and hand down his lace-draped lady without getting a drop of rain on their finery.

I coasted down the street and hung a U-turn, parking across the street in the scant shade of a Century Palm. I left the windows down rather than face a 200-degree steering wheel when I returned.

The only sound was the hiss of lawn sprinklers along the yard's boundary with Number Four Manzanillo, a little dump that probably sold for only one million dollars. Beyond a border of something that looked like bamboo, I saw a white truck with blue lettering: AquaMate Quality Pool Care, and under that, *Just Add Water.*

I pulled a leather strap beside the door of Number Three and heard three bell tones from inside the house.

Followed by a blood-curdling scream.

Chapter 3

I tried the door and opened it. As I stepped from the tier of brick stairs that skirted the massive door into a black terrazzo entryway, I felt the temperature drop at least 30 degrees in a blink.

"Hello? Is everything all right?"

I heard a noise I can only describe as whooping and then a loud slap like a beaver on a pond. "Hello?" I called again.

This time the answer was a scream and two whoops so I ran toward the sound. And that's how I first saw Margot Farr, famous film actress known for her lavish spending and carousel of husbands. Also known in recent years for her roller coaster weight gains and losses.

I couldn't help but notice she was a shade on the heavy side, thick at the waist, doughy in the legs and saggy in the boobs. I couldn't help but notice because she stood before me on a chair, buck-naked and waving a towel like a matador's cape, whipping it on the sides of her chair.

"It ran under the table! Kill it!" she shrieked at me.

"What? What is it?" My first thought was a mouse, but my second was … a rattlesnake. I froze just in case, raking my eyes over the floor like a laser scanner to see what scared the pants off Margot.

"A scorpion!" she screeched. "It's that deadly kind from Arizona! I saw it in a magazine! They bring them up here in palm trees." She pulled the towel around her and squatted on the chair, peering under the parquet tabletop toward hardwood claw feet the size of combat boots.

I took off my right shoe, then thought better of being barefoot and put it back on. I gave a quick look around the room and grabbed a copy of *Town & Country*, rolling it into a weapon. Giving the table a bruising shove with my hip, I dislodged the tiny light brown scorpion from its blind and administered a killing swat with a smart backhand.

"He's dead." I started to ask if she'd seen just the one, but figured she would have climbed the chandelier had she thought there were multiple killer scorpions in her house.

She stepped down from the chair, modestly clutching the towel to her breasts as if her naked rear were invisible, bringing to mind a western film town with elaborate facades nailed to junk-lumber shacks. At second glance, Margot Farr was more than a "shade" on the heavy side. The skin on her thighs looked like pork rinds. Or cottage cheese, large curd.

"He was in my deck shoes," she said, craning her neck to see the far side of the table. "I just tossed them in from the patio. And then I saw him run out. Thank goodness you came in when you did." For the first time she looked at me. Spreading the towel around her midriff and tugging it down to cover her butt, she said, "Who are you?"

"Olivia Wright. Here to see you about helping with your memoirs..." She made no sign of recognizing my name. "Alicia Cormer said she would call you and say I would be here."

"Today?"

"Yes. I met her today for the first time, and she said she couldn't come, that she wouldn't be able to help you with the project. And I have a lot of writing experience, even ghostwriting experience. I can provide references, of course."

"Well, she didn't call me. But I suppose we can talk about it, since you're here." She tossed her head, a trademark gesture from when she tossed her coppery-red hair at a dozen of the biggest stars in Hollywood, men she kissed both on and off screen, if legend had it right. Her hair was dull now, the roots black, and the red brassy and over processed. She wore no makeup, a grievous loss. The curve of her two chins matched bags under her eyes.

I was genuinely surprised. I'd seen her picture on the cover of *Redbook* just weeks before, and she looked sensational. The article, I recalled, raved about Margot Farr's successful weight loss and exercise regimen, formed from interviews with her now-famous cook, Kim somebody-or-other, and her private exercise coach.

Three or four of Kim's recipes were included to whet readers' appetites for her forthcoming *Celebrity New Life Cookbook*. And Ted Landers gave a few pointers on firming up, just enough to make readers sweat with anticipation for his fitness video. Built like the ubiquitous hero-model on bodice rippers, but with a boy-next-door smile, Landers could make a lot of readers sweat with anticipation for his next breath. I wouldn't deign to stand in line with them, but I'm sure he will survive the disappointment should he ever discover my disinterest.

"I'll go get some clothes on." With as much dignity as she could muster while tugging the towel down over her ample buttocks, Margot left the dining room. How times change, I mused. Four or five hundred years ago, Margot's body would make a painter swoon.

I picked up the dismembered scorpion in two tissues and disposed of the body in a wastebasket, then returned to the entryway and closed the front door, retrieving my purse from an ornate credenza.

I made another entrance to the living room, this time noticing the lush, spotless ivory carpet. I slipped my shoes off and stepped into the deep pile. My toes curled and I moaned aloud with sensual delight.

On my left was the dining room, with the parquet table crowned by a flower arrangement at least three feet high, birds of paradise as its focal flora and other tropical flowers I didn't know by name. The riot of color and the fragrance of the flowers, combined with the happiness of my 10 toes, were almost too much to bear. I'd been rich myself before, thanks to husbands one and three, and I rarely missed those days, but Margot's magic carpet took me back, just for a moment.

To my right, at the far end of the living room, shone a black grand piano, set apart on a one-step-high dais. Floor-to-ceiling windows curved around the keyboard and seat.

Halfway down the right-hand side of the room, which was about a hundred feet long, a white marble fireplace atop a matching dais counterbalanced the piano.

One of the French doors from the dining room to the patio stood ajar, and I walked out to the garden and heart-shaped pool. Palm trees and bamboo plus a dozen kinds of flowering bushes gave the yard the illusion of total privacy. In truth the windows and balconies of the house perched like box seats on the pool area. Furthermore, the top of the 10-foot stucco walls that formed the exterior of the yard could give an agile viewer a good look at the lifestyle of at least one rich and famous person.

In Mexico I'd seen such walls topped with broken bottles embedded in stucco, but here I was pretty sure they had some kind of sophisticated motion detectors. On the plate glass window beside the French doors I found the kind of emblem I expected to find, a shield with the words Vista Security and a phone number.

"Let's talk in here," Margot said from the doorway. She espied the patio apprehensively, as if expecting imminent attack by lethal arachnids. Her Moroccan-style caftan hung from her breasts, concealing her meaty thighs on the way to revealing her gold and black sandals. A quick application of foundation, blush, and mascara rallied some of her beauty. A black net snood, a nod, perhaps to Scarlett O'Hara, improved her hair. A half dozen brass bracelets jingled on each of her fleshy arms.

I closed the door behind me, snatched up my shoes, and followed Margot to the most magnificent kitchen I'd ever seen. Skylights and stained glass windows showered light into the room, and copper, silver, steel and brass surfaces reflected it onto ebony counters and blue tiles that could pass for lapis lazuli. The bleached oak floor gave more cushioning than a Dr. Scholl's. My feet were having a wonderful time in Margot's house. Reluctantly, I stepped back into my shoes.

Above the gigantic cooking island, track lights and a mirror angled down so spectators could watch the food preparation. Two video cameras up on the walls expanded the potential audience for the magic fingers and herbal incantations of Kim the cook.

Her book contract, I'd read in the *Redbook* article, gave her a $1.5 million advance against royalties, and that was only for the North American English language rights. That scarcely skimmed the meringue off the no-fat confections Kim was reputed to have substituted for Margot Farr's beloved thousand-calorie desserts. Kim's mantra of "No Fat" was bringing her a lot of gravy. Judging by Margot's midriff, however, Kim's claims and Margot's zealous endorsement were both overstated.

Margot opened the mirrored door on the right-hand side of the doublewide refrigerator and took out a crystal pitcher of pale tea. The left door, which had an ice and water dispenser built-in on the outside, was ebony-black and nearly as reflective as the mirrored door. Looked like a brilliant idea to me, a last-minute flash of reality to a dieter:

Is this trip necessary?

"It's Kim's day off. You've undoubtedly read about my cook, Kim Kaylyn?" She slid two crystal goblets from a wooden groove under a cabinet where dozens of glasses hung upside down, poured tea in both, and slid one toward me. "This is Kim's fortress."

She gave me a "follow me" nod and we carried our tea out the other end of the kitchen, past a walk-in pantry bigger than the average person's kitchen. It appeared to have less food in it than a specialty market, but not by much.

A long hallway led away from the living room/dining room arena. The ceiling curved, and green tinted windows every eight feet or so bathed the walkway in deceptively cool sunlight, nurturing a semi-tropical forest of philodendron, ferns and elephant ears.

"This is my bedroom," Margot said, stopping in the doorway of a scene from *The Sheik*. Pale gold silk fell from a brass ring suspended from the ceiling and draped over the head of the bed. The headboard was leather, with an Egyptian design in bas-relief. The bedside tables featured ceramic Bactrian camels with flat platforms on their double humps, and one drawer beneath each platform.

One wall, about 25 feet long, was made of panels of lattice, an intricate pattern of X's and O's like the screen used in movies to hide the sultan's harem from prying eyes. Five or six Oriental carpets gave the room too much color and pattern to suit my taste.

I sniffed, trying to place the fragrance.

"It's 'Cairo,'" Margot said. Her bracelets clattered as she raised a wrist to my nose. "My signature fragrance for Soto Voce."

"Very nice," I said politely. The scent could be described with several adjectives, but fragrant wasn't one of them. The words cloying and insipid came to mind.

"The office, where you'll work, is beyond that door," she said, pointing to her right. "It has its own bathroom. My bathroom is the other direction." I looked to her left, where beads hung from a Mid-Eastern pointed arch, concealing the room beyond.

"I'll show you the exercise room first." She turned away from her bedroom and I padded behind her down a narrow hallway with an arched stucco ceiling. A red Oriental carpet snaked down the hall and dropped in shallow steps every three or four feet.

The hall opened into a fish bowl of a room with a dozen pieces of Cybex equipment on the left half and carpets on the otherwise bare right half. A large-screen television sat high on a stand perfect for viewing from the two Stairmasters, the treadmill and the two stationary bicycles. The carpeted area had mirrors along the wide side and ballet barres on the other two walls. A *trompe-l'oeil* mural on one of those walls showed a line of Degas ballerinas dancing into the distance.

The rest of the house was heavily air conditioned, but the exercise room felt downright frosty. I must have rubbed my hands together, because Margot gave a laugh as cold as the room. "Ted Landers wants it this way. Says if I move 'faster-harder-longer,' that I'll warm up. And whatever Teddy wants – Teddy gets. The only thing I hate more than exercise is listening to Ted when he doesn't get his way."

I wanted to know what she meant, but discretion was undoubtedly the better part of interviewing for the job. Something else I wanted to know was, where was Margot's much-ballyhooed-in-the-tabloids husband? Not that I ever bought tabloids, but only Yukon dwellers who ate wild berries and bear meat could avoid seeing pictures of Aronn Young's full pouty lips and single eye. Well, he probably had two eyes, but his hair always covered one, making him appear to be an asymmetrical Cyclops.

"I'll show you the office. I have a computer but I hate to type. I prefer to write longhand or dictate into a tape recorder and look over a typed copy later."

I trailed her back up the tunnel to the wide hallway that led to her bedroom and, presumably, other bedrooms. As if reading my thoughts, she said, "My suite of rooms, the bedroom, bath and office, is in this wing. There are guestrooms in a separate wing behind and above the garages. And there's a maid's room there, too, but I don't have a live-in maid just now. My daughter, Esmé, has been staying here for a month while her house is remodeled."

"I'm staying with my daughter until I find an apartment," I volunteered. "In fact, I looked at one today, in her apartment complex. I like it, but maybe it's too close for her comfort."

We walked past her bedroom door to a closed door on the same side of the hallway. She turned the knob but it was locked. "We'll have to go in through my room. I don't remember locking this."

We retraced our steps and entered her Bedouin boudoir with its assaulting scent of Cairo. She crossed to a set of louvered doors and sprung them open.

The office was done in ersatz 1940s Casablanca, with a sisal floor covering, two ceiling fans, potted plants that touched the ceiling and threatened to grow through it, and rattan furniture. Along one wall, custom white wood and rattan office furniture supported a computer, printer and fax machine.

"The computer looks like an anachronism," I observed.

"Oh, all computers look alike to me," she said with a toss of her hair as she unlocked the door to the hall. "I'll want you to use the hall entrance, and absolutely nothing leaves this room without my say-so! I've had my lawyer draw up a tight contract to protect my rights to my own story. I tried to stop that bitch, Philly Mitchell, from writing about me, but there was nothing I could do. The next best thing to luring her into a dark alley and choking her to death, and that's definitely my first choice, is to publish my story in my own words."

She showed me where she kept her tape recorder and yellow legal pads full of late-night reminiscences. There didn't seem to be much order to the written notes, and I'd need a key to the abbreviations. "Dinner with B. and A. at BH" was a bit too concise for any publisher I knew of.

She settled into a high-backed rattan chair like royalty granting an audience in some country where they pronounce quinine as kwineen. "I've been going through old photos, too. Studio shots and snapshots." She lifted a cut glass rectangular box, etched to look like a cigar box, from the shelf and gently folded the top back on its tiny hinges. "Look, this was Esmé as a little girl in Paris. Good God, but she hated the Madeline outfit."

I looked at the photo. A sullen, angry child stared back from beneath a straw hat.

"Some of these are marked on the back, but not many. I've pulled out a few I want to use. They're in a folder over there."

She held out her hand expectantly, so I shuffled quickly through a stack of manila folders until I spotted the one marked PIX. Tucked inside was another folder marked Contract Form.

She slid out the contract folder, glanced over a paper inside, and held out her hand again. "A pen," she said. Again I jumped to meet her need.

"How do you spell your name? Oh, never mind, you can fill that in." With a flourish, she signed at the bottom of what appeared to be a boilerplate contract. "What's the date?"

"April 11." I examined the computer books and reference books above the monitor, propped up at both ends by wooden elephants.

She propped the contract folder, with the signed paper, upright beside the computer and looked again in the photo box. She set it back on the desk just as the phone rang. She rose, jingling like a reindeer, and took the call in her bedroom. I looked through the legal pads for any reference to dates, preferably years, so I'd have a clue how to organize the material. Although I found six pads, each of them was just partially used.

I paid no attention to what Margot was doing in her bedroom, except to notice one long conversation apparently ended, since the phone rang again, and she answered it. I booted up the computer, pleased to see it had all the bells and whistles I liked.

My inattention to Margot changed abruptly when I heard her voice rise in volume and intensity. "You can rot in hell!" she yelled into the phone. Maybe it was a long distance phone company soliciting her business, or an aluminum siding salesman, but I'd bet it was someone she knew well. *Mighty darned well.* "Don't you dare!" she added. "Don't you... I'm coming right now. And you'd better be there."

She slammed the phone down so hard the plastic might have cracked. I backed up two steps and saw her storm out of the room, her caftan billowing behind like a parasail. I had a sense of a shock wave roll past the office's closed door to the hall, an indication she'd headed toward the living room and all points west.

I did a quick read of the formulaic contract for a Work For Hire, an autobiography of Margot Farr. My name would not appear on the work, unless she got generous and acknowledged me in the typical Christmas card list of names after, "I also want to thank..." The contract was detailed on restrictions but vague on compensation. I filled in my name, social security number, and Candace's address, and signed the bottom, but if the pay stunk, I could always tear the contract in half on my way out the door.

The phone rang again; three rings, then silence. I counted the micro cassettes in the top desk drawer by the tape recorder. Nine micro cassettes, seven in little clear plastic holders and two loose. I arranged them by the dates, starting with Oct. 9 and ending with April 8. It was just a guess since the year wasn't marked. April 8 could have preceded Oct. 9, but I guessed Margot had started the project a few months before and made the most recent recording four days before, or even more recently if she'd used the tape inside the recorder as well.

I heard two women's voices, both yelling, but I couldn't make out any words. It might have been on television; the sound was muffled by distance in the huge house. I opened the door to the hall and cocked my head in the standard cartoon stance that supposedly attracted sound waves. I still couldn't make out words, but I could tell one of the two, or possibly three, voices was Margot's. And she was one angry woman, of that I had no doubt.

"Get out," she shrieked. Or maybe it was "Butt out." A door slammed and there was a crash like pottery breaking. I stepped back in the office and closed the door noiselessly.

"I need this job," I muttered under my breath, but it came out sounding more like a question than a firm statement.

And that's when I heard the first gunshot.

Chapter 4

Running toward someone with a firearm would be stupid, and I didn't get to be 50 years old by being stupid. Well, actually, I did, but not stupid about guns.

I stood back from the door and put my right hand over my heart, as if pledging allegiance might keep it from leaping out of my chest, or at least muffle the sound. I backed toward the office phone/fax machine and stretched my hand toward the receiver when the machine gave one ring followed by an electronic cough, and a wide white tongue oozed from its mouth.

A gunshot? Or what? I wracked my brain for anything else that might sound like that. Then I heard it again, from behind the house, by the pool, I guessed – and this time I was sure I heard a woman scream.

Hoping the bedroom phone was a separate line from the fax, I darted beside the bed and snatched the black phone from the two-humped camel table close to the closet. As I did, I thought I heard someone coming down the hall toward the bedroom. I froze, then exhaled as the sound receded.

I pressed 911 and listened through the longest three rings imaginable. By extending my right foot and hooking it on the lattice I managed to slide the closet door open about two feet. A glance at the stash of clothes crammed inside was all it took to rule out hiding in the closet.

At the precise instant a voice in my ear said, "What is your emergency?" I was sure I heard someone coming down the hall. I only had time to say, "I'm inside Number

Three Manzanillo and I heard two gunshots," before I lobbed the receiver onto the phone cradle and dove like a torpedo under the bed.

The thick bedspread absorbed the gasping sound that escaped my cupped hands. But, on the bad-news side of the coin toss, it deadened the sound of anything, or anyone, in the room. As my respiration slowed, I became aware of the musty dirt from the carpet I'd stirred up in my quick dive, dirt that had lain in the carpet all the way from Persia. I clamped my fingers to my nose to stifle a sneeze and lay still, willing the dust to settle.

A few minutes later I lifted the bedspread with one finger, at the speed of the minute hand on a clock, and pressed my left cheek into the carpet. I heard someone in the office but it was out of my arc of vision. There was a thump, like books and something else falling. The row of books held upright by the butts of wooden elephants had looked none too stable, I recalled.

Closing my right eye and scooting my face two or so inches closer to the peephole I'd formed with my unsteady finger, I looked toward the office. I still couldn't see anyone, but movement across the room made me bite down on my tongue. I almost dropped the bedspread, until I realized I'd caught sight of the movement in a mirror. I made out a person of medium height, a man I guessed, but couldn't be sure. I only saw his or her back, and only for a moment. Then the person vanished, probably out the door from the office to the hall.

I lowered the bedspread and rested my finger and face for a few minutes. I could hear absolutely nothing, so I repeated my slow levitation of the thick cloth. Quicker than I could spell cardiopulmonary distress, I was looking at leather shoes the color of pecans, parked twenty-four inches, max, from my rapidly blinking eye. The hands attached to that apparition did something on the bedside table. I tried to see legs with stockings or pants, anything above the shoes, but he or she glided out of my narrow line of sight.

I heard a drawer slide, stick, and then slam. The bed sagged into the too-few inches above my back, pressing on my right shoulder and making my life pass before my eyes, which didn't take long, further proof that I needed more time to make something of myself. The backs of the shoes were a scant twelve inches from my bugged-out eyes, and suspended in the air between the shoes (or so it appeared from my bizarre viewpoint) menaced the shiny barrel of a snub-nosed revolver.

At that moment I suffered clear recall of Dr. Bostwick's braying laugh and his almost papal pronouncement that I would live a long, long time.

I lowered the bedspread to the floor and curled my lip silently, in lieu of a bitter laugh.

That's what you get with managed care.

Chapter 5

About 10 seconds later, I felt the weight lift off the bed. The time on my lighted watch face read 4:55. I'd been in Margot Farr's house an hour and 25 minutes. I didn't need an MBA to know: As *a job interview, this was not going well.*

About 15 minutes had elapsed since I called 911. I couldn't hear any sirens, but in my fuzzy hideaway I couldn't even tell if the person or persons I'd seen (and felt) were still in the room with me. I opted for near-catatonic stillness and waited.

Gradually I heard more and more noise, first sirens that sounded far off but were probably close, then a tapping. I lifted the bedspread again and could tell there were people in the house, their shoes tapping in the entryway, then talking in the hallway. I heard a man saying, "I'll be there in a second," and walking toward the bedroom.

"Police!" he called at the door. "Is anyone in here?"

I raised the spread enough to be heard clearly. "I'm under the bed. I thought I heard two gunshots and I hid under the bed."

"Come on out."

He didn't have to tell me not to make any sudden moves. I squeezed painfully under the metal frame, amazed I'd gotten under it so fast before. I'd been pretty highly motivated. Standing up a little too fast, I swayed slightly and a strong arm took my elbow.

"I'm the one who called 911." I looked up into eyes the color of Colorado columbine with the kind of long, thick lashes women said were wasted on a man, but in this case they were wrong. I'd seen eyes of that startling shade of blue before, and just as up close and personal as I was to the eyes in Margot Farr's bedroom. In fact, I'd seen *those* two eyes in *that* face before. It had happened in San Diego. And that occasion had also been in a bedroom – mine.

"Mace!"

"Olivia?"

"I called 911."

"You said that. So what happened here?" I noticed without moving my eyeballs that his light blue chambray shirt and diamond patterned tie in dark blue and eggshell brought out the blue in his irises. I glanced down, quickly cataloguing his taupe silk sportcoat and navy gabardine slacks, probably from a store for big and tall men, the best place to fit his athletic frame. Not a lock of his wavy, tobacco-brown hair strayed out of place. It wouldn't dare.

"I just moved to Las Vegas, and I came here to talk to Margot Farr about a job. She needs someone to help with her memoirs."

"Needed."

"What are you saying? Did someone shoot Margot?" My hand flew to my mouth in the international sign for "Omigosh!"

"Detective Emerick," a uniformed officer said at the doorway. "Excuse me, Detective. The medical examiner is on the way, and the crime photographer just arrived."

"Wait here," Mace said to me and stepped into the hall to confer with the officer.

Talk about mixed feelings! I didn't know which event shocked me more, Margot's sudden death or Mace's reappearance in the universe I knew as my life. How I'd loved that man, and how I'd hated him. *Still do hate him*, I reminded myself.

The officer listened to Mace's instructions and said more officers were on the way. Mace returned to the bedroom and took his notepad out of his pocket. "How long have you been here?"

"Since, uh, 3:30. Yeah, 3:30, that's right, that's when I got here." I looked at my watch as a way to tear my eyes off his face.

"Did you see any other people?"

"Here? Oh, sure, yeah. No, no, I didn't meet anyone, or see anyone, during the time Margot took me on a tour of the house." I gave a quick exposition of my interview with Margot, starting with the scorpion scenario and ending with my counting micro cassettes. "I remember she said she didn't have a maid just now, and Kim Kaylyn, her cook, is off today."

"Does the cook live in?"

"No, but she said her daughter, Esmé, is staying here while her house is being remodeled." I looked at my feet and concentrated on inhaling all the way to my diaphragm and forcing my lungs to empty before inhaling again.

"What about her husband? Where's he?"

"She didn't mention him at all. She did speak of Ted Landers, her exercise coach, but she didn't say where he was or when I should expect to meet him. He wasn't in the exercise room when she showed it to me." My mouth answered his questions, but my mind was lost in minute examination of Mace Emerick's sideburns, salted anew with flecks of gray, and of his cheeks, and of the tiny nick on his chin where he'd shaved too close. I looked again at my watch and reminded myself to exhale. *Last time I had this much trouble breathing, I had my feet in metal stirrups, waiting for the order to PUSH.*

I described what little I'd seen from underneath the bed,

the glimpse via mirror of someone in the office, and the shoes and gun inches away from my face.

"I don't think anyone knew I was at Margot's house, except Alicia Cormer. I don't know how to reach her, except through the Stardust. She'll be working there, starting Monday."

"You didn't tell anyone else you were coming here?"

"No, the chance to work for Margot Farr just fell into my lap and I came over. I'm staying with Candace."

Mace nodded, murmured, "Um, with Candace," his attention on the spot on the floor where I said I'd seen the shoes. Abruptly, he squatted beside the bed and noted the line of sight from the floor to the mirror and the door to the office.

I wondered if he remembered Candace. She had been a sassy teenager when Mace and I had worked together in the San Diego County Sheriff's Office. It hadn't helped our romance any that I had two children still at home, daughters 14 and 9, each fixated on the idea that life would be bliss if I would only get back together with her father. Since they were my children by my second and third husbands, respectively, one or both of them were doomed to disappointment.

My first child, Cable, Son of Brock, never had any fantasy of my playing kissy-face and huggy-bear again with his father. I was only slightly more to them than a surrogate mother. Once I had produced Brock Willsen's son, I was extraneous. It was sort of like *The Sound of Music* in reverse: I started off as the wife of a cold, self-absorbed man and became, in effect, a nanny to his son, a royal man-child who had, by some cosmic coincidence, issued from my womb.

Mace walked over to the open door between the office and the bedroom. I could see books and papers on the floor. "You say you counted the tape cassettes right before you heard a gunshot?"

"Yes. I had them in order. There were nine on the desk top plus one in the tape recorder."

"And no one saw you," he repeated to himself. "Wait here," he ordered. "Don't move, don't touch anything, and don't talk to anyone. I'll be right back."

Waiting for Mace Emerick to return, I counted back by the mental touchstones of what grade Candace had been in when we lived in Escondido and how long I'd worked for the San Diego County Sheriff's Department. I factored in how long before I met Mace that I had given up on the myth of joint custody and sent Cable where he'd wanted to be all along, alone with Brock the Father. The math worked out to 11 years since Mace Emerick had last told me to wait for him.

Our romance had been uneven from the start. I was 39, no youngster by the world's standards, but I felt about 25 and looked 30. If I had hidden my children in a closet – a frequent temptation as Candace entered adolescence and began to use her mouth as a semi-lethal weapon – I could have passed myself off as younger. My age made more of a difference to Mace than it did to me. Five years older than I, he seemed to obsess on his age and, by association, on mine. I wanted love and marriage; my three disasters had softened rather than hardened my heart. Tears pooled in my eyes whenever I read Robert Browning's poem that starts, "Grow old along with me, the best is yet to be..."

Mace Emerick, however, had some bizarre idea that women shriveled when they hit the big four-o. I don't know when he thought the great decay happened to men. Probably the big six-o.

I couldn't read his mind, but I could read the footnotes. I guess he believed the vaccination against getting old was to marry a younger woman. "Stay young along with she, the worst won't have to be." I base my guess on what happened while I waited. The butthead (which is how I thought of him afterwards) married SueEllen Hoffman, a soccer-playing and nubile young patrol officer.

His real name was William, but by the time I met him, the nickname "Mace" had completely overtaken his identity. He got it as a rookie patrol officer when he'd spotted an erratic driver out in Vista, a rural part of the county. Calling it in, he found out it was a stolen car, and took off Code Three, lights and sirens, and chased the guy about ten miles. When he got him stopped and out of the car, he had to fumble in his pocket for the card to read the guy his rights, read them, and realized the guy didn't understand English. So he read the rights in Spanish, while getting the guy handcuffed, and the suspect, who acted like all he wanted to do was go to sleep, suddenly became Hercules and took off, handcuffs dangling from one wrist.

Officer Emerick called it in and took off across an orchard after the guy, a man who couldn't stay on the road while driving but was running straight as a 400-meter sprinter, and almost as fast. Emerick got to a fence and hurdled it, only to discover a 150-pound German Shepherd coming at him on his flank, muzzle flared and teeth bared like a hound from hell.

Emerick pulled his mace from his belt and pivoted toward the onrushing watchdog. As he did, he stepped into a leaf-covered depression, just a few inches down, but enough to throw him off balance. As the dog lunged toward him, he sprayed the can of mace to stop the dog before he became another notch on Killer's collar. The bad news was, the wind direction was toward him, and William the rookie cop went down – out cold. The farmer called in on 911 that an officer was "down" – which he technically was, thanks to gravity. And the combined forces of the California Highway Patrol, the San Diego County Sheriff's Department, the City of Vista and four nearby communities, and six officers from private security companies responded – helicopters and all. When the smoke – or, rather, toxic fumes – cleared, "Mace" he was and Mace he would remain.

By the time I left San Diego, nursing my broken heart, I never expected, or wanted, to see Mace Emerick again.

"You think I'll ever speak to that jerk, that butthead again?" I'd ranted to a sympathetic girlfriend who brought over a bottle of cheap wine and a bag of tacos. "Me speak to Mace Emerick again? *Over my dead body!"*

And now here he stood, and I was speaking to him. But it wasn't over *my* dead body after all.

Chapter 6

Mace stepped in from the hall, interrupting my trek down memory lane. "Come with me, please. Olivia! God, I can't believe you're here in Vegas, let alone at a murder scene."

"Yeah, doesn't happen every day." I'd harbored a few fantasies of seeing Mace again, but none of them included crawling to him on my hands and knees as I'd just done.

"I'd like you to look at the rest of the house and see if you notice anything different from when you got here."

"Where's Margot?"

"She was face down in the pool. Bloody mess. Good thing there are no sharks around here."

Or at least none in the pool, I wanted to hiss. "Was I right, about the gunshots?"

"Oh yeah. Two shots, two wounds, head and abdomen. Either one would probably be fatal. The medical examiner has her out of the pool. You can stay in the house until the body's removed, if you'd feel better."

"No, I'm okay. I've seen corpses before. As long as they're in one piece, I'm okay." While working in the sheriff's department I'd completed my associate's degree in criminal justice and done an unofficial but intensive apprenticeship in criminal investigations, mostly evidence collecting and the paperwork end of every chore. Mace hated paperwork, and was only too glad to have me spend my spare time covering his ass. Covering, not coveting, although both terms applied.

In the process, I had great on-the-job training. Mace got

nearly all the credit, but at the time I didn't mind. *Oooo, I wish I could go back in a time machine and kick my butt soundly. And his!*

The doors to the patio stood wide open, tasking the air conditioner with an unreasonable assignment. The pool water, I couldn't fail to notice, was a nauseating shade of pink. Margot's body lay face down on the patio, draped in a saturated caftan. A crime technician tied paper bags on her hands to protect evidence that might be under her long nails, and a diver with a facemask examined the pool from the surface and occasionally dove with a strong kick.

"Bullet," Mace said with a nod of his head toward the diver. "One went in and out. Might be in the pool."

In the deep end of the amoebae-shaped pool, the automatic pool cleaner, the type I knew as an Oscar, butted its round, floating blue body against the side, kept from its appointed rounds by the waves from the diver. In its ideal state, an Oscar is an efficient, low-maintenance sweeper, keeping dirt from settling on the bottom by spewing water from its dangling tentacles. The suspended dirt is sucked efficiently into the filter.

I noticed a smudge of bright red on Oscar's sun-scorched top. "Did you see that?" I nudged Mace in the arm with my elbow and pointed to the pool cleaner. "He must have been at the scene of the crime."

We sidestepped around a technician on his knees, apparently examining some evidence on the rough concrete patio surface, and got closer to Oscar, who was beating his plastic rim against the Mexican tile border like an autistic robot. I noticed the tile needed scrubbing, thanks to the notoriously hard water of Las Vegas.

"Oh, I just remembered. When I got here there was a pool service truck parked next door, in front of Number Four."

"Not there when I got here," Mace said absently, his

eyes on Oscar's bloody top. "What company?"

I had to search my memory. It had seemed so unimportant when I arrived. "I'll have to look in the Yellow Pages to jog my memory. Have you found out anything about why the guard shack was empty and the gate up?" Before he could answer I got lucky. "Mace, look, under the diving board."

He followed my intense stare, squinting until he saw it, too. "Bullet hole," he called. "On the bottom of the diving board." The technician who had been placing bags on Margot's hands turned her attention to the diving board and was joined by the crime scene photographer.

"Good eye," the technician called to Mace, with a smile that belonged at an audition for a Carnival Cruise ad, not at a crime scene.

Mace gave her his "Oh, shucks, ma'am" smile in return and a modest shrug that made me want to hurl. *Hell, yes, it's a good eye that spotted the bullet hole. Mine!*

I turned on my heel and walked closer to Margot's body. I had exaggerated how cool and professional I felt around corpses. Yes, I had seen quite a few, and some of the deaths had been more tragic than Margot Farr's. Babies, for example. Children, teenagers after prom night, one young couple on their honeymoon. There was a pregnant woman too young to have a baby, let alone too young to stop living. She'd died in a carjacking.

But Margot's death hit me hard, because I'd been right beside her just minutes before she died. The perfume from her wrists was still in my nostrils when I heard the gunshots. I wanted to know what bastard had killed her.

Mace walked up behind me. I felt his palm barely brush my shoulder, then a gentle squeeze to show he knew it was hard for me to look at Margot. "Say, let's go inside," he said softly. "I want to talk to you about something before I call my captain."

Another technician was in the kitchen, lifting fingerprints off the refrigerator, the counter, and the glassware. I longed for some iced tea to wash the adrenaline taste out of my dry mouth, but the tea was off limits. We sat on the couch at the far end of the living room, fingering our respective antimacassars with more than a physical distance between us. "You said you don't have a job yet," he began.

"Technically, no. Margot and I had almost defined a professional arrangement, when events took a turn for the worse."

"So, you need a job, and, at the same time, you'd like to see the police nail her killer fast."

"True enough," I said, not seeing where this was going.

"If I can get the captain in charge of homicide to hire you on a temporary basis, sort of an unofficial assistant, would you take the job?"

"Why would anyone hire someone to investigate a murder when that someone was present at the time and scene of the crime?" I turned toward him.

"Well, you know that, and I know that, and of course the captain will know that, but nobody else knows you were here. You'll be a secret witness. My secret weapon inside the investigation." He grinned, totally taken with the brilliance of his idea.

"Alicia Cormer knows I was here. Or at least that I said I was coming here."

"Let me worry about that. How did you say I can find her?"

"If what she told me was the truth, she'll be starting at the Stardust Monday, in publicity."

"Why do you say, *if* she told the truth?"

"Because she also said she'd call Margot and tell her I'd be coming to see her. Margot Farr had never heard of me."

Mace tugged on his right ear lobe, a quirk I once found endearing but now found annoying. "We've got a lot of ground to cover."

"We? *We?* You got a frog in your pocket?"

"Come on, don't kid yourself. This murder is right up your alley. You're itching to dig in, and it's not like you've got five other job offers."

"I don't have this job offer either, remember? I will consider it if the position is offered by your boss, and not otherwise. A paying job. I can't afford to donate my time."

He held up his hands. "Whoa! I'm with you all the way on that. Now, why don't you go home – where did you say, to Candace's place? – and I'll call you as soon as I talk to Capt. Asswacker. Uh, that's Capt. Avery S. Wacker to the public and to his face."

"I'd better call you, in the interest of keeping this under wraps." I sighed, wondering how he'd gotten me to go even this far with such a harebrained idea. "Look, I know less about Margot Farr than the average woman in the express line at the supermarket. I think you're wasting investigation time by even talking to the captain about me."

"Not so. Trust me." When he saw me roll my eyes, he added, "That was not a cue."

A woman about 60 years old, wearing a lab coat, came in from the patio and said, "Oh, there you are, Detective. We're taking the body out now. You can call me tomorrow after 3:00 p.m."

Mace rose and shook her hand as he introduced me. I struggled to get up from the spongy couch without splaying my legs apart and shook the hand of the county medical examiner, Dr. Gale Rodgers. She held the handshake longer than is standard, and I wondered if she might be checking for a pulse. Casting about for business, perhaps, like a Mary Kay saleswoman eyes dry skin or pale eyelashes.

"Glad to meet you." She weighed and measured me with her eyes as if staring through a surveyor's transit, another habit I put down to her work with clients in need of rubber bags with zippers. I felt relief when she turned her attention to Mace. "Could I speak to you by the front door, Detective? There's a crowd gathering."

I watched them move to the foyer, beside the body bag on a gurney. On the left of the fireplace, which was on the street side of the living room, I pulled a curtain away from the wall and peered out. The crowd was still small, but I spotted two TV station trucks.

Mace spoke to Dr. Rodgers and to two uniformed officers, then helped wheel the gurney to the medical examiner's truck in the driveway. From the window I watched the truck pull away and the policemen move the TV cameramen back from the lawn.

Mace returned to the living room carrying a yellow bundle in both hands. I let the curtain drop from my fingers and asked, "How secret is a witness whose departure from the scene of the crime is broadcast on the evening news?"

"No problem," he said, grinning broadly. With a flourish, he shook out the bundle. "Wear this."

Chapter 7

Letitia, the invisible roommate, was gone by the time I got back to the apartment. Candace was in the shower, thank goodness, gaining me a few minutes to collect myself before dishing out the necessary lies about where I'd been and what I'd been doing. If I put my suitcases back in my car and drove straight back to New Mexico, would all this not have happened?

"Oh, you're here," Candace called cheerfully.

I leapt to my feet, a reaction out of all proportion to the tiny surprise of Candace coming out of her own bathroom in her own apartment, but she was toweling her hair and didn't see me. "Uh, yeah. I just came in. A minute ago."

"Did you hear about Margot Farr?" Candace snatched the remote control off the coffee table and zapped on the news.

"What? No, what? Who? Margot? Farr?" I squeaked as though speaking in tongues. Apprehensively, I turned toward the TV screen. And there I was, my body encased in coveralls the color and size of a liferaft. There was Mace walking me to the criminologist van and opening the door, then closing it behind me and heading back toward Margot's house. The movement was just generic crime scene footage to the average viewer, who was probably fixated by the reporter who was saying, "Shocking... grisly... gunshots... police... neighbors." The words whizzed out of her mouth and past my ears like flying toasters off a computer screen. My attention was riveted on the criminologist van behind her head. In only a few seconds

I might be seen stepping out in my street clothes and scurrying like a rat down a gangplank toward my car.

Before that magic moment, the camera panned to the entrance to Margot Farr's "estate" as they called it, past the five-car garage, all doors closed and only police cars in the driveway. An ambulance pulled away from the front door, no emergency lights on. No reason to hurry.

Candace returned to the bathroom and raised her voice to continue the conversation. "They're looking for her husband – what a creep! He probably did it for the money! – and they can't find her live-in maid, either."

I opened my mouth to say, "She didn't have a live-in maid anymore," but managed to turn it into, "She, oh my, way-oh." It's a good thing Candace was in the bathroom when I looked back at the TV screen. My mouth and eyes bulged like a grouper spotting a 10-pound shrimp as I spotted my VW drive past the back of the reporter's head, appearing to zip in one ear and out the other as she continued.

"Ms. Farr's nutritionist and cook, Kim Kaylyn, just arrived and we're hoping to talk with her before she goes inside. Ms. Kaylyn, excuse me," she said as she thrust the microphone in the face of a perky brunette, "how did you hear of Ms. Farr's death, Ms. Kaylyn? Did it come as a complete shock? Where were you when you heard the news?"

Candace's hair dryer drowned out her answer. I changed channels and saw Kim Kaylyn arrive again, this time introduced by an earnest-looking black reporter who was facing the street, the *porte cochere* behind him appearing to be a pointed red hat sitting lightly on his dreadlocks. At least he didn't have traffic driving in and out of his ears.

My supposedly-surreptitious trek from Margot's house to the van in the clever disguise of a crime scene technician, and my subsequent hop out the door and over to my car, dressed again as myself, had been the brain-child of Mace Emerick. He must have had a lobotomy since I knew him in California. At his behest, I had sneaked away from the scene of a homicide.

Kim Kaylyn put very black sunglasses over her eyes as she stepped out of the car. Her denim shorts bordered tan, shapely thighs, and a white lace camisole said "virginal" and "sexy" at the same time.

"I'm sorry, I just can't talk now. This is a horrible, horrible shock. Margot Farr was like an older sister to me. Please excuse me." She waved away the microphones and a uniformed police officer steered her toward the front door.

"Her husband is a creep," Candace said again. She was clad in a bra and panties with enough material to properly clothe a modest chihuahua and was unrolling her pantyhose as she gently tugged them up toward her waist. She did a deep knee bend and shot her legs out one at a time like a Russian dancer to get each gam properly gloved in transparent nylon. "I met him, Aronn Young. A certified jerk. Made a pass at me!"

"How did you meet him? And I'm not surprised he made a pass at you. You're gorgeous."

On her way to her bedroom she called back to me, "All right, all right, you can stay here, Mom, but only as long as you flatter me."

Galls me to admit it, but Candace owes most of her looks to her father. He was in many ways a certified son of a bitch with a serious alcohol consumption problem, but then and now he could be mistaken for Tom Selleck. Candace is five feet 10, about 130 pounds, and she has a cloud of thick, shoulder-length auburn hair. Her eyes, though, are a clone of mine, as brown as mahogany, with flecks of gold.

She headed for the bedroom and came back out in a

midnight-blue floral dress, long in the back and tied in the front to show some leg, Polynesian-style. "I've got to go. Kenneth has a tennis tournament to look over for tomorrow and he can't be at the film premiere until late. I've still got to let the florist in and check the ice sculpture."

"You didn't say how you met Margot Farr's husband."

"Oh, at an Arabian horse show. Kenneth and I were checking everything in the food tent and Aronn Young mistook me for an heiress or something. Then Philly Mitchell, the slasher of Hollywood, spotted Aronn and hopped after him like a frog on steroids." She set her giant purse on the dinette table and stretched open its maw. Carefully, so as not to break one of her long sculptured nails, she retrieved select scraps of paper, a leather business card holder and her wallet, dropping them in a blue cloth evening bag.

"Was Margot Farr there, at the horse show?"

"Oh, no! She's been pretty much a recluse the past year. I hear she was into meditation and health, stuff like that. Didn't like to travel or go to parties. Her 'loving' husband was the opposite."

"Did you ever meet her cook? Kim Kaylyn?"

"No, but our chef, Gaston, says she's a fraud." She paused thoughtfully. "To be fair, however, Gaston says everyone is a fraud. He believes he's the only person in North America who can cook. And he's about eighty pounds overweight with no sign of stopping. Kim Kaylyn's claim to fame is getting Margot Farr back her figure."

"Fame and *fortune*," I added, but I was thinking about the lumpy mashed potato body I'd seen on the dining room chair. That was nothing to advertise on the cover of a potential best-selling diet cookbook. Kim Kaylyn's career was better off with Margot's mouth closed, albeit permanently.

Candace snagged her cell phone off the kitchen counter

with her red talons and called, "See you later."

I poured a tall glass of tea, dropped in ice cubes, and examined my own nails. They needed work. I pulled a card out of my suit pocket. "You bastard," I muttered as I punched the numbers on the wall phone. Ring, ring... then a tone. I punched in the seven digits of Candace's home phone number and hung up. About one minute later, the phone rang.

"Hello?"

"Olivia?"

"Yes, it's me." I wished Mace were there in person so I could put my hands around his neck and choke him. I'd probably black out from the effort before his thick neck muscles were even tired, but it would feel so good to try.

"Little Greek restaurant on Spring Mountain Road. Mom and pop place." He gave me the address. "I'll be there in 30 minutes."

"Mace, I just saw myself on TV..."

"In 30 minutes. We'll talk about it."

I heard the phone click and hung it up, more forcefully than the innocent plastic deserved. Tossing my suit on a chair in Candace's bedroom, I darted into her bathroom for a quick shower. I toweled dry in front of her closet where I'd squeezed in my clothes on hangers before I left for my abortive interview at the Stardust. A seersucker skirt and blouse had traveled better than the rest, so I put them on with sandals and touched up my makeup. I dabbed some of Candace's Poison behind my ears, wishing it were as good as its name. *Lean over here, Mace Emerick, closer, closer, now take a deep breath!*

*****

To say Mace and I had some history is like saying something happened at Gettysburg. I was the best wife Mace Emerick never had.

On the way to the restaurant I conducted a quick review

of my romantic past. I didn't expect any movie offers, unless they did a remake of *The Good, the Bad and the Ugly*.

For me in marriage, not even the third time was a charm. Three up, three down.

"Uh-oh," I muttered. Unable to change lanes fast, I missed the left turn Mace had told me to take, and ended up making two right turns, a U-turn and a detour through a parking lot to get back to it.

Where was I? Oh, yeah. Three up, three down. It's hard to say who-left-who in the case of Willsen, Mason, and Vale. Brock Willsen and I shared an intense love of Brock Willsen when we married. His devotion remained intact, but I lost mine. *C'est la vie.* I've been accused of being a lousy mother because I gave him custody of Cable, but to keep them apart would have been heartless, thankless and ended in a lifetime of hate directed toward me. Brock was as generous as he could be, which isn't saying a lot, but I had enough to get by, go back to college, and bury a little nest egg.

It's harder to explain my marriage to Del Mason. A charming professor, a romantic poet, a world traveler, a fascinating conversationalist. And on the rebound, as I was. Our marriage was more a chance collision of two sticky but inert molecules than a combination of elements resulting in something better than either one alone.

Our union did, however, produce Candace, which was good, but our divorce hit her hard. She learned distrust early and never let go. Although she blamed me for the breakup, it was men she distrusted on a cellular level. Our relationship has always been prickly, every episode of warmth shadowed by the knowledge that she would find an excuse – any excuse – to pull away from me. Stasis for Candace and me was the classic stance of two bull elk in a nature documentary, antlers lowered, eyes fixed by the upstart on the old fart and vice versa, their feet moving in a wary circle.

Candace inherited the best of Del and the worst of me. Or maybe it was the other way around, I forget. In either event, I was getting tired of the blame game. I was ready to dance at her wedding – though it was beginning to look like it would be held at a nursing home, if at all. Candace liked to attract men, but she liked even more to reject them. I guarantee – she didn't get *that* from me.

Valerie was the product of my third marriage. A sunny child, a tender girl, a serious student who would probably win the Nobel Prize for peace if not for science, Val was enrolled at Northwestern University. I didn't see much of her, but it was a healthy distance. Her father, airline pilot Captain Russ Vale, always called Cap, was a better pilot than he was a father, and a better father than he was a husband. We parted as friends, and have remained so. He had the good grace to marry a woman my age when he did marry again, and the four of us, Val included, get along famously.

But Mace Emerick left me for a younger woman, and ever since then I've wanted him to be a kidney donor. A double kidney donor.

*****

The food in the storefront Greek restaurant was good, but the ambience detracted measurably. The décor was, *in toto*, a sun-faded poster of the Aegean Sea, courtesy of a travel agency. It could be changed to a Chinese restaurant, or Thai, before we ordered coffee.

Mace was well into his hot moussaka before he turned his attention to the murder investigation. He used his fork to indicate I was the subject of his contemplation. "You went to the office, then Margot's bedroom, then down the hall to the gym."

"Not exactly. I followed her into her bedroom and she

sort of pointed toward the office. We were in her room less than a minute. She said her bathroom was through the hanging beads, to the left of the bed as we faced it, and then we went down the hall to the gym." I stabbed a piece of romaine and mopped up some feta cheese and dressing with it. "Are you going to eat your olive?"

"Of course I'm going to eat my olive. I'm saving it for last." He sawed ineffectually at a hard roll, then gave up and stabbed the dull knife into its flank and worried it open enough to stuff with butter.

"I didn't see Ted Landers anywhere. The gym was freezing, the TV was on but the sound was way down or muted. The lights were fairly dim, too. Soft anyway."

"Tell me again exactly what you saw when you drove up." He bit into the tough roll and tore away a mouthful. A raven-haired beauty in a green apron, worn over a pathetically tight, short black skirt, poured coffee for both of us without taking her eyes off Mace.

"Would you like some dessert?" she said.

"Yeah, sure, thanks, Lacey. Bring us some baklava, if you would. How come you're here? Aren't you dancing tonight?"

"It's my night off. And my sister is going to have a baby any minute, so I got drafted to help here."

She glided toward the kitchen and I watched Mace watch her. She stopped and bent over gracefully to retrieve a napkin, and her skirt rode up her thigh, high enough to show her panties, but nothing showed. Well, no panties, anyway.

"It's going to be, uh, interesting to work with you again, Olivia." His eyes were still riveted to Lacey's thigh. "I'm used to working by myself. I guess you could say I'm a lone wolf."

"You've got that half right," I said dryly.

Lacey finished advertising for whatever show or porno

film she danced in and disappeared into the kitchen. Mace looked back at me. "Uh, where were we?"

"In answer to your question, and at the risk of interrupting your reverie, when I arrived there was no guard at the gate and the red arm was in the Up position. A silver BMW was parked in front of the garage, and all the garage doors were closed. I didn't see any people."

"No gardener?"

"No. In front of the house next door, Number Four, there was a pool service truck."

"Oh yeah, I remember you said that." He mopped up the remains of his moussaka with the last piece of his roll, swallowed, and pushed his plate away. Then he got up and reached behind the cash register to pull out a thick Yellow Pages book. He leafed through it quickly and plopped it open in front of me. I looked at the ads and alphabetical listings for Swimming Pools, Maintenance. "That's it, AquaMate."

He wrote the address and phone number on a napkin and stuffed it in his pocket. "So, you didn't meet Margot's daughter, but she said Esmé was living there for a month?" He was covering ground we'd been over before.

"Never saw her. The thing is, Margot was going off like a smoke alarm when I arrived, and if Esmé or anyone else were around, I'm sure they would have run in, too. She said the maid's room was in the wing above the garage, but that she didn't have a live-in maid just now."

"Right. I looked into that. Woman named Carmen Espiña, worked for Margot 14 months. Margot fired her ass three weeks ago for taking pictures of her looking like a whale. Word is the maid was trying to get pictures of Margot's weight gain and sell them to a tabloid. If the maid were the one found dead, I don't know who'd have the most motive – Margot, Kim Kaylyn or Ted Landers. Those two are making seven figures, thanks to whipping Margot into shape. Pictures of her looking like Elvis in drag could send them back to a car wash in Pasadena." The waitress returned with two small plates of baklava, the delicate pastry glistening with honey, and a carafe of coffee. "Thanks, Lacey. That's all we'll need. Everything was great, as always."

"Come back soon. Dad will be sorry he missed you." Her smile almost included me, but not quite.

I stirred cream into my coffee as I considered what Mace had said. "So the maid, Carmen Espiña, was probably pretty ticked about being fired."

"Good theory. I'm working on that."

"On the subject of working, as in paycheck procurement, did Capt. Wacker offer to hire me, or did he enjoy a hearty laugh as he wrote up your reprimand?"

I was sorry I said the word the instant it came out of my mouth. The pained look that crossed Mace's face reminded me of trouble he'd had with a reprimand in San Diego. A woman detective had been promoted to head of his section, 10 percent on ability and 90 percent on affirmative action, and had then proceeded to get even with every man in the department for slights, some real, some imagined – or at least blown out of proportion. Mace's charm was not only wasted on Ms. Whittier, it was an affront to her feminist agenda. He suffered through a sexual harassment suit and settled for a reprimand he didn't deserve in exchange for a transfer to another department.

"Capt. Wacker, while not the brightest bulb in the chandelier, saw the advantage of keeping your name out of the press. He wants to meet you before he signs anything, but I'm sure he'll go along with it. I told him how fast you transcribe tapes, and we need the information off Margot Farr's audio tapes as fast as we can get it."

I changed the subject. "When did you move to Las Vegas, and why?" As angry as I could get at Mace for personal reasons, I had nothing but admiration for his detective skills. Whatever caused Mace to leave California was California's loss.

"You remember Hornet Armstrong?"

"Sure." The chief of police in the City of San Diego had been Mace's best friend since police academy days. Hornet got his nickname from a massive, intricate sting operation he'd worked to expose corruption in the Los Angeles Police Department. For once, superior ability was rewarded, and Hornet moved up quickly as an administrator. Everyone knew San Diego was temporary for Chief Armstrong. Meanwhile, as Hornet's career thrived, Mace languished under the thumb of Ms. Whittier. Hornet, Mace and I had spent a lot of days racing sailboats together, and cooperating on joint task force drug busts. That Hornet Armstrong said I had the makings of a top-notch criminalist was one my proudest achievements.

"Las Vegas made Hornet an offer he couldn't refuse, and he's the chief here now. All it took was a call from him and I packed my duffel."

"So you must be a lot happier, with Hornet as your boss." I sipped my coffee.

"Yes and no. Wacker has been here a long time, 15 years as a detective, one of them as captain. He was real thick with the previous chief, who was forced to resign, so – as you'd expect – he's not Hornet's biggest fan. But all that is below the surface, way below. Capt. Wacker knows which knife butters the bread."

"So what's the problem?"

"I'm the red-headed stepchild in the detective department. Wacker wouldn't disagree with Chief Armstrong if Hornet said cows can fly, but he's got it in for me. Oh, he's subtle, I'll give him that, but I have to keep my eyes open." He warmed his cup from the carafe. "Great coffee, huh?" I nodded absently.

"Anyhow, you don't have to worry about Wacker. You'll be working, uh, under me." He grinned and winked.

I grinned back through clenched teeth, then cleared my throat. "That reminds me, how is SueEllen? She still got those taut nipples and no tan line?"

"I haven't seen her in a couple years. Still looked fine last time I saw her. Her new husband is an architect."

It was my turn to grin and wink. "Oh, a younger man? Or just richer?"

"Who knows?" he shrugged as if the thought had never crossed his mind. "I've got to get back to the station. You're staying with Candace? How is she, by the way?"

"Doing well professionally, vice-president of Royale Catering. Physically, she's gorgeous. You make a pass at her, I'll consider it incest and stab you with an ice pick."

"Incest? That's outrageous and you know it!"

"Well, yes. And I'd feel awfully guilty after I stabbed you. Probably cry for an hour. Well, half an hour."

"You've always been direct, Olivia. Perverse and emotionally unstable, but direct. That's one of the things I like about you. One of many."

I smiled and tucked my purse under my arm. "I'm going to Candace's place to unpack. This has been a hell of a first day in town."

"Call me early in the morning, okay? We'll get to work."

*****

I made up the sofabed and propped myself up, just in time for the late local news. I watched as Margot Farr's husband, Aronn Young, was pummeled by news crews as he arrived at her home, presumably *their* home, around 8:00 p.m. He wore black leather pants and a white T-shirt that looked like underwear to me. He had a five o'clock shadow, from five o'clock day before yesterday. With him was a short balding man in a white dinner jacket, looking like he'd been called away from the baccarat tables at

Monte Carlo. The same woman reporter who'd introduced Kim Kaylyn while I made my getaway introduced Charles St. John, Margot's agent.

"No comment at this time," St. John said into the glare of lights. He kept one hand on Aronn Young's elbow to show he was speaking for both of them. "This is a horrible shock. Excuse us, please. We will talk to the press at an appropriate time, but we need privacy now. Thank you."

The camera backed off to show another car arrive. Kim Kaylyn, dressed in a hunter-green evening pantsuit, stepped out. She ran the gauntlet and caught up with Charles St. John and Aronn Young. They entered the house together.

The camera centered on the reporter, and her name, Mindy Random, appeared across her right breast. "Norman and Dixie, I'm at the Las Vegas home of actress Margot Farr, who was found dead this afternoon. Her body, I am told by police, was floating face down in her swimming pool, and the cause of death is believed to be gunshots. I'm told Ms. Farr's husband, Aronn Young, whom you just saw arrive at the home, was in Los Angeles today and raced back to Las Vegas when he heard the tragic news. The police said they will have no further comment until they have the results of an autopsy."

The words "Earlier today" appeared at the top of the screen and Mindy gave a quick recap of activity at Margot's house as footage rolled of the gurney being wheeled out and Kim Kaylyn's first arrival, in shorts and camisole.

"Thank you, Mindy," the co-anchor named Norman Pierce said ponderously. "In the studio with us we have Philly Mitchell, author of books on Frank Sinatra, Steve McQueen, Marilyn Monroe and other stars."

In my opinion, Philly looked older on the local news set than she did on national TV where lights and cameras had a wider range of kindly effects. Lately I'd noticed the anchors on network news were looking better than they did 20 years ago. Sure, they were getting plastic surgery, the best money could buy, but there is also something about a diffuse, golden light from below one's face that does wonders.

Norman Pierce continued. "Philly Mitchell has been working on a biography of Margot Farr, a book that is said by some to have angered Ms. Farr. What can you tell us, Philly, about this controversy over your book?"

"It's true my book, *Going Farr*, is an unauthorized biography, but it's not true that Margot Farr was angry about it. We were close friends for many years, and Margot respected me as a journalist. But, like all stars, she sometimes had an overreaction to public interest."

"So when will your book be out?"

Philly folded her hands prettily, showing the sculptured nails to best advantage. *Damn,* I thought, *that does it! I'm getting fingernails!*

"The book is almost finished," she said, "but of course this changes everything. My publisher wants me to write about Margot's death. I can't say just when it will be out, but it will be soon."

"Do you have any idea who would shoot Margot Farr?" the other anchor, Dixie Valdez, asked.

"It could have been someone who knew her, or a random act of violence. We all know of famous people who have been murdered by some crazy fan. The police have asked me to help, and I'll help any way I can, Dixie. I'm devastated by this horrible, horrible crime, the same as Margot's other friends."

"Thank you for joining us, Philly Mitchell, author of a biography of Margot Farr, murdered today in Las Vegas," Norman said to wrap.

The next news was from the state capital, Carson City, and I turned off the TV. I took a spiral notebook from my purse, found a pen by the phone, and wrote the word, Suspects, and underlined it twice.

Under Suspects I wrote: maid, husband, daughter, cook, and exercise coach. On the next page I wrote, "Who was beneficiary of Margot's will?" and added "What about life insurance? Beneficiary? How much $$$?" My mind wandered from the issue, however. I chewed absently on the end of the pen.

This crazy "secret witness" idea and the even crazier "work with Mace again" idea could still be jettisoned. I could easily say, "No! I'm a witness – take my statement, tell it to the press, and say good-bye." Then I'd march out and get myself a good job, meet new people, some of them men. Who needs this insanity known as Mace Emerick in her life? Not me!

But then another thought wormed its way into my mind, and I felt my resolve evaporate. *So, Mace and SueEllen split up.* I sighed and tucked the pen behind my ear. *How interesting. How very, very interesting.*

I had the distinct impression – in my mind's eye – of a metal door with narrow bars sliding shut behind me, and the clang of a lock. Dumb idea or not, I was in this adventure for the duration.

Chapter 8

"Olivia Wright," I said, extending my hand to the captain. Mace had been closeted with him for half an hour while I watched detectives and uniformed officers breeze past my chair. At last I was summoned to the private office at the far end of the big room. It was 9:00 Thursday morning, about 24 hours since I'd arrived at Candace's apartment.

"Avery Wacker," he said giving my hand a firm shake. He was tall and thin, with an unattractive pallor, hooded eyes, and a nose so long it had to start almost even with his eyebrows. If Capt. Wacker had gone into politics, cartoonists would have thought they'd died and gone to heaven.

"Please, take a seat. This case is a hell of a mess, phones ringing off the hook from every newspaper and magazine between here and Vladivostok. ABC, NBC and every other damn C is dogging us every step of the way." He rested half his bony rump on a corner of his desk and looked down his beak at me with the cold eyes of a raptor. "Have you told anyone – *anyone* – that you were in Margot Farr's house yesterday?"

I was glad I had no misdeed to hide, as I would have confessed readily under his piercing glare. "No, not even my daughter, and I'm staying with her."

"But I presume your car was parked in front of her house?"

"Actually, it was across the street and around a curve. The sprinklers were on at the house next door and the wind was blowing the water toward the sidewalk in front of Margot's."

"What about this Alicia Cormer?" Wacker's eyes darted from me to Mace and back again. "She knew you were there?"

"I'd say she probably knew. She's the person who gave me the address and told me to go around three-thirty. But she said she would call Margot to introduce me, and Margot didn't have any idea who I was."

"Or so she said?" He shrugged. "Detective Emerick makes much of your experience in investigations." The clear implication from his tone of voice was that Mace made *too* much of my experience. Wacker lifted my résumé from his desk and made a show of studying it. I noticed he held it by the edges, as if it were evidence not yet tested for traces of blood.

"I don't know that I'd call it a lot, but yes, I have some experience." There was no place on a résumé to put "plain old horse sense" but that was my strongest suit. A lot of success in law enforcement came from paying attention and keeping one's mouth closed, two skills I'd honed working with Mace in California. I practiced the latter just then by clenching my teeth.

Capt. Wacker placed my résumé under an agate paperweight. He paused, giving Mace a dagger-look. I knew that look, having perfected it myself two-and-a-half husbands ago. I had to restrain myself from looking at Mace at all. Why had I so readily believed what Mace told me, that Capt. Wacker would think this was a great idea, the police having a secret witness inside the investigation? If I were a cartoon, there would be steam rising from my collar.

From his center drawer, Wacker pulled a single typed

sheet and slid it over to me. "This should cover the bases while I shove paperwork through the system." If Mace had to go to bed without his supper, it would be decreed out of my hearing.

I read the simple contract quickly. I was on the payroll of Las Vegas P.D. on a temporary, special-needs basis. The money wasn't good, but it was a start. Mace handed me a pen and I signed under Wacker's signature.

"Do we have your fingerprints yet?"

"Yes, sir. I gave them at the crime scene yesterday."

"Good. If you're ready to start, Mace will get you set up." We rose in unison and I shook hands again with Wacker. I hoped Mace could feel *my* dagger-look in the back of his head as we left the office.

*****

"He didn't look very happy with the arrangement," I said as I gingerly pressed the hot metal of the seat belt into its latch.

"That's just the way he looks all the time. Like he's next in line for the proctoscope."

"How did you talk him into hiring me?"

"I didn't. Hornet did, by phone." He rolled his window down and turned the air conditioner on high to blow out the hot air.

"Oh, that's nice. He'll consider me to be forced on him by the boss he resents."

"That pretty much describes how he feels about me, so what's the problem? Hornet wants me, Hornet wants you. Capt. Wacker is all out of chips in the crap shoot."

I had a very uneasy feeling about the political maze I'd wandered into, but I changed the subject. "When is the funeral?"

"Not settled yet. Baron's Funeral Home will take Margot's body after the autopsy, which is being done this morning, but there's a battle between her husband and her daughter over who is in charge. I have a call in to her lawyer to see if she left any instructions. Of course, I also want to know who stood to gain from her will."

So far, it was a cool day in Las Vegas, 10:00 a.m. and only 85 degrees. Must be a cold front, was my guess. "Have you talked to Ted Landers yet?"

"Naw, he's in deep mourning on a handball court. Has a one-third interest in a coed fitness complex, Sinbad's." I must have reacted visibly. "What?" he asked.

"Nothing, or anyway, not much. Candace happened to mention that she and her roommate both go to Sinbad's."

"Yeah, it's a happening place, as they say. All the really big stars supposedly go there when they're in Vegas. And all the richest singles. Personally, I think it's like those, what do you call them, urban legends? Where you hear that someone's friend's cousin saw Barbra Streisand there, saw her with his own two eyes, and 30 people retell it, but nobody can ever quite identify the one person who swore he saw Streisand." He shrugged. "It was probably Ted Landers or his partners, trying to boost the value of their investment. Streisand, yes! And Garth Brooks, and Whitney Houston!"

When I let myself laugh I felt a knot in the back of my neck start to release its hold on my muscles. Good grief, but I was tense. "So you didn't talk to him yet?"

"Only to a receptionist at Sinbad's, three times, and Landers' voice mail, twice. I'll track him down today. I figure, how far can he run, on a treadmill?"

We pulled into the driveway of Margot's house and Mace parked in the shade of the entryway. Crime scene tape criss-crossed the front door and stretched across the wide expanse of the garages. An officer nodded to Mace as we let ourselves inside.

"I took the micro cassettes, tape player, and several pads of paper with what I presume was Margot's handwriting to the station. You can listen to the tapes and try to decipher her notes there. I want to take a look at the maid's room and the daughter's room, and then have you walk through what you saw and heard."

"Was Esmé in the house last night?"

"Briefly. An officer accompanied her to her room to pack enough for a couple days away from the house." As he spoke, he headed up a set of stairs and entered a bedroom suite done in white eyelet and lace. A dozen pillows in ruffled shams topped a fluffy comforter, leaving less than half the bed a flat, uncluttered surface. It was lovely to look at, but the pits for convenience.

"This is the daughter's room," he said. "She says she has been staying here for a month while her house is being remodeled." He picked up an antique perfume atomizer and gave the cloth bulb a squeeze.

"Where is she now?" I looked inside the walk-in closet at two rows of dresses and gowns draped with clear plastic. The drawers of the bedside table were empty.

"She's staying with Margot's agent, Charles St. John."

"I saw him on TV with Aronn Young. Does Young stand to inherit a lot?"

"I would only be guessing." He leaned the pillows forward and looked beneath them. "And that's not why they pay me the big bucks. Come on."

We did a quick turn through the maid's room. On the floor behind the dresser I found a snapshot of four Latina women, each of them holding a baby. The exuberant smiles of the women made me smile, too. Neither names nor a date was written on the back.

"The maid's name is Carmen Espiña," Mace said. "She came from Tijuana to work in a clothing factory, but somehow she started working for Margot Farr." He looked over my shoulder at the photo. "Been here a little over a year, according to Esmé."

"When will we talk to her?" I asked. "I mean, to both of them?"

"To Esmé today at 3:00. I want *you* to find the maid. Come on, let's go to the other wing."

We padded down the carpeted hall and the stairs from the guest and maid's wing to the expanse of the living room and dining room, then down the Oriental carpet, under the arched green glass to the exercise room. It looked just as it had the day before, ballerinas continuing to twirl off into the distance. And it was still cold enough to keep lettuce fresh.

In Margot's bedroom I recounted my misadventures, recalling nothing new, and stepped into what would have been my office, had fate been kinder to Margot and, by extension, to me. The front of the white drawers and the area around the computer and fax machine still had black dust from the fingerprint tech's work. Mace pulled two thin latex gloves out of his jacket pocket, gave me one, and tugged the other on his right hand.

With my hand gloved, I slid open each drawer in turn. The tapes and small tape player, as well as the legal pads, had been removed as he said. I was eager to work on them.

Mace had not shown me the fax that came in at the same time Margot was shot. He'd bagged it, of course, when he packed the tapes, and he'd taken messages off her answering service. I asked him about the fax while I leafed through the books above the computer monitor.

"It was from her husband, in Beverly Hills. He said he'd be home around 8:00 p.m."

A business card slipped out of a computer manual and fluttered to the floor. I picked it up and read aloud, "Vicente Amis, Consultant." A local number, no address, was printed below the name. On the back was a 10-digit number. I handed it to Mace. "It looks like a phone number to me, starting with the country code for Mexico."

Mace bagged it and slipped the bag in his inside coat pocket. "I'm thirsty."

I shook out the pages of the last book. "There's cold water and ice in the door of the refrigerator."

This time I led the way, pouring us each a glass of ice water. The deep blue of the tile counter bore a few marks of fingerprint powder.

"Why would anyone need a kitchen this big?" he muttered. His idea of a cooking extravaganza ran to burritos and microwaves.

"It's as much a studio as a kitchen." I smiled at the thought of Mace giving a televised demonstration of unwrapping the burrito, being careful not to get his fingers burned by the steam. "Kim Kaylyn worked on her special recipes for Margot here, taping segments to be used on TV shows or whatever. The cameras are right . . ." I looked toward the two corners where I'd seen small video cameras the day before. "Two cameras were visible yesterday when Margot showed me the kitchen."

I set my water glass in the sink and wriggled my fingers into the latex glove. First I looked in all the drawers of the butcher block cooking island. The control panel and tape deck were inside what was once a garbage compactor. "Aha!" I said triumphantly. I pressed Retract and the cameras appeared in two corners, the tiles in front of them folding up like little garage doors to the barely audible whirr of a motor. I pressed Retract again and the cameras disappeared like shy birds, covered at once by the tiles. The cameras were again invisible.

I pressed Eject and another tiny motor hummed, but nothing came out of the VCR.

Mace pulled out the antenna of his cell phone and punched in a set of numbers. "Detective Mace Emerick here. Who was the officer in charge of the crime scene at

Margot Farr's house last night?" He paused, swearing under his breath. "Yeah? And where is Billings now? No, I can't hold on, I'm on my cell. Tell him to call me here, right away." He gave the number and stabbed the End button.

I used the time to examine the walk-in pantry. Each spice and herb was meticulously marked. There were a dozen different kinds of flour. I heard Mace's phone ring and took two steps backward so I could hear him.

He snarled at Officer Billings and described the cameras. "The cameras were retracted before I got here today. No, I didn't see them yesterday, but I have a reliable witness that says they were visible before Ms. Farr was shot. Did anyone but a crime scene tech or a detective go in the kitchen after I left here?" I continued to snoop in the kitchen drawers and cabinets with my gloved hand while keenly aware of Mace listening intently to the officer's list.

"Yeah, I know her daughter came in. She had permission to get a few things from her bedroom. Yeah? So what did Kim Kaylyn want?" To me he said, "Kaylyn went in the pantry and got the author's galley of her cookbook."

Back into the phone he said, "Then what? She sat in the living room with St. John and Aronn Young, and that's all? Then they left?" He listened, shaking his head in disbelief. "Oh, for crying out loud, and you let her go back in the kitchen unescorted? Tell me she was never out of your sight." He paused, then said, "Shit!" and closed his phone.

He looked at his watch and turned the pages of his small notebook. "Here it is. Let's go see Kim the cook."

*****

Two calls on Mace's cell phone directed us to Ms. Kaylyn's present location, a TV studio on Industrial Road. The receptionist directed us down the hall to a window on the studio. A red light above the closed door said ON AIR. Sound came from a monitor on the wall farther down the hall, so we watched Kim Kaylyn's and the host's lips move in front of us, but heard them behind us. Strange.

"I know there were rumors," Kim was saying, "and I don't like to dignify them with a comment, but I must! Yes, Margot Farr had put on a few pounds, five or six I would guess, although I never, ever weighed her. That would have been a violation of her privacy, as it would be of anyone's! She was neglecting to drink as much water as a person should, especially in this climate. And she ate a little more than I recommend, because, frankly, she was under a tremendous strain the weeks before her murder."

The host, whose name I didn't know, smoothed his mustache and stroked his pony tail against his shoulder like a pet ferret. "Kim, I understand how loyal you are." He spoke with a slight lisp that grated on my nerves. Understand came out *under-thtand*.

"I *under-thtand* how loyal you have *alwayth* been, to Margot. But Kim, *theriouthly, wath Margoth'* weight gain a threat to the *thuk-theth* of your diet book?"

"Certainly not!" she said. I had to give Kim Kaylyn credit. I would have answered, "Thertainly not!"

"Margot lost a lot of weight by staying on the tasty, nutritious diet plan I prepared for her this past year. Of course, I can't take all the credit," she went on, in a tone that meant, "I most assuredly *can* take all the credit, but I am magnanimous to a fault."

"Margot Farr's personal trainer, and my dear friend, Ted Landers, helped her find an exercise program and level she could stay with, and anybody who says dieting is all there is to weight loss is trying to pull the wool over your eyes." Kim Kaylyn had charisma, I'd hand her that. I looked at the young man operating the camera, and guessed he had just fallen in love.

Kim was petite and just as perky as Katie Couric. In fact, I wondered if her mother (or Kim herself) had chosen her name in some kind of subliminal homage to Katie.

"No, Richard," she was saying in answer to another soft-pitch question from the host, "my publisher's decision to move up the publication date of my cookbook has nothing to do with Margot's tragic death. The decision was made some time ago, a couple weeks ago, I think, to go to press more quickly. My publisher says he's just *buried* with orders already."

Richard made nice for the camera, about how grateful he was for Kim Kaylyn taking the time, *et cetera*, and just after the tragic death, *et cetera*, and wishing her well, and so on. The red light went off and they came into the hallway, with fervent thank yous and air kisses and promises to do this again soon. *Do thith again thoon.*

"Ms. Kaylyn," Mace said in his official police voice, "I'm Detective Mace Emerick. We met yesterday evening at Margot Farr's house. I need to ask you some questions." In the car, he'd retraced her arrival at Margot's a few minutes after my exit. He said he'd tried to question her then, but she broke down crying and left. When she returned two hours later with Charles St. John and Aronn Young, Mace wasn't there.

"I have some time this afternoon . . ." she began in a dismissive tone.

"I have a full schedule of interviews and I'd appreciate it if you could answer a few questions now. I can find you later if I need any clarification." He had placed himself strategically between Kim, Richard, and the exit.

"Detective, I'm Richard Gable," the host said, extending his hand. I watched his eyes widen slightly as Mace gave him a handshake more manly, perhaps, than he was used to. "Uh, you could *uth* my *offith*. Right here."

"Thanks. This will just take a few minutes, Ms. Kaylyn."

She looked at her watch and gave a sigh of annoyance. "I have a phone conference scheduled in 30 minutes with my literary agent, from New York."

"The sooner we get started, the sooner you'll be on your way." Mace stood his ground and crossed his arms, poker-faced. *I'll see your annoyance and raise you two aggravations.*

"All right," she conceded with another sigh, "In Richard's office."

We trooped single file to an office dominated by a poster of Judy Garland in *A Star Is Born.* Mace gestured to the comfortable chair behind the desk and Kim sat down. I tugged the other chair as far away from the desk as was possible in the small room and pulled a steno pad and pen from my purse. Mace introduced me as Linda, with a dismissive gesture and a mumbled, "going to help me with some notes."

Richard stood at the door as if looking for some way to make himself useful, and therefore included. Mace said, "Thanks," and closed the door, then half-sat on the edge of the desk, blocking Kim Kaylyn's view of me. Out of sight, out of mind, as the saying goes.

"Ms. Kaylyn," he began, "when was the last time you saw Margot Farr?"

She had expected the question and answered quickly. "As I told you yesterday evening, the last time I saw Margot was Tuesday evening, the day before she died, at 7:00 or 7:30. I fixed her a grilled chicken and mandarin orange salad with Belgian endive and frisee and flambéed orange liqueur dressing." She even talked like a cookbook.

"Did you videotape the preparation of the salad?" he asked.

I leaned forward enough to see her face. She was surprised by the question. "Um, no, I didn't. Margot wanted to sit in the kitchen and watch me fix it, and she was dressed informally. I didn't think it would make a good tape."

"Did Margot look fat? Is that why you thought it wouldn't make a good tape?"

She bristled and narrowed her eyes, and I retreated behind Mace's bulk so she wouldn't see me smile. "Margot lost a lot of weight when she ate only the food I prepared and when she followed Ted Landers' exercise program. She was so thrilled with her new body and her new energy level that she wanted to do anything she could to help others with weight problems dogging their lives. Yes, she had put on a few pounds in the weeks before her death, but she was determined to lose them and I have no doubt she would have. I won't participate in any trashing of Margot Farr to you or to the press."

"You didn't answer my question," Mace persisted. "Did she look fat and is that why you didn't videotape your cooking in her kitchen Tuesday evening?"

"I did answer your question, Detective. I felt protective of Margot Farr that night, and I'm protective of her memory now. She didn't look her best, and I did not tape us in the kitchen."

"She didn't look her best Wednesday afternoon either," he went on. "Do you have any idea who might have been angry enough to kill her?"

"Of course I've been wracking my brain with that question," Kim said. "Margot could be aggravating, setting the extremely high standards for people around her that she demanded of herself, but she had a heart of gold, and I can't imagine a person so cruel as to kill her. No, I have no idea."

"Did you take anything out of Margot's kitchen last night?"

She smiled, ready again for the question. "Why, yes, the police officer at Margot's house let me take the manuscript for my cookbook. I explained I had to check my copy against the galleys. It was on a shelf in the pantry. He watched me take it."

"Did you take anything else?" Mace sounded like that question had simply come, unbidden, into his mind, sort of like Lt. Colombo's famous, "Just one more question," technique.

Kim looked thoughtful, as if searching her memory, trying so hard to be helpful, then shook her head. "No. I just went back in the living room, chatted a few minutes with Charles St. John and Aronn Young. Margot's daughter, Esmé, came through just for a moment, with a suitcase, and I expressed my condolences."

"Where were you yesterday afternoon?"

"I was at Charles St. John's house, in The Lakes. He was giving me a second opinion of some contract work my literary agent was doing for me."

"How long were you there?"

"About two hours. About 3:00 to 5:00, I'd say. When I got home I got a call from Ted Landers telling me Margot was dead. I couldn't say exactly what time it was. I was in shock, of course."

"Did Mr. Landers say how he'd heard about her death?"

She stopped to consider the question. "No, and I didn't ask him."

"You didn't go back in the kitchen last night, after you say you picked up your manuscript?" Mace said, standing and opening the door.

She looked slightly flustered. "I don't recall. Oh, wait, I did step in for just a moment while Esmé spoke to Charles St. John, to get a key to his house, I think."

"And did you remove a videotape, or make any changes in the taping equipment?"

"No," she said, puzzled. "Oh, I looked in the video machine, and there was no tape. I might have, just by habit, closed down the cameras. Yes, I think I did. It's better for the lenses." She stood, too, and Mace allowed her to precede him into the hall. I followed along behind, by now completely unnoticed by Kim Kaylyn.

"Thanks for your time, Ms. Kaylyn." He read a phone number from his notepad. "Is that your correct phone number? And do you have a cell number?"

Reluctantly, she gave him her cell phone number. I knew from Mace that the other number was just a message service, a way to never take a call she didn't want to take. *A lot of that going around*, I'd said to him earlier. *Everyone in the whole damn country is "out, so please leave a message."*

Candace dealt with a lot of Hollywood-types, and she'd once explained to me what "Call me" meant in Hollywood and its distant suburb, Vegas. "No one calls anyone who is beneath them," she had said, "and they only take calls from people who are above them in the food chain, or the ladder of success, so the only way to reach anyone is to reach their 'people.' And that's not easy, either."

Kim took another look at her watch and registered "Oh, horrors!" on her expressive, TV-friendly-face and said a hurried good-bye to Richard.

Outside we watched her drive off in a white Chrysler Sebring convertible with its top up. Mace's cell phone rang in his pocket and he said in a singsong tone, "Social strata, bottom floor." Into the phone he was all business. "Emerick here." We walked to his car as he listened. "We're on our way. ETA five minutes."

He unlocked my door and opened it, saying, "Damn!" at how hot the metal was. As he got in his side and slipped his cell phone in his breast pocket, he said, "I was wrong. There is a lower floor on the social strata, and that was who called."

"Capt. Wacker?" I guessed.

Mace laughed. "Yeah. We have time for lunch on the way."

*****

I thought Mace was being insubordinate to tell the captain we'd be there in five minutes, and then say we had time for lunch, but I had forgotten his idea of lunch always came through a window in a paper bag.

I ate my Whopper in my cubicle in the homicide department while Mace met with Capt. Wacker. His quadruple Whopper or whatever he had was lukewarm by the time he returned.

"He wants Margot Farr's tapes transcribed by this time tomorrow." He folded back the paper and took a humongous bite of burger. He seemed deep in thought, or maybe it was ecstasy over his burger that made him close his eyes and place his left hand on his forehead. I waited, sipping my Coke.

After he'd eaten, an indelicate process that took three minutes, tops, he pulled out his notepad and flipped through the pages.

"The micro cassette tapes have been speed-copied on a master. I'll show you where to work on them. I'm going to line up Charles St. John, Esmé and Aronn Young for this afternoon. And before that I'm going to nail Ted Landers down to an interview time and talk to Margot's lawyer. Think you could be ready to roll by 3:00?"

"Sure. I can work on the tapes 'til then, and tonight." *Heh, heh heh,* I chuckled soundlessly. I had been afraid Mace would see all those people without me along, and I'd be left to pry information out of him, which was tougher than getting a reliable stock tip from an astrology column in the paper. I was relieved to learn I'd be along for at least part of the investigation.

In a booth near the evidence room I made sure the electrical cord to the laptop computer was snug and created a new file, Tape One, and typed in the current date and time. Then I tugged Mouseketeer-sized earphones over my head and pressed Play on the console. Anticipating Margot's smoky voice, coming from beyond the morgue – though not yet from beyond the grave – I shivered, took a deep breath, and placed my fingers on the keyboard.

Chapter 9

"Anything so far?" Mace asked me as we drove to Sinbad's to talk to Ted Landers. It was 3:15 Thursday afternoon.

"On the tapes? No, just Margot's gilded memories of her first starring role." Transcribing the tapes was going faster than I'd expected, as Margot had let the cassette continue recording even while she poured a drink and thought about what to say next.

We had been planning to go first to Charles St. John's house and interview Aronn Young, Esmé, and St. John. Ted Landers still hadn't returned Mace's phone messages, so I gave it another try right before we left the police station.

The receptionist transferred me to Tyrone, a desk attendant with a voice like the bass in the Oak Ridge Boys. "Mr. Landers is having a massage, ma'am. I'll transfer you to his voice mail."

"No thanks, that won't be necessary," I said, smiling at Mace across the phone. "The medium is the massage."

"What was that?" Tyrone asked.

I wanted to ask him to sing a few bars of "Elvira," but of course I did no such thing. Instead I said, "Nothing, thank you very much," and hung up the phone with a nod to Mace. "Let's go to Sinbad's and catch Landers with his pants down."

Mace rolled his eyes. "If memory serves, you give a hell of a massage yourself."

"Memory will have to serve. I'm working with you on a

strictly professional basis, remember? This is a murder case."

Ted Landers was lying face down in a small room near the sauna at Sinbad's. His rump was draped discreetly with a towel, but the rest of his magnificent body glistened with oil. "Mr. Landers," Mace said as he displayed his badge to the Asian masseuse and gestured to the door, "I'm here on police business."

"What the hell are you doing coming in here?" Landers snapped.

"Oh, don't get up," Mace said, with a straight face. The masseuse slipped quietly out the door and closed it behind her. I stood in the corner. Landers had caught a glimpse of me behind Mace as we entered, uninvited, but I stepped quickly out of his line of sight. From my vantage point at his feet I had an excellent view of the musculature in his legs. They had enough hair to be masculine, without crossing the line to gorilla. I couldn't help but think how long it had been since I'd given a man a massage. My skill at the art of massage was not, and never would be, on my résumé. Massage, to me, was foreplay. Unless I took a career detour into porno flicks, it would remain my secret weapon.

"I'm Detective Emerick, Mr. Landers. I've been leaving messages for you, but I haven't heard back. I thought it would be best to save us both some phone tag and meet – in the flesh, as it were. Now, Mr. Landers, where were you yesterday afternoon?"

"I resent the implication of that question!" The muscles in the back of Landers' legs tensed. Nicely, I might add.

"I'm sorry," Mace replied. "But part of a murder investigation is to pin down where everyone related to the victim, whether by family ties, business, or romance, was at the time of the murder. The sooner we know where you were, the sooner I can leave. I have a lot of work to do, Mr. Landers, a lot of ground to cover."

Landers snatched the towel around to his groin as he rolled over and sat up. He glowered at me from beneath his black eyebrows, then turned his glare to Mace. "Esmé Mott and I had a late lunch together, at Spago's. Then I gave her a lift home because she needed her car. I drove straight to Sinbad's and I was here the rest of the afternoon," he said, enunciating clearly. "I worked in my office on paperwork. Later I played racquetball."

"When was the last time you saw Margot Farr?" Mace asked.

"Tuesday morning. I worked with her in her home gym from 10:00 to 11:00. I remember I'd blocked out two hours for her, but she quit shortly after 11:00. In fact, she didn't get started until about 10:20."

"Did that make you angry?" Mace asked. "Did you feel you were wasting your time?"

"No, I wasn't angry." He combed his fingers through his wavy, sun-bleached hair and shrugged. "I was disappointed that she was falling behind in her exercise program. Every step backward takes two steps forward to stay even. I always tried to encourage her to exercise every day. Margot needed a lot of encouragement."

"Had she put on a lot of weight in recent weeks?" I asked, my steno pad in front of me, and my face down.

Landers glanced at me and back to Mace. "Not a lot, but, yes, she was letting pounds creep back on. We had a heart to heart about it Tuesday morning. She got all teary and sad and promised to get back on her program."

"But then she quit after, what, 40 minutes?" Mace prodded.

"Margot would have lost the weight and firmed up. I'm certain of it!" he said. "After all, she had the best personal trainer in the business." He held his hands out, palms up, as if making an amusing exaggeration.

"Was her weight gain any threat to your exercise video

deal?" I inserted.

"Absolutely not! The public loved Margot Farr, and they identified with her struggle to lose weight and keep it off. My video would sell out the minute it went on the market, and the producer knew it." He stood, holding the towel strategically over what romance writers call his "manhood" with his right hand, and favored us with a boyish smile. "I want to find Margot's killer as much as you do, probably more, so let me know what I can do to help."

I thought it would be helpful if he'd drop the towel, but I kept that to myself. "Do you have a cell phone?" I asked. "So Detective Emerick can reach you more easily?"

Like Kim Kaylyn, Landers clearly disliked giving us the number, but he did so. Mace stuck out his right hand to shake, and Landers deftly transferred responsibility for his modesty to his left hand (*darn!*) and gave Mace a hearty, manly handshake.

"One more question," Mace said. I had to look at the floor to hide my grin. *Colombo, again.* "Do you have any thought of who had a motive to kill Margot Farr?"

Ted Landers started to speak, stopped, started to speak, stopped. He appeared to be tortured by indecision. "I hate like hell to say this, to cast aspersions on anyone, you understand, but I know Margot had a big fight with her agent, Charles St. John, right before I saw her on Tuesday. She was still steaming, furious. Margot believed Charles had been embezzling money from her. I'm not saying I believe that, but Margot thought it was true. And Esmé, Margot's daughter, is no angel, if you get my drift."

"No, I don't," Mace said. "Was there some trouble between Margot and her daughter?"

"There was nothing *but* trouble between them," Landers said with a laugh. "Ask Esmé. I don't know anything first hand, just how Margot groaned and moaned about Esmé treating her like last week's garbage. And how she suspected Esmé was sleeping with Charles St. John."

It seemed to me that for a man who hated like hell to cast aspersions on others, Landers was pretty free with the tar brush.

Mace thanked him again and followed me out. The masseuse was sitting in a pedicure chair, reading *People,* her feet straddling the plastic feet-soaking container. She watched us without expression, then rose, graceful as a dancer, and returned to the small massage room.

*****

"I don't like the way Margot's agent and her daughter and her husband have linked arms like best friends," Mace said en route to Charles St. John's house. We turned left at the main entrance to The Lakes, the upscale suburb of Las Vegas so named because a large bank and credit card company, the anchor of the community, didn't want "Las Vegas" in its address.

"They've had plenty of time to compare alibis, I'll give you that." I read off St. John's address and watched street signs. "There it is. Backs on that — body of water." It was like no lake I'd ever seen. It had an unnatural color, like Ty-D-Bowl. I read aloud a sign saying Absolutely No Swimming and added, "They've got that right!"

St. John's house was a combination — a bad combination — of art deco and California mission. The side toward the driveway was white stucco with red tiles. So far so good. But the two-thirds that faced the "lake" was a curved structure with glass bricks and silvery metal. There were two balconies that wrapped around, affording a magnificent view of a fountain in the lake that spewed the queer blue water up and back into itself. The upper balcony probably had a good view of the megawatts of Las Vegas after dark. I actually liked the two-thirds of the house done in art deco. But it should have been in La Jolla, looking out over the Pacific, not over an ersatz lake the color of a water treatment lagoon.

I recognized Margot's agent, Charles St. John, from the TV news. The bright Vegas sun reflected off the water and, in turn, off the mirrors along one wall of the living room and his mostly bald head, fringed by too little hair to comb. I know men who call that a receding hairline, but they lie about other attributes, too.

We said thanks to his invitation to come in out of the heat, and yes to his offer of lemonade. A Latina woman he called Rosa brought a pitcher and tall glasses, straight from the freezer so they'd frost. Red linen napkins were tucked under a plate of biscochitos. St. John thanked Rosa and poured five glasses of lemonade. "Excuse me, just a moment," he said. "Oh, here you are."

A woman about 35 or 40 years old came down the stairs. Esmé Mott bore a slight resemblance to Margot, mostly in the heart-shape of her face and her leonine eyes. She had a direct, almost confrontational appearance. Her slender figure showed to advantage in white crepe slacks and a matching V-neck sweater. Heels at least three inches high put her close to six feet, and a wide, beaded choker emphasized her long neck. There must have been a lot of her father in her.

She tossed her straight platinum hair back. I was sure the hair didn't come from her father any more than it came from her mother. Unless her father owned stock in Clairol.

Aronn Young came in from the deck wearing bikini swim trunks. He didn't have the body of Ted Landers, more the body a mother would look at and say, "Eat! For pity's sake!" Mace had said Aronn was 33, but he could pass for 23. He'd gotten his start in celebrity circles as a model for Calvin Klein underwear. He had a great tan, and dark, brooding eyes that went with his full, almost feminine lips. He had a two or three-day growth of beard and a really unattractive clot of hairs clinging to his chin that might be the starter for a Van Dyke or a Fu Manchu. His height put him roughly at Esmé's collar bone (with her heels on), but still a head above Charles St. John's shiny pate.

As Esmé did, Aronn looked me over and dismissed me as no one worth knowing. That's okay, I thought. I much prefer it this way.

"If we can all sit down," Mace said, "I'd like to ask you a few questions."

Charles made like a host and gave everyone a glass of lemonade and a coaster. Esmé and Aronn settled gracefully on a pale green divan. Esmé crossed her legs and dangled a backless shoe in the air. Aronn slung one arm over the back of the couch and propped one leg up on it, displaying his crotch.

"I'll just sit over here, Mr. St. John." I placed my glass, coaster and notepad on a game table behind Esmé and Aronn.

"Please, call me Charles." He turned his attention to Mace. "Now, what can we tell you? We are all just devastated and shocked at Margot's death."

They looked to me like they'd get over it, if they hadn't already.

"Where were each of you yesterday afternoon?" Mace asked.

"Aronn was in Los Angeles. . ." Charles began.

"I'll get to Mr. Young in a minute," Mace interrupted. "Where were you, Mr. St. John?"

"Please, call me Charles," he repeated. "I was here at my house with Kim Kaylyn from about 3:00 to 5:00 or 5:30. Maybe a little later. As soon as I heard about Margot, I got on the phone to Aronn. That was around 6:00, but I can't nail the time, sorry."

"Okay, thanks." Mace rested his right ankle on his left knee and brushed a little lint off his slacks. "Mr. Young, when did you go to Los Angeles?"

"Tuesday morning. I flew out around 10:00."

"How long did you plan to stay?"

"Well, I wasn't sure, you know? I had some business, and I didn't know how long it would take, you know? As it happened, I wrapped things up yesterday afternoon and sent Margot a fax saying I'd be back around 8:00 that evening." He sipped his lemonade, then stood abruptly and strode to the glass-front liquor cabinet. He poured in a shot of vodka, took a sip, and tossed in another shot. This time when he took a sip he looked satisfied.

"Do that for me," Esmé said, stretching her arm way back over the couch so Aronn could reach her glass.

Charles looked a trifle piqued, but turned back to Mace, an earnest look on his face. "Do you have any idea who shot Margot?"

"No, I wish I did."

Mace continued. "Do you know of anyone who was feuding with Ms. Farr? Somebody with a grudge, or a score to settle?"

"Margot was a sweet, trusting soul. Here's what I'm thinking, you might think about this. Margot could have befriended someone, an insane fan or something like that, and let him in her house. Him or her, a woman can be crazy, too." Charles shook his head in disbelief. "You know, she had a security system, but I swear, she never had it on. Am I right?" Aronn nodded.

"It was more complicated than she needed," Esmé volunteered. "She'd forget it was on, and she'd go out to the pool and set it off. She got so she hated it."

Mace caught my eye and I pantomimed picking up a phone and acting shocked. He gave a slight nod and leaned toward St. John. His voice was dripping with compassion. "How did you hear about her death, Charles?"

"Don't you know? The worst way! I called her house about 5:30, you know? Maybe 5:45. And a policeman answered. I told him who I was, Margot Farr's agent, her best friend, for God's sake! And he told me she was dead, and asked me to help them locate her husband." He pulled a handkerchief from his back pocket and wiped his eyes.

"Where were you?" Mace turned to Esmé. "Who told you about your mother's death?"

"I was shopping all afternoon, after a long social lunch. A policewoman called me on my cell phone about 5:15. My number was written next to Mother's phone, I guess. I didn't have the phone on just then, so it went to a message service. I didn't retrieve it until about 5:45. By then there was a frantic message from Charles, too. The first message was to call the police department, Officer – oh, I can't remember her name now." She let her shoes slide off her stockinged feet and tucked her legs under her, then continued.

"So I called and the officer met me outside Sinbad's. I was on my way in. Of course, I ran in immediately to tell Ted Landers. The police just barely told me before I would have heard it on the news."

A phone rang on the deck and Aronn got up lazily and walked toward it, no "Pardon me," or "I'll just be a moment." We waited silently; I noticed Charles and Esmé exchanged tight, humorless smiles.

Mace spoke in a friendly tone to Charles. "If you will excuse us for just a few moments, Charles, I need to ask Esmé a couple questions."

Charles St. John looked blank, then said, quickly, "Oh, of course, I understand. I'll be in the kitchen."

As soon as he was out of hearing, Mace moved to a chair close to Esmé. "Have you and Mr. Young settled on the funeral arrangements?"

"Excuse me?"

"Perhaps I was misinformed, but I heard you were not in complete agreement on the matter."

"Aronn and I are never in complete agreement, Detective, but we know when to compromise. My mother will have a closed casket funeral at Desert Palms Mortuary at 10:00 a.m. Saturday."

"Hmmm, good. Another question, if I may, Ms. Mott. Did your mother tell you she might divorce Aronn Young?" Mace sipped his lemonade.

"No, she didn't, but it wouldn't surprise me. *L'enfant terrible* was hardly ever around." The three of us noticed Aronn drag himself into the room, still focused on his phone conversation.

"Well," Esmé concluded with a curl to her lip, "here's my stepfather now. I think I'd like to change the subject." She drained her glass. "Will you excuse me?"

"Yes," Mace said, rising as she did. "Thank you for your time, Ms. Mott."

"Uh, for our records," I blurted, "what is your cell phone number?" She bent her head toward Mace as if he'd been the one to ask her, and he copied down what she said on his notepad.

Aronn seemed to be having trouble ending his conversation, which was full of chatter such as, "I was like, no way. And she was all, whatever. And I go, yeah, right." The kind of vernacular that makes English teachers drink Scotch whiskey.

Mace motioned to Aronn to get off the phone, pantomiming snapping it shut and pointing to his watch. Sullenly, he said, "I'll call you later," and set the tiny phone on the coffee table.

"A couple questions and I'll be out of here," Mace said. "I hate to intrude on your grief." He crossed his arms.

Aronn mirrored Mace's stance, legs apart, knees stiff, hands on his elbows. "All right. What?"

"Did you sign a prenuptial agreement before you and Margot Farr got married?"

"It was no big deal," he shrugged.

"What would you get if she divorced you?"

"She didn't divorce me. So I guess we'll never know."

"Did she threaten to divorce you?" Mace spread his legs a little further apart, as if he were digging in and preparing to lob hand grenades.

Aronn said nothing for a moment but held Mace's gaze without flinching. "No," he said at last, "she didn't."

"Then I have just one more question, for now, Mr. Young," Mace said, retrieving his glass from the coffee table and relaxing his stance. "What flights were you booked on to and from Los Angeles, and can you prove you were on them?"

Chapter 10

It was almost 8:00 p.m. when Mace dropped me back at the police station, after dinner and two cups of strong coffee at Denny's Restaurant on the Las Vegas Strip.

As soon as we had ordered our dinner, I called Candace and left a vague message about running into an old friend at Denny's and said I'd see her later. I put on lipstick and fresh mascara, then returned to the table.

Mace was drawing a grid on a sheet of paper he'd torn off my steno pad. At first I thought it was tic-tac-toe, but there were too many lines for that. I said nothing, not wanting to interrupt his train of thought. He doodled outside the grid, stars and triangles joined by arrows. Every once in a while he'd set down the pen and rub his earlobe.

His cell phone rang just as the waitress placed chicken fried steak in front of him and a chef's salad in front of me. "Detective Mace Emerick," he said, his attention still on the blank grid he'd drawn. "Yes, Mr. Champion." He sat up straighter and shoved the grid aside as he opened my steno pad to a clean sheet. "Thanks for calling me back. No, I can't go into it on the phone. Yes, I thought you'd understand, thanks. Tonight, if at all possible." He looked at his watch. "Good, 8:30, at your office. I'll see you then."

"Margot's lawyer?" I asked.

"You betcha. I want to know about the pre-nup and Margot's will. Can't ask the right questions if I don't already know the right answers."

The thought crossed my mind that maybe that

explained the screw-ups in my life. Maybe I never got the right answers because I didn't ask the right questions. Or was it that I asked them of the wrong people?

"I'll be back in a minute," Mace said, setting his phone on the table. "Tell her I could use some more coffee, will you?"

He walked stiffly toward the men's room, looking as tired as I felt. My "wrinkle-resistant" gray suit had surrendered unconditionally around 6:00 p.m. and now looked like I'd slept in it on a lumpy couch. I rested my elbows on the table and massaged my forehead with my fingertips.

While Mace was in the restroom, his phone rang. "Hello, uh, Detective Emerick stepped away for a few minutes, may I help you?" There was a long pause. "Hello? Would you care to leave a number?"

"This is Esmé Mott," she said. "He has my number."

"Yes, Ms. Mott, I remember he wrote down your cell phone number. I'll have him call you."

"Well, I'm out with some other people tonight. Uh, why don't I give you a message, and he can call me tomorrow."

"Sure, if you'd prefer that, I'll be glad to."

"I've been thinking about my mother's live-in maid, Carmen. I can't think of her last name just now. Anyway, my mother fired Carmen about three weeks ago, and the more I think about it, the more I wonder. Maybe she was so mad . . ." Her voice trailed off.

"Why did your mother fire her?" I asked.

"Because she was a thief for one thing, took my sapphire earrings and a ring! And she had taken pictures of Mother when she didn't know anyone was watching her. *Very* unflattering pictures! Mother was afraid she would sell them to a tabloid."

I wondered if firing her wouldn't *guarantee* her selling them to the highest bidder, but I said nothing.

"I don't know where Carmen went. I tore up the pictures and the negatives myself, so I know her scheme fell apart. I never trusted her. She pretended to understand about ten words of English, but she knew every word we said." I heard another voice in the background and could tell Esmé covered the receiver. Then she came back on the line. "I've got to go. I'll call Detective Emerick tomorrow."

I closed the phone and started eating my salad. I hadn't been hungry when I ordered, but suddenly my stomach woke up and shouted, "Yes! Yes!" My eyes locked on a table tent of a hot fudge sundae. I told my stomach, "No! No!"

As soon as Mace returned, I gave him Esmé's theory of the Raging Maid. He tossed it back in my lap, reminding me that finding Carmen Espiña was high on my "To Do" list.

Esmé's strange clue, lobbed to Mace like a badminton birdie in a headwind, intrigued me. I could readily believe that photos of plus-size Margot – looking just as I had seen her on her dining room chair – would be grabbed by tabloids and plastered all over. Who could forget the paparazzi shot of a bloated Liz Taylor settling into the back seat of a limousine? I wondered how one made contact with such "magazines," if they could be called that, and how deals were struck.

My vivid mental picture of Margot on the chair totally displaced my desire for a sundae.

". . .wants to see you," Mace said.

"I'm sorry." I was running down like a cheap watch. "Who wants to see me?"

"I told you. Hornet." I must have looked blank, because he added, "Chief Armstrong."

If I continued to look blank, it was an honest projection of my dismay. "Why? Why in the world does he want to see me?"

He shrugged. "I don't know. For your eyes only, I

guess."

"Where? When?" I asked automatically, still focusing on *Why?*

"Tomorrow night. He wants you to meet him at his slip at Callville Bay Marina. I'll draw you a map."

"How big is his sailboat?" He'd had a 25-foot racing sloop in San Diego. Mace and I were his crew. Not only were we good hands, but we could withstand Hornet's withering denunciations of our gross stupidity and clumsiness if we fell one percent off perfection. If he'd been as nasty on shore as he could be on board during a race, he'd never have made it through the police academy, let alone rise to chief of police. But Hornet was one of those people who vent like a geyser, quickly, and forget all about it. I once heard him describe Mace and me to another skipper, and I didn't recognize those paragons of seamanship as anyone I knew.

"He doesn't have a sailboat anymore," Mace said. "Probably couldn't find anyone else on earth crazy enough to crew for him. He sold the Shetland when he took the job in Vegas. But he missed being on the water, so he bought a 24-foot power boat to doodle around the lake."

"Aren't you coming with me?"

"I'm not invited." He finished his chicken fried steak and ate a few french fries with ketchup.

I thought about what he'd said. "Is Hornet still married?"

"Not *still* married. Married *again*. That's another reason he had to sell the Shetland. Betty was entitled to half the money." He signaled for the check.

As we walked to his car I took in the glitter and crowds around us. "What's the new Mrs. Armstrong like?" I asked, dreading the answer. I had thought Betty and Hornet were very happy. The words to a song crossed my mind: "Doesn't anybody ever stay together anymore?"

Mace said exactly what I expected to hear. "Younger,

firmer, tanner, with legs that start somewhere near the ground and go up to the second floor. Name is 'Vanitsa Noble.' Probably made up. Hey, with names in Vegas, it's 'don't ask, don't tell.' Her real name is probably Mildred Jones."

Something he said rang a bell in my tired brain, but slipped away to wherever clever thoughts hide. In this case, it probably slid behind the image of SueEllen Hoffman kissing Mace Emerick in the parking lot outside the San Diego County Sheriff's Department, squeezing his firm butt with her hand and giggling provocatively. A wave of nausea made me stop walking and pretend to enjoy the lights. *What was I doing walking around and riding around with Mace Emerick, a man who treated me so shamefully? Did I have no sense, or no pride?*

He dropped me at the police station at eight and I went in to get a couple more hours of Margot's tapes out of the way.

At 9:30 I had two breakthroughs in the case. One was on a tape Margot had recorded one month before her death. She was languidly describing the house she bought at Malibu and how much she loved the surf, when the ring of the phone interrupted her. As she habitually did, she set the small tape recorder down and forgot it. I kept transcribing every word.

"Hello? Yes, this is Margot, who's this? Oh, yes, I've been expecting you to call. God knows I'm paying you enough you could pick up a phone from time to time. . ." Her words were imperious, but her voice showed warmth toward the caller.

"So are you in Los Angeles again? What did you find?" A pause, then she continued.

"Damn! So their divorce was legal? Damn! I was so hoping the little shit was a bigamist. It would have saved me a lot of trouble." The tinkle of ice cubes and an unladylike slurp dragged on a full minute.

"Yes dear, yes dear," she said sarcastically. "You warned me not to marry him, and I wouldn't listen. I know, why do I hire a top drawer lawyer to advise me and then piss on his advice?" Her voice changed from strident to sad, almost defeated. "I'm sorry, Reid, dear. I know you're right. I'm just so damned angry with myself. I wish he'd do us all a favor and drop dead, but that's not bloody likely." She laughed a little bit. "He's probably wishing I'd do him the same favor. And he has company. Esmé and Charles would like to dance at my wake." Another pause, another slurp.

"Oh yes, they would." She sniffed loudly, said "hold on," and blew her nose.

"Reid? I'm tired. I want to go to sleep. I was having such a nice evening, dictating for my memoirs, about my house in Malibu. Remember, with the deck right over the beach?" She apparently listened for a while, softly saying, "Yes," and "Um-hmm" several times.

"I don't want a big protracted fight with Charles, Reid. Just get him the hell out of my life. He thinks being an agent gives him more power than God, and I'm sick of it! I just want him gone!

"You do whatever you have to do. Get a court order if you must. That bastard has drained me so dry there's not enough for Esmé and Aronn to have a catfight over." She yawned loudly. "Reid? Sorry, I can't keep my eyes open. Call me tomorrow? Well, as soon as you know something, okay? Please? Pretty please?" She laughed and kissed the air. "You too. Goodnight."

The tape ran five more minutes with no speaking, just the clink of a glass near the tape recorder and a hum that might have been Margot snoring softly. Then the tape ran out.

I took off the headphones, saved the transcription to a

disk, then sat in the silent cubicle, staring cross-eyed at the pattern in the acoustic tile. I decided to jot some notes and go home, or to as much a "home" as I had just then. *Maybe tomorrow I'll sign a lease for my own place.*

That's when the other breakthrough occurred, as I glanced over my notes on my steno pad. What was it Mace had said about the hokey name of Hornet's new wife? "With names in Vegas, it's don't ask, don't tell."

So who was Aronn Young, really? I wondered. And Kim Kaylyn? and Charles St. John?

Who, for that matter, was Margot Farr?

Chapter 11

When I snagged a Visitors Only parking space behind Candace's apartment, at 11:00 p.m., it was my intention to shower and fall in bed, but my plan was derailed for an hour.

Candace had just arrived home, accompanied by Kenneth. He was opening white plastic containers of food as Candace set plates and forks on the table beside them. "Olivia! You're just in time," Kenneth said as I entered. "You can eat like the rich without having to put up with them. Gourmet leftovers!"

"Our chef, Gaston, was magnificent tonight," Candace added as she took a third plate from the cabinet. "It was a buffet for the most expensive bar mitzvah I've ever seen. I only worry that he was *too* good. I heard some New Yorkers asking questions about him. I don't like that."

Letitia came out of her bedroom in black silk crepe pants and a gray cashmere sweater. She wore boots with a heel no more than two inches, but she was still as tall as Kenneth, six-three, maybe six-four. I'd spoken to Letitia on the phone, but as she had moved in after my last trip to Las Vegas, I introduced myself.

As if her height and figure were not enough to stop traffic on eight lanes of freeway, Letitia had perfect skin, as pale as a porcelain doll, and sleek, almost sculptured, black hair that cupped her face as it tucked in toward her neck.

"Do you have time for a snack?" Candace asked.

"Gaston's finest! Try the medallions of veal. Try the shrimp."

"Just a bite," Letitia's makeup and false eyelashes made her green eyes seem large and luminous. I watched her insert a small bite of veal into her mouth and slide it off the fork with her teeth, careful not to mar the perfect color and gloss of her lipstick. "Umm, my compliments to the chef. Thanks. But I've got to go. I'm meeting Liam at Caesar's."

She turned to me as she dropped her keys in a black Luis Vuitton bag. "I'm glad to meet you, at last."

"Yes, me too." When the door closed behind her, I turned to Kenneth. "How are you?"

"Just fine. I don't know day from night, but what's new, huh?" He stabbed some medallions of veal, placed them on his plate, and spooned some braised julienned peppers, green, red, yellow and purple, beside them.

"We don't know summer from winter anymore either," Candace added. "It's April, and we're booked solid for November, December and January." She took her plate to the couch and propped her feet on the coffee table. "My feet are throbbing! And to think we asked for this. No, we *begged* for this." She turned on the TV with the remote control.

The late news was already on. I recognized Philly Mitchell, being interviewed outside Margot Farr's house. The interview had been done in late afternoon sun, causing Philly to squint and shade her eyes.

"We've been talking to author Philly Mitchell," the reporter was saying. "We're in front of the home of famous actress Margot Farr, victim of a tragic murder yesterday afternoon. Thank you, Ms. Mitchell, for being with me today. This is Mindy Ransom reporting."

"Isn't that a shocker?" Kenneth sat at the dinette facing the TV. "Did Letitia say anything about it?" he asked

Candace. "Her boyfriend was very close to Margot Farr," he added for my benefit. "Liam Kiley, the photographer."

Candace yawned. "No. Well, the two minutes I just saw her was half the time I've seen her all week." She turned to me. "Mom, any luck on the job search?"

I was expecting the question. "I've got several interesting possibilities. I'm doing some temp work, transcription, mostly, while I look around."

"Hey, that gives me an idea," Kenneth said enthusiastically. "Would you be willing to lend a hand Saturday? We're catering Margot Farr's wake at her agent's house, and we're desperately over-committed and under-staffed."

"Kenneth's right. We took it on even though our schedule is full. Gaston will be cooking all morning and I need help serving and removing everything at Charles St. John's house. Can you do it?"

I was surprised that Candace liked the idea. "Saturday? What time?" My mind was racing with pros and cons. Mace might love the idea.

Candace quickly calculated, ticking off time on her fingers. "The funeral is at 10:00, and people will go to Charles St. John's house for a buffet lunch. I'd need you there from 11:00 until 3:00." I didn't answer right away, so she added, "It'll be more interesting than transcribing for doctors or whomever you're working temp for."

"I'll need an outfit," I said, wishing I could consult Mace about it.

"No problem. We've got your size. I'll pick it up tomorrow and have it here for you." Candace smiled and I couldn't say no.

I returned her smile. "Yes. I'll be glad to. Don't forget to give me directions to his house. What did you say his name is? Saint somebody?"

"St. John," Kenneth laughed. "Charles St. John. But

he's no more a saint than I am."

I smiled at his joke, but I was thinking Candace would not be amused if I announced I'd been to Charles St. John's house already. And that what I had been transcribing was Margot Farr's recital to her lawyer of St. John's sins. *No saint, indeed!*

*****

Friday morning I got an early start on items one, two and three on my To Do list. Thanks to Margot's records, I'd located the address and work number of Carmen Espiña's aunt, Eva Belize, and I'd gotten lucky. She worked the morning shift in housekeeping at the Las Vegas Hilton. She told me Carmen Espiña was staying with her sister in Los Angeles and had an application in for work as a hotel maid. She said Carmen's sister didn't have a phone, and she refused to give me any information on where Teresa Belize worked. I understood why, of course. Employers did not welcome calls from the police. I persuaded her to give me Teresa's mailing address, however, and I said I'd write to Carmen care of Teresa.

The airline Aronn Young had supposedly flown on Tuesday and Wednesday, April 10 and 11, had no record of him traveling. I left a message on his voice mail to call Officer Emerick at LVPD and gave my extension.

Number three on my list was to finish transcribing Margot's tapes, but I put that off while I compared what I already had with Margot's cryptic notes in her desk diary. Appointments and lunches with "CSJ" were most likely with Charles St. John, and "RC" could be Reid Champion, her attorney. Esmé she always spelled out, and "Ar" was probably Aronn. I was interested in the six entries since January first for "LK." I recalled what Kenneth had said the night before, about Letitia dating Margot's photographer, and I looked up Liam Kiley in the Yellow Pages.

There was no ad, just his name, an address on West

Sahara, and his number. I dialed. Of course I got voice mail. I hung up, unwilling to give the police number, and uneasy about giving my home number, which was also Letitia's.

"What's up?" Mace asked. He set a small paper bag and a cup with a plastic cover on my desk. "Double latté and a scone."

"Thanks. You go first. What did Reid Champion have to say last night?" I had hated to miss that meeting. I guess at heart I'm a control freak. I want to be everywhere, hear every conversation, log every clue. I've been told that this "control" trait showed up early – in first grade, when I got written up as "not willing to share with others."

"He was very helpful."

"Good, helpful is good. So what about Margot's will?" I took a bite of scone and the damn thing crumbled, dropping chunks on my chest and lap. I ended up picking crumbs off my clothes and eating them, looking, I am sure, like a baboon grooming herself.

"Margot's will, which will be entered for probate in a week or 10 days, leaves half her estate to Aronn Young – no surprise in a community property state – and half to Esmé. But they have no reason to celebrate, Champion says, because Margot was broke. Her big house had a major new mortgage on it. Her net worth was probably less than zero."

"No way, how can that be? I thought she had millions!" I gave up on the smallest crumbs and vigorously brushed myself off.

"Remember what Ted told us, that Charles St. John had been embezzling from Margot for years? Well, according to Reid Champion, that was true. Margot only discovered it about six weeks ago. Champion was preparing to bring criminal and civil charges against St. John. The lawsuit would have been for $5 million."

"How can anybody not know they're missing $5 million?" I was incredulous.

"You know the old saying, 'The rich are different.'"

I handed him a printout of my transcription of Margot's tape, the one I'd listened to the night before. While he read I finished my latté and took our two paper cups and lids to a wastebasket down the hall.

"What do you think?" I asked.

Before he had a chance to answer, my phone buzzed. "Olivia Wright," I said.

"Detective Emerick said for me to call," a man said. I recognized his voice as Aronn Young.

"Yes, is this Mr. Young?" Mace reached for the phone but I covered the receiver and said, "Let me take this."

"Yes, I'm Aronn Young. What does he want?"

"Uh, Mr. Young, Detective Emerick asked me to ask you again about your trip to Los Angeles on April 10. The airline you said you traveled on, American Airlines, can't find your reservations. Same for the return on April 11."

There was a long pause. "Oh, I just remembered, I used another name for the trip."

"You used another name?" I said aloud for Mace's benefit. "Didn't you have to show identification at the gate?"

"Oh, yeah, sure. But I have an ID in the other name. I just do it to avoid the press. You know."

It was my turn to pause. "What name did you travel under?" Mace nodded his approval of my question.

"I used a friend's name, with his permission. Liam Kiley."

My eyes widened in shock. "The photographer?"

"Sure, we're old friends. Look, I've got to go, I've got to meet somebody."

"Detective Emerick will be in touch later today," I said, and hung up. I took a deep breath and filled Mace in on the reason I'd called Aronn Young — the problem with the airline not listing him – and what he said about the fake ID. Then I added what I'd learned about Liam Kiley the night before, my guess about the "LK" entries in Margot's desk diary, and Kiley's address on West Sahara.

"Let's go," he said.

Chapter 12

The one-story green stucco and glass brick building on West Sahara looked like a lone holdout against the four- and five-story buildings all around it. Whoever owned that land was looking at a whole lot of capital gain, I'd wager. Above the glass brick front was a tasteful sign: Liam Kiley, Photography. A white Chrysler Sebring convertible, top down, was parked in front.

I was pretty sure I'd seen that car before. I was not surprised, therefore, when Kim Kaylyn flounced out the door of the green building, slid into her car, and slammed the door. Before she could back out, Mace and I were right beside her.

"What do you want?" she snarled.

Now, snarling is not a good way to greet any police officer, and in particular not a wise move when the officer is Mace Emerick. He leaned down to sniff her breath and made a face. "Step out of the car, please."

"I'm in a hurry, and you have no reason to order me out of my own car. I'm not stupid, you know." She turned the key in the ignition.

"My, my, my. Aren't we in a bad mood today?" Mace opened her car door and with a swift, practiced motion turned off the ignition and removed her keys. "If it's true, as you say, that you're not stupid, you'll get out of the car." She still didn't move. "Now!" he barked.

"Look," she said in a kinder, gentler voice as she slid out of the Sebring and stood beside it, "this is just a, uh —

misunderstanding."

Mace looked at me and shrugged, an exaggerated look of puzzlement on his face. "A misunderstanding, Ms. Kaylyn?" To me he added, "Was I not speaking clearly?" I shook my head, stifling a laugh.

He turned back to Kim and said, "What part of 'Step out of the car' did you not understand?"

"I want an attorney," she said, her chin lifted defiantly.

Mace burst out laughing. "She wants an attorney! That's great. Usually people wait until they're under arrest and I break out the rubber hose before they demand an attorney."

She glared at him, an imperious "We are not amused" look on her face. "Well, Detective? Am I under arrest or not? And what crime are you going to come up with?"

"While I think about that, let's see your driver's license and car registration," he said. All humor had evaporated from his voice, replaced by cold, businesslike menace. I halfway expected him to say, "Go ahead, make my day." His eyes said it for him.

She seemed to vacillate between confrontation and backing down. I was glad she chose the wiser path. Sliding back into the car, she opened her handbag. Holding it suspiciously close to her body, she darted a hand into the bag, fumbled around inside, and came out with a small wallet. While holding it open to display her driver's license, she kept her purse clutched tight.

Mace took the wallet in his hand and examined the license closely. "This says you need glasses to drive."

"I was about to put them on when you practically assaulted me, Detective. They're in my purse." She was so annoyed she opened the purse wide to get out her glasses. Wider than she intended.

"Whoa, hold it right there," I said, looking over her shoulder. "Do you have a concealed weapons permit for that?"

She snapped the latch on her purse – fast, but not fast enough. Mace had his hand in and out of her car faster than a rattlesnake's tongue. He opened the purse and made a "Tsk, tsk" sound.

All the fight went out of Kim Kaylyn. "Okay, no, I don't have a concealed weapons permit. Big deal! Usually I keep my gun at home, where I could get to it if an intruder broke in. There's no law against that. But my dear friend was murdered two days ago, and nobody knows who did it. I want some protection with me!"

Mace said nothing, just looked into the purse, took a handkerchief from his pocket, and gently lifted out the gun. Handing me the purse, he rolled the cylinder open and removed the bullets. He dropped the bullets in a plastic bag and slipped the gun into a larger bag, wrote a few words on both bags, and locked them inside the glove compartment of his car. Then he said I could return the purse to Ms. Kaylyn.

"I apologize, ma'am, for thinking I smelled alcohol on your breath. I know now it's just some godawful perfume. Same stuff Margot Farr's house reeks of." He handed her the car keys he'd dropped in his pocket earlier. "You're free to go, Ms. Kaylyn. I'll be in touch."

With shaking hands, she started the ignition. Opening her purse again, she took out her sunglasses, and adjusted her rearview mirror. Without a word, and without looking at either of us, she backed out onto Sahara Avenue and headed east. Smiling and shaking his head, Mace turned away and locked the door of his car.

"Vegas is a big city," I said with a chuckle, "but the way you run into people you know, it's still like a small town."

"Let's go make a *new* friend," he said as he held the door of the green building open for me.

"At the rate I'm making friends in Vegas, I'll be looking

to move somewhere else in about a month."

A bell rang softly as we entered the reception area of Liam Kiley, Photographer. "I'll be there in a minute," a deep voice called from down the hall.

We perused the gallery of beautiful people on his walls, each framed photograph lit by tiny but powerful lights mounted against the ceiling, each light angled just right to pick up the color in the skin, eyes and faces of his subjects. The most stunning was a matte photo of Letitia Farrell, looking into the camera lens across an enormous bouquet of scarlet roses, the exact color of her high-gloss lipstick.

"Hello, I'm Liam Kiley." His voice had a very slight lilt, as if he were Irish or a damn good actor. His thick, black shoulder-length hair, a jumble of unruly curls that wouldn't hold a part, shone in the light of the mini-gallery. With skin-tight black jeans he wore a black silk shirt with sleeves rolled up above his elbows, and open all the way to his navel. His chest was buff, hairless and tan. I dragged my eyes from his thighs to his chest to his face, glad his gray eyes were focused on Mace's badge and handshake instead of my flushed cheeks.

He'd probably think I was having a hot flash.

He'd probably be right.

I noted his height in his high-heeled leather boots and guessed he'd be eye to eye with the statuesque Letitia. He had the same dancer's grace she had. I halfway expected Liam Kiley to suddenly place his hands on his hips and break into faster-than-the-eye-can-see Irish tap.

"And you are?" he said, holding his hand out to me.

"Olivia Wright, glad to meet you." He shook my hand and held it a moment longer than necessary.

"You have wonderful cheekbones," he said. Try as I might, I couldn't recall ever hearing that from a man before. I smiled stupidly and murmured my thanks.

"What can I do for you, Detective Emerick? Would you

both like some coffee?" He gestured toward the Mr. Coffee on a built-in cabinet. In front of the cabinet sat an elegant reception desk with an ivory French telephone.

"Yes, thanks," Mace said. "Black for me. Cream, no sugar for Olivia."

Liam poured coffee in three pedestal mugs and added half-and-half from the small refrigerator beneath the coffee pot. "Would you like to come into my office?"

We said yes in unison and followed him down the hall. His office was a room about 30 feet by 30 feet, with eight computers, an enormous light table, and slanted drafting tables. Metal file cabinets lined one wall and custom wood cabinets lined a second wall. The third wall was just four feet high, then large panes of tinted glass reached another six feet and joined panes the same size angled in about 20 degrees to where they joined the ceiling. The expansive view, however, was of nothing but a concrete patio, a tall cinder block wall, and a lone cottonwood tree. Liam pulled two comfortable chairs up to a massive desk topped by a computer with possibly the largest monitor I'd ever seen. Close beside it and joined by cables was a smaller monitor. Liam brought his chair out to the side of the desk so he'd be closer to us. Before he could sit down, though, the entry bell sounded again.

He looked at his watch. "I'm expecting a client. Please wait here. I won't be a minute."

Mace used the opportunity to phone the medical examiner. "Dr. Rodgers? Detective Emerick. Have you finished the autopsy on Margot Farr yet?" The doctor had expected to do it the day before but had been delayed.

Mace looked at me and nodded. "Good. Can I come talk to you in, say, one hour? Fine, good. I'll see you then." He disconnected, then made another call.

"Yes, thank you," he said. "Who is this? Sergeant, this is Detective Mace Emerick. Is Capt. Wacker available? Oh,

I see. Well, here's the deal. I'm supposed to brief him at 1:00, but I'll be with the medical examiner then. Please tell him when he comes back that I'll call to reschedule." He thanked the sergeant again and gave his cell phone number.

"I need to tell you . . ." I began, but Liam Kiley came back into the room. I still hadn't had a chance to tell Mace I would be working at Charles St. John's house after Margot's funeral.

"Now, what can I do for you?" Kiley said. A few reckless curls threw themselves over his forehead and he shoved them back with his fingers.

"I am investigating the murder of Margot Farr, and I heard you did some photography work for her. Is that correct?"

Kiley propped one boot on the other knee and sat back. "I thought that might be why you were here. Yes, Margot had been my client for years. Six years – ever since I moved to Las Vegas from Los Angeles. I think I can safely say I'm the only photographer she has worked with the past year and a half."

"Did you do the *Redbook* cover shoot?" I asked.

"Well . . .not exactly."

"Please explain," Mace said, his eyebrows knitted in confusion. I was equally puzzled.

"Margot made up excuses to postpone and cancel every shoot the magazine scheduled. They wanted to send their own photographer, which is pretty standard. But she stalled, until they were up against the wall on time. Then she had me send them the photo, the one they used."

"So you *did* do the photo shoot after all?" I asked.

"Uh, no. I used a photo I'd taken of Margot a year ago, one that hadn't been published anywhere." He rubbed a smudge off his boot with his thumb.

"Let me guess," I said. "A picture taken when she was

slender."

Kiley put his foot back on the floor and leaned forward, resting his forearms on his thighs and clasping his hands together. "I'd rather that didn't get into print. It would be bad for her memory, and frankly, it could be bad for my business. I have a lot of clients who rely on my discretion."

"On your discretion to do what?" Mace asked.

"To – improve on nature just a little. Thanks to these computers, I can work miracles." He stood and swiveled the large monitor a quarter turn toward us and placed his chair at the keyboard. Mace scooted his chair closer to the desk and I stood beside him where I had a good look at the screen.

Kiley typed a few keystrokes and the screen saver of enormous red lips blowing kisses disappeared and a plain blue background showed up. He moved his fingers to a second keyboard and a menu appeared on the smaller monitor. He typed rapidly and various windows opened and closed.

"Here," he said, as the image of the beautiful, sultry Margot Farr appeared just as it had on *Redbook*. The resemblance was only slight between the glamorous star on the computer screen and the woman I'd met in the flesh some 48 hours before. The woman I had seen could pass as this woman's much older sister.

"And you say this photo of Margot was taken only a year ago?" I said incredulously.

"The photo, yes, an image on film," Kiley said. "First, I use a soft, forgiving lens, I backlight her hair. No, let me go back a step. First Margot got her makeup done by a theatrical expert. Then I did the best I could do with photographic equipment. And then I did a little, uh, painless plastic surgery. Hey, if I can print a picture of a person cheek to cheek with a polar bear, so real you'd swear on anything she was really with a bear, how much easier is it to erase a few crow's feet?"

Mace and I wanted to see more of this wonder, but Liam Kiley abruptly shut down his computer. "If there is anything I can do to help find Margot's killer, I want to. But I have a client cooling her rich heels in the photo studio and I need to get to that right away." He lifted a business card from a holder on his desk. "Feel free to call me. Preferably not tomorrow as I have a funeral to attend."

Mace examined the card. "Sure, thanks for your time, Mr. Kiley. I will call you."

"There is something we need to know right now, though," I added.

A look of annoyance crossed his features, but Kiley stopped walking toward the door and looked at me. "Yes?"

"Does Aronn Young use your name, and identification, sometimes?"

"Yes, he prefers to travel under another name occasionally. As a favor, I let him get a driver's license in my name with his picture. We're about the same age, roughly, and only about five inches difference in height. Police never look at that," he smiled, then realized his *faux pas*.

I pursued the subject a little further. "Do you know if Aronn Young used that identification to fly to and from Los Angeles Tuesday and Wednesday of this week?"

He continued toward the door without breaking his stride. "I haven't seen Aronn in several days. I don't know anything about a trip to Los Angeles. Sorry. Now, please excuse me. You know the way out."

He turned left at the hall, entered a room just down the way and gushed, "Please forgive me," as he closed the door behind him.

Mace followed me back to his car. He unlocked and opened the passenger door and I rolled down the window to let some of the heat escape. He got in, started the engine, and turned the air conditioner on high. After a couple minutes the temperature dropped below "excruciating" to just "hideous." I rolled up my window and we backed out onto Sahara Avenue.

"Let's go see the medical examiner," he said. "And then, for dessert, we can go see Capt. Asswacker."

As we pulled away I noticed a car parked in the scarce shade beside the green building. It was a silver BMW.

Chapter 13

At sundown I tucked Mace's hand-drawn map under my right leg and put the top down on my Cabriolet. I'd returned to Candace's apartment long enough to eat some cottage cheese and tomatoes, take a shower, and change into white cotton slacks and tennis shoes. A long-sleeved V-neck sweater was all I might need for the early evening, but I brought a matching red windbreaker for later.

I hadn't seen Hornet Armstrong for eleven years, as long as it had been since I'd seen Mace. I still couldn't believe Hornet and Betty were divorced. Mace didn't know where she lived or anything else about her. What did he say the new wife's name was? Vanitsa Noble. *With legs that started at the ground and went all the way to the second story.* I hoped I never had to meet the new Mrs. Armstrong. Hornet's name had plunged a few places in my list of "men I admire."

I fought crazy traffic east on Flamingo Boulevard. As I passed over I-15 I had a strong urge to turn onto it, to just turn south and keep driving, south, then west into California. I didn't much care where in California. Just away from Mace and the mess I had walked into in Vegas. Although the garish lights of Las Vegas burned in every direction, I thought of Robert Frost and two roads diverging in a yellow wood. At every junction in my life, it seemed, I'd taken the road marked "Unknown," my good sense left like roadkill as my curiosity sped recklessly on. And once again, here I was, following a map to a mysterious meeting with

Chief Hornet Armstrong.

I detoured through a McDonald's and got a Coke, took the ramp to I-515, south, and accelerated to 75 miles per hour. To my right, I saw that the sun had dropped below the horizon, its rays still illuminating swirls of clouds to create a beautiful desert sunset. Sparkling like rhinestones against the pink sky, a steady line of planes lined up on an aerial highway, each one bringing more people to Las Vegas. "A nice place to visit," they were known to say, "but I wouldn't want to live there." *Me neither.*

It had been a hell of a day. After Mace and I left Liam Kiley's studio, we spent an hour with Dr. Gale Rodgers, the county's assistant chief medical examiner. There were no surprises. Margot had been shot twice by a .38 caliber pistol. One bullet entered her abdomen, went through her stomach and one kidney, and exited low in her back. The other, which killed her in a few minutes, lodged in her brain. The drug screen would not be back for a week at the earliest, and it might take as long as a month. There was no alcohol in her system at the time of her death.

She had been a relatively healthy woman, age 61. Her height – or more accurately, the length of her body – was 66 inches. Five-feet-six. My height.

Margot's last occasion to visit a scale was noted with none of the euphemisms we like to use. Margot Farr was no longer "big-boned, thick-waisted, a little heavy-set," nor was she "voluptuous, fleshy, chubby, plump." In black letters on white paper she was not said to be "puffy, full-figured, plus-size," or "a beautiful woman who'd put on a few pounds." Medical fact was as icy-veined as a dead body on a metal scale. Margot Farr weighed 179 pounds at the time of her death, about 50 pounds more than I weighed, and about 50 pounds more than she wanted anyone to know. The *Redbook* article said she was a size eight.

When we returned to police headquarters, Mace took Kim Kaylyn's revolver and bullets to the evidence room for safekeeping. "Probably no connection to Margot's death, but we'll keep it for a few days at least."

We agreed that he'd go see Capt. Wacker without me, so I gave him printouts of all the transcription I had completed on Margot's tapes. Then I spent two tiring hours in a cubicle finishing the last ones.

Mace was gone when I emerged, rubbing my forehead and looking for aspirin. A sealed envelope with my name was propped against my coffee mug on my desk. Inside was a note from Mace, a map to Callville Bay Marina, and a key to the gate on the dock.

"Two docks. Go to the one on the right; key needed halfway out. He'll be there from sundown on – boat is Vega Star, tied up at slip #123. See you at the mortuary, 0900 tomorrow."

I left I-515 in Henderson and headed east on Highway 146, away from the lights of so-called civilization. About 15 minutes later I stared open-mouthed like a Beverly Hillbilly at the lavish, extravagant new development to my left. A sign surrounded by dozens and dozens of palm trees told me I was overlooking Lake Las Vegas Resort. I'd heard from Mace that the resort's lake was formed by pumping Lake Mead water to the highest elevation of the resort, letting it water all the emerald golf courses and flow into Lake Las Vegas. Having served humanity, the water passed by the earthen dam at a carefully controlled rate, and continued in a picturesque stream toward Lake Mead. Kind of made me proud to be a taxpayer. Too bad I wasn't rich enough to own a little piece of paradise. Hell, I wasn't even rich enough to rent it for an hour.

I paid five dollars for a seven-day pass to the National Recreation Area at one of its entrances and turned left on Northshore Scenic Drive. As I drove toward the Callville

Bay turnoff I recalled with a smile how Mace had reacted to my upcoming job with Royale Catering. On the way from Liam Kiley's to the morgue, I told him I had agreed to help with the after-funeral luncheon at Charles St. John's house.

"Absolutely not!" was his reaction. His overreaction.

"It'll be . . ."

He didn't let me get a word in edgewise. "Do you want to blow this investigation apart? How much are people going to open up to me when they notice my 'assistant' serving canapés at a very private party?"

"They won't notice," I insisted.

"They've all seen you already! What makes you think they won't recognize you?" He was shouting even though we were both in the car with the windows closed.

I tried twice to answer but he went on ranting about what a dumb idea it was. Finally he wound down. "May I say something? Without interruption?" I asked quietly.

He glared at me but didn't say anything further. "They won't recognize me for two reasons. One, I'll be in the standard black pants and white blouse of a catering employee. People look right through "servants." And two, I am a 50-year-old brunette of average height and weight. I am as close to invisible in our society as a woman gets. The only one of the people we've interviewed who gave me more than a cursory glance was Liam Kiley. I'll stay away from him. And I'll be in an excellent position to see how all these purported friends and relatives of Margot Farr behave when they're all in the same room. Even if you attend, you won't see them act natural. Whereas, I can be the fly on the wall."

"Fly in the ointment is more like it," he snapped, but I could tell he was considering the idea.

By the time we got to the morgue I'd brought him around to my way of thinking. In fact, he'd gone me one better by saying I should help seat people at the funeral, as an employee of the mortuary.

"Tomorrow will be a bitch," I muttered aloud as I spotted the turnoff to Callville Bay Marina. When I made the sharp turn to the southeast, I saw the water shimmer in the fading sunlight. The part I could see from the top of the hill was only one small part of the massive lake. The marinas and public boat launches ahead of me, in Boulder Basin, were among the closest access points to the lake from Las Vegas. Across the basin I could see the yellow-orange lights atop Hoover Dam. A conga line of traffic wound down the canyon walls in Nevada to the narrow top of the dam, crossed the state line to Arizona halfway across, then climbed once again to the desert plateau. Five minutes later, I knew from experience, the landscape of Arizona would be so desolate that a driver could easily believe the lake had been just a grand mirage.

I parked at the marina on the north shore of Boulder Basin and used the restroom in a building that housed the harbor master's office, a snack bar, and a cocktail lounge. I followed the path to the dock on my right and strolled out to the metal mesh gate. As expected, the key Mace left for me gave me access to this yachtsmen's holy of holies. Finding the Vega Star was easier than I anticipated. "Hello!" I called from the dock.

"Hold on," came the answer, a man's voice from the cabin. I looked the Vega Star over from stem to stern. She was a gleaming beauty of a boat, paint so fresh I wondered if it might still be wet, and hardwood decking and trim varnished to a mirror finish.

"Olivia!" Hornet called. "Come aboard." He held out a hand to steady me as I straddled the water en route. He looked me over and I wondered if I looked a lot older to him. Well, if so, there was nothing I could do about it. "You look great!" he said.

What else could he say? I thought. Still, it was nice to

hear.

Hornet Armstrong was the same age as Mace, fifty-five, and although he'd put on some weight, especially at the waistline, he looked as handsome and virile as he had at forty-four. *What is it with men? Damn! Life is unfair, and you can quote me on that!* "Whatever elixir you've been drinking," I said with a laugh, "it's working. You look great, too."

Whatever elixir, indeed! Hornet was drinking from the same fountain Mace was, the one marked Younger Women Only.

"If you think I look good now," he said with a chuckle, "wait until I retire. When I get this stress off my back, I'll look years younger. Everybody tells me that." He opened an ice chest. "You want a beer? Wine? Soda?"

"Have you got a 7-Up? Or a club soda?"

"Both. You still like your club soda with a twist of lime?"

I nodded, amazed that he remembered such a small detail about me from our sailing days. All I ever drank then was soda or wine coolers.

"Come on, get comfortable." He patted the vinyl cushions on the bench. He poured my drink, handed it to me, and twisted the top off a Heineken. He took a swallow, then placed a wedge of cheese and a small loaf of French bread on a cutting board. He stabbed the cheese with a serrated knife and set it down next to me. "Help yourself."

We munched and made small talk, how was Candace, how long had he had the Vega Star, did I have an apartment yet. Two subjects floated like storm clouds just over us: his trophy wife, and the reason he wanted to talk to me. Both subjects made me edgy and uncomfortable. Gradually our small talk got smaller. I concentrated on slicing bread and cheese as if each were an extremely complicated task.

"I guess Mace told you Betty and I are divorced," he

said after a long gap in our conversation.

I felt like pointing out his choice of words. "Betty and I are divorced." Passive voice. As if a natural, unavoidable event had simply happened to them, like one might say, Betty and I are ill, or Betty and I are older. I thought I might respect him more if he came right out and said, "I divorced Betty. I hired a lawyer, served her with papers, insisted she sign them, and it was over. I did it. Me!"

No, I wouldn't respect him more. And I *shouldn't* respect him less. Who knows what goes on inside a marriage? I of all people should value each person's right to seek fulfillment. How was it the Declaration of Independence put it? Our *inalienable* right to the pursuit of happiness?

I had a rare moment of clarity and saw that my attitude toward Hornet vs. Betty was about 90 percent transference of my old anger at Mace. I hadn't felt half the pain in my divorces that I did when Mace married SueEllen. I said nothing, just nodded to show that, yes, Mace told me about the divorce.

"I planned to stay single, really. But I met a terrific woman, Vanitsa, and . . .we got married."

"Are you happy?" I asked coldly. My rudeness surprised me as much as it surprised him. The question hung in the air.

"Yes. I am. We are."

"I'm sorry. I shouldn't have asked that. I really hope you're happy, and I'm glad you are. And it's none of my business."

The silence dragged on. I'd really put my foot in a can of worms, as Mace liked to say.

"Apology accepted. I'm just so used to people kissing up to me I don't know what to say when anyone speaks her mind. You want some more soda?" I hesitated. "I'm going to have another beer. And then I'll tell you why I dragged you clear out here."

While he poured my drink I put my windbreaker on. A breeze was freshening across the lake. He offered me a cigarette, said he was trying to quit, and lit one. When he sat down, I noticed again that he had a little paunch and what people always call "love handles" on a man, and "fat" on a woman. His hair was going gray, but it looked distinguished, even sexy. Richard Gere was gray. Harrison Ford was gray. I could go on and on. *Ad nauseum.*

"I'm down to half a pack a day," he said. "Doctor's orders."

"The doctor ordered you to smoke half a pack of cigarettes a day?" I grinned.

"No. If you must know, the doctor ordered me to quit. So I'm meeting him half way. I know how doctors are. If I manage to quit completely, I'll gain another 30 pounds, and he'll say, 'Fine, now quit eating.'"

"In the immortal words of Gilda Radner," I laughed, "it's always something!"

"Look." He pointed toward the east, where the moon, past full but still more than a quarter, rose over the craggy rocks that formed the bowl of Lake Mead. It seemed to peek over the rocks, creep slowly skyward, then suddenly it popped all the way up, above the horizon. A shimmering white line extended on the lake surface from the beam of the Vega Star as far as I could see, a straight line to the moon.

"It would be a great night for a sail." The steady breeze would just fill a sail, easy enough for a beginner to sail a boat single-handed. I recited a line from a poem I've always liked. "'And all I want is a tall ship, and a star to steer her by.'"

A 30-foot Bayliner I'd admired on my way to Hornet's slip backed up and aimed for the open lake. The driver hit full power before clearing the marina and sent a wake that rocked us hard. "Asshole!" Hornet muttered.

"I'm waiting to hear why you invited me out here," I said as the Vega Star settled down.

"Okay." He seemed to struggle with what he wanted to say. "Okay. I have an ulterior motive for getting you into the Margot Farr investigation."

"And that would be?"

"I don't trust Capt. Wacker. Something is going on, and it stinks, but I don't have any proof. I think you can look around without drawing any attention to yourself. That's what you're really great at. You and Mace are the only people currently in the department that I trust absolutely."

"And Mace is too high profile," I added. Capt. Wacker sensed, correctly, it now seemed, that Hornet Armstrong was his enemy. He'd be extra cautious concerning Mace Emerick, Hornet's fair-haired boy. He didn't like having me hanging around, either, but as a threat I probably ranked somewhere beneath the newest rookie on the roster. "Just what is it you think the captain has been up to?"

"I think he took over the former chief's lucrative recycling program. And I don't mean putting aluminum in separate trash cans."

"Hmm . . . what do you mean?" Although I studiously kept any sign of annoyance out of my voice, I was getting weary. It had been a hideously tiring day already, the next day promised to be worse, and I had a long drive back to Las Vegas.

"Okay. The previous chief was allowed to resign rather than face criminal charges. He had been removing drugs from the evidence room – with help from someone inside – and selling it back to dealers."

And I'll bet he neglected to pay income tax on the profits, too, I couldn't help thinking. Sadly, I realized corruption in politics and bureaucracies failed to surprise me anymore. "Why on earth did they let him just resign?"

"The usual reason. Political fallout." He lit another

cigarette and took a long drag, holding the smoke in his lungs, then finally exhaling through his nose. "At least four powerful politicians had invested their capital in hiring him and building him up as a paragon of law enforcement. It was expedient to avoid the scandal, and he agreed to go quietly."

I thought about that. "So now you think Wacker picked up the reins, as it were?"

"Yes, I do. I just need to know who in the evidence room is participating. Then I swear I'll bust Wacker's ass clear out of Nevada. I was hired to pour oil on the water, but this cop doesn't DO oil on water."

"What, exactly, do you want me to do?"

"You're great with computers, Olivia. You've always been able to track money and find people who don't want to be found. Remember all you did on the Lasker case in San Diego? I know Mace got most of the credit. . ."

"ALL of the credit," I interrupted.

"Your point is well taken." He stubbed out the cigarette in a beanbag ashtray. "But that was then, this is now. I want you to conduct a private investigation of the people in the evidence room, as well as Wacker's financial dealings. I think that's where we'll pick up the trail."

I said nothing, just studied the moonlight on the water.

"I managed to lay my hands on some details of how the chief sold the cocaine. Internal Affairs did a pretty good job of documenting that. I can give you everything I have so far." He lit a third cigarette.

For some reason – maybe seeing Hornet ignore his "doctor's orders" and continue to pollute his lungs – I thought of unctuous Dr. Bostwick in Las Cruces. Was it less than three weeks ago he'd cancelled my cancer diagnosis? And I'd reacted by deciding to have more adventure in my life? Now here I was, working on a murder investigation and being asked to add an undercover police corruption investigation to my To Do list. How much more adventure did I want, anyway?

"I'm willing to look at what you have, and I'll do some computer searches, poke around and see what moves. But I can't guarantee anything."

"I know, I understand. I feel better already, though, knowing you'll give it a try. You should have been born a bloodhound, with your instincts, Olivia."

"Some men really know how to give a compliment. You, unfortunately, are not one of them."

"Sorry. Well, you know what I mean. I'll be right back." He put out that cigarette and went below. In less than a minute, he climbed back on deck with a legal length brown envelope. From the thickness, I guessed I'd just added hours of unpaid labor to my full schedule. *Oh well, there are those hours between midnight and six a.m. Hours that I'm just wasting in bed.*

In bed alone, I added ruefully.

I drove back to the city with my top up, my windows down, and my old cassette player on loud. I joined the Beach Boys for "California Girls," "I Get Around" and "Little Deuce Coop." I turned the volume all the way up, the tape volume and my own, for the last song on the tape.

"And she'll have fun, fun, fun 'til her Daddy takes her T-Bird away-ay-ay." *Ah, they just don't write songs like that anymore.* I laughed aloud at an image of myself doing the same thing at age 80. *Geezer boombox music. Yeah!*

Candace was asleep in bed when I returned from Lake Mead at 11:00. I folded out the sofabed quietly and tiptoed into her room to get a pillow. After I hung my clothes in the bathroom, I put on an extra-large T-shirt as a nightgown and poured myself a generous glass of wine. I propped myself up against an upended couch pillow plus my sleeping pillow and tugged the blanket up to my waist, then opened the envelope the chief of police had given me.

My intention to give the paperwork 15 minutes was quickly forgotten. It was after 1:00 when I turned off the lamp, and after 2:00 when I turned off my racing brain.

What have I gotten myself into this time?

Chapter 14

Saturday morning I left the apartment wearing a khaki skirt and cotton knit sweater, having told Candace I had to do some transcription before meeting her at Charles St. John's house. I placed my pressed black slacks, white dress shirt, black bow tie, and comfortable black pumps on the back seat of my car.

"Remember," she said as I left, "take a left into The Lakes, then the first right. Grab the first parking spot you see. You'll have to walk a ways."

"Got it," I called. "See you at 11:30."

I had arranged late Friday afternoon to pick up a sedate black suit and white blouse from a store the assistant funeral director recommended, and I already had that uniform stashed in my car, unseen by Candace.

I parked in one of the Employees Only spots behind the Desert Palms Mortuary and entered at the back of the building. A tall, pale young man directed me to the funeral director's office and announced me at her open door.

"Rochelle Goodman," she said, meeting me halfway across the room with her hand outstretched. "Please, come in." Gesturing for me to sit in a red leather armchair in front of her desk, she sat in one exactly like it, also in front of her desk, putting us almost knee to knee. Her slate gray suit was unquestionably a designer label. It had a rolled stand-up collar that blended into wide lapels. One large pewter button pulled the jacket to her slim midriff. Under the jacket she wore a gray silk shell. Her wide blue eyes and warm smile balanced the severity of her silver hair pulled back in a tight bun. She had skin like an airbrushed peach. "Detective Emerick came to see me yesterday," she began. "I was opposed to the idea of having you help out at Ms. Farr's funeral, partly because dealing with the bereaved is an extremely delicate profession." She paused. "Also, I firmly believe a funeral home owes it to the client to put privacy and confidentiality first." I wondered if by "client" she was referring to "the deceased" or "the bereaved."

She sighed and continued. "Everything to do with Ms. Farr's funeral arrangements has been difficult, particularly trying to balance the wishes of her husband and her daughter. And even more stressful has been the incredible pressure from the media for details. Did Detective Emerick tell you a photographer tried to break in here yesterday, right after we transferred the remains from the hospital?"

"No, I haven't talked to him since about 3:00 yesterday afternoon. We've been working on different aspects of the investigation, trying to cover ground as quickly as we can."

"Well, that's what happened. We blocked the photographer's access and called the police, but he got away before they arrived. I did, however, get his license number. That was what made me say yes to Detective Emerick, I mean about having you here undercover. We have double the usual staff here this morning, and uniformed police officers will be here any minute, but I can use your help, too."

"The police are already out front. They've set up barricades to keep fans back away from the entrance." I didn't add what she surely knew, that a scaffold had been set up in prime space across the street, a platform for TV crews.

Her phone interrupted us and she stretched gracefully to press one of the dozen buttons on the console. "Excuse me, please. Yes?"

"A Detective Emerick is in the lobby, Ms. Goodman."

"Please direct him to my office, Jillian."

A few moments later Mace stopped in the open doorway, gave me a little wave, and crossed to Rochelle, addressing her as Ms. Goodman and commenting on her style and figure with his appreciative glance. "The crowd is increasing, as you'd expect. The next best thing to the Academy Awards is a celebrity funeral."

"I took a quick look at the paper this morning," I said. "Looks like the cream of Hollywood society is coming." Or, as Mace hooted the day before, "the cream of the crap."

"Ms. Goodman, did you say you have a seating chart for some of these people?" he asked. "I don't envy you that job."

"It's awkward, I'll grant you that. Not only do we have to remember who is the bigger star, but we have to seat current wives far from former wives."

I could see her problem. No funeral director wants the body count to increase during a funeral. I excused myself to go change into my suit. On the way I passed a door marked Chapel in brass letters, its ivory double doors closed and guarded by the tall young man I'd seen earlier and by a burly fellow who looked like a nightclub bouncer in a black suit too small for his bulk.

I slipped the blouse and skirt on quickly, brushed my hair vigorously, forced it to part in the middle, and twisted it into a chignon. Sliding my arms into the black wool-blend jacket, I checked myself in the full-length mirror. I looked like librarians used to look. I would hardly notice me, and I knew me.

Mace was gone by the time I returned to Ms. Goodman's office. She had freshened her lipstick and was examining papers on a clipboard. "I'm about to sound General Quarters," she said. "I want you stand with Walter in the vestibule and seat people on the right side of the chapel, the right side as you look toward the casket. Walter will tell you and three other assistants where to seat them. I'll be out front with another assistant to escort the family and closest friends, like Charles St. John, down the hall to wait in my office."

The tall man came in just then. Ms. Goodman introduced him to me as Walter and gave him the clipboard with hurried instructions. She looked at her watch and added, "I'd better go out front. Open the outside doors to the chapel in ten minutes, please."

Walter and I walked behind her through the interior entrance to the chapel. An ornate lilac-colored casket had been placed on a marble dais, surrounded – almost buried, in fact – by flowers. Lilies, daisies, roses, mums, and more. The sprays were set in huge white wicker holders, staggered by height. A blanket of red, pink and white roses was draped over the casket. The muscular guard, who kept stretching his thick neck as if the shirt was cutting off his air supply, stood on the main floor at the front of the dais. His position – feet wide apart, massive hands clasped in front of his groin – made it clear no one was to approach the casket.

There was never any question this was to be a closed casket funeral. Someone in the press speculated that Margot's body could not be made presentable after the horrible gunshot wound to her head. That speculation was repeated and tossed around until the person who started the rumor heard it again and reported it as "reliable information, from a source close to the family." I felt sure nobody close to Margot wanted the public to see her as she'd looked even before she was shot. As if to prove my theory, a framed enlargement of Liam Kiley's "photograph" of Margot Farr, the one used on the cover of *Redbook,* had been placed on an easel at the foot of the casket.

I followed Walter down the center aisle and shook

hands with the two men and one woman assistants, all dressed in gray or black. Walter checked his watch, placed the clipboard on a wooden lectern the size of a music stand, and turned to survey the chapel. Light filtered through modern stained glass panels. I noticed that no crosses, saints or angels were depicted. Nothing that wouldn't look comforting to bereaved Jews, Unitarians, or non-believers who might come to the chapel to pay their respects. The patterns in the colored glass had no meaning beyond soothing appearance. Each mourner could contemplate his or her "higher power," or lack of same.

On a signal from Walter, the organist in the loft above us began playing a lovely piece by Vivaldi. One more look at his watch, and Walter strode to the carved oak doors at the entrance to the chapel. He unlocked them by raising metal pins from the floor and propped each door open.

I took a quick peek at the throng assembled outside and spotted Rochelle Goodman shaking hands with Angela Lansbury and Della Reese. A stretch limousine pulled up just then and the driver walked around to the street side to open two doors. Charles St. John was first to step out. He studiously ignored the crowd as he buttoned his black suit coat. Then he held out his hand to assist Esmé. As she stepped into the bright sunlight her tight skirt rode up to show shapely thighs. She modestly tugged it down as she stood and took St. John's arm.

Aronn Young emerged from the second passenger door and looked around at the crowd. He tucked his hair back from his eyes, for a change, and let the light catch his face. Slowly, he took sunglasses out of his suit pocket and placed them on his face. His grief-stricken visage was recorded by a hundred whirring cameras and would appear on television, tabloid newspapers and, if he were lucky, *People.*

Margot Farr was no Princess Diana, but she was (or

had been) a big star, and she'd died suddenly, tragically, maybe even with scandal attached. It was, for the time being, the biggest story in entertainment news. Rochelle Goodman met the bereaved daughter, husband and agent on the steps, shook their hands, and gestured to them to follow her in a side door.

I backed up, into the semi-darkness of the entryway, and waited for instructions from Walter. The line of guests surged forward, eager to take their seats.

"Third row center, on the right," he said to me in a barely audible voice. Kim Kaylyn and Ted Landers looked at my back as they followed me down the aisle. I stepped quickly, but with proper decorum around the right side of the chapel and was ready when Walter said, "Fourth row, center." Seeing him at the lectern, an unseemly comparison to a maitre d' crossed my mind. Would he be above palming a "U.S. Grant" and moving someone up in the Las Vegas-Hollywood pantheon? Good thing I wasn't in Walter's job. For 50 dollars, I'd let someone sit on the casket.

The director who had pulled an Academy Award-nomination performance from Margot Farr 15 or so years ago guided a beautiful Latina star by the elbow to the pew where I stopped. Each time I seated someone on the center aisle I walked back up the aisle so I didn't have to cross in front of Kim Kaylyn and Ted Landers. The people I most needed to avoid were Liam Kiley, who might recognize my wonderful cheekbones, and Alicia Cormer, who might also "make" me. I stayed in the shadows or seated people I'd never seen before, in the flesh, that is, as the chapel quickly filled.

Letitia Farrell and Liam Kiley arrived together when the chapel was almost full, making a stunning entrance. Walter himself escorted them to the second row, right. Ted Landers stood and shook hands with both of them, then stepped into the aisle to let them greet Kim Kaylyn and glide past her into the pew. Letitia wore a sleeveless dark-chocolate brown sheath, mid-calf length, made of soft wool – cashmere was my guess – with lighter brown calfskin boots and matching belt. She carried herself like the showgirl she was, tall and proud of it.

Before he sat down, Liam Kiley surveyed the room like a candidate and favored a dozen people with his warm and very personal smile. *Hmph!* I thought jealously. *He probably tells all of them they have wonderful cheekbones.*

Alicia Cormer arrived alone and was seated on the tenth row left, on the outside, not the aisle. She left her sunglasses on and kept dabbing at her cheeks as if to wipe continual tears.

Walter closed one of the two doors. From my vantage point, standing at the back of the chapel, I watched Rochelle Goodman bring Esmé, Aronn Young, and Charles St. John in the side door and seat them in the front row right. St. John went into the row first and Esmé and Aronn stood there in an uncomfortable pause, all eyes on them. Aronn put his hand on Esmé's waist and gave her no choice but to enter the pew ahead of him.

The last person to enter before Walter shut the second door was Philly Mitchell. The other assistants had taken seats in folding chairs, so Walter whispered to me to seat the lady on the outside of the left side, wherever I could find space. I stopped beside the tenth row, careful to stay behind Alicia Cormer, and watched the interaction between the two women. Philly Mitchell appeared peeved that I'd stopped so far back in the chapel, then she looked aghast when she saw she'd be rump to rump with Alicia Cormer. Quickly, she recovered her composure and the two of them kissed the air beside their cheeks.

A pool photographer was allowed in to shoot a dozen shots of the assemblage and the flower-draped casket. He squatted by the right side wall as a minister came in a door behind the altar and said, "Please rise." He spoke of being here to celebrate the life of Margot Farr, of comforting her family, and added, "Let us pray."

At the conclusion of the prayer he gave a nod to the Latina star beside the director and she went forward to a microphone. She waited through a musical introduction by the organist, then sang "Morning Has Broken" in English and Spanish. The photographer crept forward on his knees and snapped four pictures of her. I remembered her name just then, Raquel Costa. She'd been linked to a very wealthy African-American comedy actor, maybe she was engaged to him. Maybe she'd already married him and divorced him. I couldn't keep up with Hollywood, nor did I care to try.

Mace Emerick entered the vestibule from a door I hadn't noticed before. We made no sign of recognizing each other. He moved to the left side and watched the mourners, especially the so-called bereaved. It was possible Margot had been killed by a total stranger, just a random act of violence, maybe a foiled robbery attempt. But it was more likely the killer was someone she knew. Someone who knew her well enough to attend her funeral.

Chapter 15

The service lasted 45 minutes, longer if one counted the mood-setting organ music. When it ended, I watched from the sidelines as Esmé Mott, Aronn Young, and Charles St. John followed the casket and pallbearers down the aisle. Maybe I was too steeped in cynicism (*maybe?*), but Esmé's grief seemed to increase the closer she got to the TV cameras.

The pallbearers stopped at the top of the chapel steps and Walter took over. With help from the burly employee and the two men who had helped seat people, Walter guided the casket on its foldable legs and rollers down the steps and into the waiting white hearse. Rochelle Goodman and the minister both stood at the curb to shake hands with the daughter, husband and agent of the deceased.

The hearse moved forward about 20 feet and a matching white limousine moved forward. Before the driver opened the doors, Philly Mitchell came from the chapel and hurried to the three principal mourners. She exchanged cheek kisses with each and gave Aronn Young what appeared to be a tight embrace. Kim Kaylyn and Ted Landers emerged, as well, put on sunglasses in the sudden glare, and stood close to St. John.

The Esmé-Aronn-St. John trio stepped into the limo, lady first, and waited for the caravan to the cemetery to form before they left. Kim and Ted had parked closest to the entrance, in a handicap space, no less, and Ted pulled the Sebring convertible, its top up, behind the limousine.

The crowd oozed out of the chapel onto the stone

steps, then spilled onto the sidewalk and lawn. It was a gorgeous day, surprisingly humid, and certain to get oppressively hot by early afternoon.

Liam Kiley and Letitia moved at the front of the wave toward the limousine and the Sebring. Ted Landers came back around the car and gave Liam a hearty handshake and elbow hug, then beamed at Letitia, who had to stoop just a little to accept his cheek kisses. At the same time, Liam bent to kiss Kim Kaylyn, who looked like a dwarf next to Letitia. But a perky dwarf, nonetheless.

Ted opened the passenger door for Kim, shook Liam's hand again, and got back in the driver's seat. Liam and Letitia crossed the street and somehow folded their long bodies into a Jaguar convertible.

I went back inside the funeral home to change again, this time into black slacks, white shirt with stiff tuxedo pleats, and a black bow tie. I placed the suit skirt and jacket on a hanger, folded my tan skirt and cotton sweater, and placed them in a paper bag with my tan shoes. In the restroom I undid my chignon and dampened my hair, then whipped it into a French twist.

Instead of turning my Volkswagen out of the employee parking lot toward the queue heading for the cemetery, I turned right and drove straight to Charles St. John's house. Well, almost straight to his house. I had to suffer the indignity, first, of having a guard allow me to drive in, but telling me to use the "service entrance" to the house.

The Royale Catering truck was already in the back driveway, so I squeezed my small car up close behind it and left my keys in the ignition in case someone had to move it.

"Hi, Mom," Candace called as I let myself in the back door. "Could you take glassware out of the dishwasher, set it over there on the table by the pantry, and give this silver a quick polish? I've got to get another load in the dishwasher and – and what? Oh, set canapés on trays."

The bartenders were checking their stock of vodka and gin and swearing because the pressure wasn't right in the canisters of club soda, Coke and Sprite. "There's a spare in the truck," Candace called. "But first check the hoses on these. Maybe something is loose."

I dodged Gaston who was setting out his special pans on what was a large stove for a home, but like a toy to Gaston. His chef's hat made his large head and ruddy, jowled face seem even more fearsome. He barked an instruction to his harried assistant, a young woman I pitied mightily, something about making a roux and getting "those god-damned shrimp cleaned," and turned to glare at me, an interloper in his space. (*Sacré bleu!*) I couldn't tell if he remembered me, and what difference would that make anyway? Every day, every event was a new culinary crisis for the great Gaston. He swore in French, whether about me, or the shrimp, or the stove, I couldn't tell.

I thought, as I had before, that I detected a Cajun echo in his French. Gaston Renáud of Paris might really be Billy Bob Reno of Natchitoches, Louisiana. What's in a name? *That phrase again! What's in a name?* I made up my mind to go straight to the police station when I got off glorified KP and see what I could find about the deceased and the bereaved, information they did not mention in interviews.

I scurried out of the way as the bartenders, still in T-shirts, carried a heavy canister through the kitchen. I rubbed spots off the highball glasses and stemware and placed them upside down where Candace had said, polished a dozen silver trays and set them near the refrigerator.

Kenneth came in the back door with two big bottles of Johnny Walker Red Label. "Olivia!" he gave me a sunny smile. "How's it going? Where's Candace?"

"She's putting trays in the spare refrigerator, in the garage. She'll be back in a second."

He held out the bottles and asked, "Would you please give these to Sean and Roy, the bartenders?"

I clutched them to my chest like a proud mother of twins (*"Named them both Johnny. So much easier to remember, don't you think?"*) and looked around for the bartenders. Just then they came in from the garage, bare-chested – and built, I must say, like Chippendale dancers. They took the bottles from me and set them behind the bar.

"Please set this on the dining room table." Candace handed me a tray of tiny sandwiches and crab canapés. "And get the one just like it out of the kitchen refrigerator. Put them both at the end by the napkins."

As I did so, I saw the buff bartenders quickly put on their starched white shirts and unzip their black dress slacks to tuck their shirttails in. By an enormous art deco mirror they centered their bow ties, combed their hair, and attached their name tags. The one who looked like Brad Pitt was Roy; the one who looked like Matthew Broderick was Sean. My interest in them, even esoteric interest as artistically perfect specimens, ended abruptly when Sean leaned over and kissed Roy.

Candace and I were going over her checklist of when to serve what when Charles St. John came in the front door. "Honey, I'm home," he shouted. Candace rolled her eyes and puffed her cheeks as if she were about to hurl. I covered my mouth with my hand.

"Mr. St. John," she said, her voice cool and professional, "Everything is ready."

"Let me have a double Story on the rocks," he said to Sean. "And go easy on the rocks." To Candace he added, "Call me Charles, honey. You've known me a long time. Hey, did you get married yet, or you still on the market?"

I had ducked into the pantry so "Charles, honey"

wouldn't recognize me, and it was a good thing I had. I would have snarled at him like a mama tiger if he'd been any closer to me. Still on the market? Was this guy for real? Candace was used to schmoozing with self-important schmucks like Charles St. John. As long as they lived up to their contracts with Royale, 50 percent up front and the remainder – in full, cashiers check – within 24 hours, they could call her honey. Then and only then.

"Gaston," he called as he strode into the kitchen. "*Comment ça va?*" I backed farther into the pantry.

"*Très bien, monsieur,*" Gaston said through his nose.

The front doors opened and a half dozen people called out, "Charles!" at one time. "*Pardonnez-moi,*" Charles said with a theatrical bow to Gaston, who responded with a perfunctory bob of his buffalo head.

No one but the owner of the house dared to set foot in the kitchen during the four hours of the luncheon, and even he stepped in only once to ask Candace a question. I moved from the kitchen to the table to the bar to the extra refrigerator in the garage, to the catering truck, all the time looking like a film running at 110 percent speed. Whenever my retrieval of empty plates and glasses put me in the vicinity of anyone on my list of "suspicious persons," I loitered behind him or her, involved with pesky crumbs. So doing, I overheard several interesting tidbits I was eager to share with Mace Emerick.

Kim Kaylyn and Charles St. John put their heads together in a cloud of cigar and cigarette smoke on the deck. They confirmed that they'd both told police she was at his house from 3:00 to 5:30 p.m. the day of Margot's murder, and that she sent a fax from there to her agent in New York around 4:30 or 5:00. I emptied all the ashtrays on the deck.

Philly Mitchell sat on a window seat with Aronn Young, so close they could have shared an oxygen mask if one dropped from the ceiling. Whatever the subject of their conversation, she was doing most of it, and he was nodding a lot. I never got close enough to hear a word from them, because Philly clamped her lips tight when I, or anyone else, got near her. She was clearly in the mood for information gathering, not information dissemination.

After Candace frantically asked me to find toilet paper for the guest bathroom on the main floor, I did a quick survey of the other bathrooms. As I stood in a large linen closet off the upstairs laundry room, trying to get the outer wrapper off a giant package of toilet paper, I heard Philly's voice. She seemed to be coming up the back stairs with someone. I tugged the closet door closed and stood in the dark.

It took me a minute to recognize the second voice. Someone with a sardonic tone. A woman, certainly. *Oh, Esmé, that's who it is.* I had noticed her many times in the course of the fashionable get-together. She'd been tossing back a lot of martinis. Since she sat still and said little, I couldn't tell if she was getting sauced or not. She might be getting drunk and sick. Or maybe she was a heavy drinker, even an active alcoholic, and the martinis just maintained her at the level she preferred. I needed more data.

"Lay off the gin, damn it," Philly was saying. "You're going to spill your guts and I don't mean just throwing up!" The doorknob in front of me turned.

"That's not the bathroom!" Esmé giggled. "That's a closet. In here. Here's a bathroom."

I heard them through the wall on the other side of the closet, peeing like mares, flushing, and talking about hairdressers. Then Philly got down to business. "I'm going to drive you home."

"No! I'm like the – the guest of honor. I'm not leaving. She was *my* mother." She said it without emotion, just like she'd probably say, "He was *my* gardener," or "It was *my* car."

"Well, suit yourself. But don't be surprised if you become the murder suspect of honor."

There was a pregnant pause, then Esmé had a fit of coughing. In a raspy voice she said, "What the hell are you talking about? You oughta be locked up."

"I didn't say I think you killed your mother, for heaven's sake. But somebody killed her . . ."

"Oh, way to go, Sherlock. Is that why the police want your help, because you're so smart?" Esmé laughed until her voice squeaked, then was taken by another coughing spell.

"As a matter of fact, yes. I think Kim Kaylyn did it, even though that detective said she had an alibi. I'll be very surprised if her alibi doesn't fall apart." She sounded smug.

"Well, I don' know." Esmé's speech was definitely slurring. "I told them I think Mother's maid did it."

"Why would she shoot Margot?" Philly sounded annoyed at such a notion.

Another pause. "I don' wanna talk about it anymore. I'm gonna take a little nap."

"I think that's a good idea." The bathroom door opened and I couldn't hear what else they said.

A couple minutes later I heard one set of footsteps go down the back stairs. Slowly I shoved the door open wide, and stood there as if I'd just that moment arrived at the closet. I took out toilet paper, hummed a little, and walked into the bedroom near the laundry room. Esmé was sprawled on the bed, her nose mashed sideways against the bedspread, making what was a soft snore into a gorilla-in-the-jungle snore. I stepped quickly into the bathroom, placed the new roll on the spindle, and headed back downstairs.

At the landing I heard someone coming up, and lowered my head. "Olivia!" a friendly female voice sang out. I looked straight ahead of me, eye level to Letitia, who was two steps down. I smiled broadly, more than a little relieved, and greeted her.

"Candace told me you'd be here, helping out Royale," she said. "Are you sorry yet that you moved to Vegas?"

I matched her smile for smile. "Uh, let's say I'm having second thoughts." *And third. And fourth.*

"I didn't know Margot personally," she said, lowering her voice. "I'm here with Liam Kiley. He was pretty close to her. Well," she added as we exchanged steps and she once again towered over me, "I know you're busy. See you later."

Candace caught my attention as soon as I reached the ground floor and asked me to get more clean glassware to the bartenders. "These people never heard of moderation," she whispered. "Charles St. John is paying for the open bar, and I think some of them are trying to even some old score with him."

The party noise had increased while I was upstairs, and so had the crowd. It is generally accepted etiquette that, at an open house, some will *arrive* and some will *leave*, but Margot's mourners only understood the first part. Apparently a few tasteful recollections of the dear departed Margot Farr had given way to raunchy tattle-tales. As I floated in and out of the living room with trays of stemware and hors d'oeuvres, I overheard snippets of parties, affairs and misadventures presumably from Margot's past. I was not above wanting to hear more salacious details, but my humdrum life didn't seem so bad to me, just the same.

The most hilarious stories centered on a Venezuelan rancher, Fernán Ortega, who had fallen madly in love with Margot Farr on the screen, and had come all the way to Hollywood to propose marriage. I noticed Alicia Cormer at the center of a knot of people laughing companionably about Ortega's folly. She looked elegant in a silvery-mauve suit, the peplum jacket emphasizing her figure. Her hair again was her best feature, a cloud of blond folded under at the ears. The skin on her neck and deep lines beside her mouth gave away her age. She looked like she'd gone in for a facelift but run out of money before the doctor finished.

I made sure I stayed out of her line of sight. The downside of that was I never got to hear the punchline of the Fernán Ortega story, a punchline that sent listeners into spasms of laughter.

On my way to the truck for more prosciutto I saw Mace arrive. He started up the driveway, then angled toward the truck. We intercepted each other on the far side of the catering truck.

"I've only got a minute," I said. "Alicia Cormer is in the living room; silver suit, blond hair. Esmé is upstairs sleeping off about 10 martinis. Don't ever challenge her to a drink off. Charles St. John should be charged with first-degree boorishness. Oh, and I think you should have police set up a checkpoint at the exit to The Lakes. I'm the only one here still sober enough to be a designated driver."

"That's kind of a shame." He grinned. "You're more fun when you've had a couple drinks."

I curled my lip in disdain. "Yeah? *You're* more fun when I've had a couple drinks, too."

"Hey, how would you like to go to Los Angeles tonight?"

"Alone? And not come back? Sounds great."

"No, with me, on business, and we'll be back in the morning."

I bit my lip, thinking that over. "What business?"

"Check out Aronn Young's alibi, and find the maid." I didn't answer, so he continued. "It won't cost you a dime. I've got it all on expense account. I've already called LAPD and told them I'd be there. Come on, you'd be a big help with the maid. Your Spanish is better than mine. And you're a woman."

"What time are you going? And when do I have to decide?"

"It's 2:00 now. I thought we'd catch the 6:30 flight and be there in time to see people tonight."

I noticed how well his charcoal silk blend sportcoat fit him through the shoulders, and how crisp his lighter gray slacks looked. I concentrated on his shoulders to keep from looking into his eyes. I could never think clearly when I looked in Mace Emerick's deep blue eyes. "I can make it," I said with a sigh of misgiving. He told me where at the airport to meet him.

I took the prosciutto in to Gaston, who was almost apoplectic that I'd taken so long. I suddenly recalled urgent business elsewhere. Now, in addition to avoiding Liam Kiley, the man most likely to remember me as Mace's sidekick, and Alicia Cormer, I had to avoid Mace and hope Candace didn't see him.

Candace! I froze in mid-motion of emptying a large chrome ashtray. *What the hell am I going to tell her about me being gone all night?* I dismissed it from my mind and concentrated on removing glasses and plates. Sean's and Roy's congeniality was beginning to ebb, as was mine, in direct proportion to the pain in my feet, and they made a last call for the bar. At three Candace joined them to do an inventory. Charles St. John was going to owe Royale a lot of money. But then, Royale had already paid a small fortune to alcohol distributors and other purveyors to bring the supplies. After they paid for supplies and employees, the profit for Kenneth and Candace would be modest.

Gaston left before three and his assistant left shortly thereafter. Candace and I bumped into each other in the pantry and were too tired to say a word. Luckily for our feet and aching arms, Kenneth and four Royale employees arrived, having finished the other event.

"Ah!" Candace said in greeting. "Fresh blood!"

"Not fresh," Kenneth amended, "but less anemic than yours. Why don't you take off?" He included me in his nod.

"Gladly!" Candace and I said in tandem. As we walked out the back door she said, "Oh, I almost forgot to tell you, Mom. I'm invited to a guest ranch tonight and most of tomorrow. Old friends. I'm leaving right from here." She leaned over and kissed me on the cheek. "Thanks for helping today. You were great."

I debated whether to go to the police station first, then back to the apartment to shower and change for the quick trip to LA, or the other way around. I needed about two more hours than I had. I backed slowly out of the driveway, watching out for lingering and maybe staggering guests. As I left The Lakes, I looked at the clock on my dashboard. *Only three hours until the plane takes off. Well, I'll just have to use my time well.*

Instead of the hot bath I longed for, I took a speed shower, put on a casual but lovely sundress with matching cotton jacket, and decided to let my hair air-dry in the car. In an overnight bag I stuffed underwear and makeup, a soft nightshirt, jeans, shirt and running shoes.

I used my identification to get into the police department and headed for "my" computer. I'd only had it for three days, but I'm territorial by nature. In the center drawer I found what I had asked Mace to leave me: the birth dates and social security numbers of Margot Farr, Aronn Young, Kim Kaylyn, and Ted Landers. While I waited for the computer to boot up, I added two names with question marks. "Liam Kiley?" and under that, "Alicia Cormer?"

It took a lot of work, searching data bases in six states, but my hunch paid off when I discovered that Ted Landers, a.k.a. Ted Rucker, built up his excellent physique the old fashioned way – in prison.

Chapter 16

Ted Rucker served three years of a six year sentence in the Michigan State Penitentiary, was paroled to live with a brother in the Upper Peninsula, and dropped out of sight about a year later, in 1995. His sentence was for possession and intent to distribute cocaine. Compared to serial rapists, child killers, and people who sent bombs in the mail to judges, Rucker was of no more interest to the Michigan correctional system than a stray dog. Chances were 49 to 1 he was somebody else's problem by the time anyone noticed he'd missed three meetings with his parole officer.

I downloaded all I could get on Ted "Landers" and ran the others. Kim Kaylyn had changed her name so many times the post office had to keep an index card on her to know alternate names under which she would accept mail. It looked like all the changes but one were to a husband's name, then back to her maiden name, Kimberly Stuart. She'd been Kimberley Atkins, Burkett, and Cabrini, which made me speculate she was working her way through the alphabet like Sue Grafton, but her last change (or last change so far) to Kaylyn seemed to be for show biz purposes rather than connubial convenience. She'd gone through the legalities of changing it just recently, three months before, although she had apparently used the name for at least two years.

Her previous job was as a weight and nutrition counselor at the Oasis Spa in Scottsdale, Arizona. Her reason for leaving, some 18 months before, was "to start my own business." She had done so immediately, in Las Vegas, thanks to a $10,000 loan from Margot Farr. "Forever Slender" incorporated in Clark County, Nevada, and now had an extremely fat bank account.

I managed to look online at her statements for the current and previous month and could see exactly where the huge balance came from. In a day the account went from just under eight thousand dollars to four hundred thirty thousand. A look at a miniature copy of the deposit slip showed a wire transfer from Barnard Cohen Literary Agency in New York City. That had to be the advance on her cookbook, minus the agent's commission.

I didn't have time to search for information on Aronn Young, Liam Kiley or Alicia Cormer, but I did access Margot Farr's bank accounts and looked at the period shortly before Kim Kaylyn left the spa in Arizona. Sure enough, Margot had been a client of the ritzy fat farm during that time frame. She must have been so impressed with Kim as a counselor she lured her to Vegas.

I went to the Las Vegas Police Department on the web and tried accessing the database with Mace's old PIN. Sure enough, he was still using 36-24-36, the perfect bust-waist-hips measurements. I looked through evidence entries, but couldn't find everything. Apparently there was another level of security, and I couldn't gain access.

I could find Kim Kaylyn's gun and bullets, logged into the evidence room on Friday, April 13.

The list of items bagged at Margot's house was so long I almost decided to skip it until Monday, but an anomaly caught my eye. In a prescription bottle, removed from her bathroom, was "unknown white powder." The name of the prescription drug was Zoloft, a common antidepressant.

But Zoloft comes in tablets, not a white powder. I made a note of the item number and went to the evidence room. The few people I'd met in that department worked weekdays, day shift only. A young woman whose nametag read "Juanita Peron" closed a paperback when I came in and set it front-cover down on her desk. I could read the words ETERNAL DESIRE on the back cover, written in ornate purple letters against a background of flames. "Can I he'p you?" She sounded bored. In spite of her two Hispanic names, she had the coloring and features of an African-American.

I introduced myself, explained my official interest in the Margot Farr evidence, and asked to see the item. She moved her book into a drawer and rose with a stretch. "I'll go look," she said pleasantly, and disappeared behind a solid door.

I looked at my watch and calculated again how long it would take me to drive to the airport, park and get inside to meet Mace. I had no luggage to check, and he had the tickets. All I had to do was show my photo identification and jump on the plane. I could afford to stay at the police station 10 minutes, no more.

Juanita was back in five. "That item is missing. Or else you got the number wrong." She'd jotted down in a small notebook what was in the evidence bags numbered right before and right after the prescription drug bottle. They matched my list.

I thought about the information Hornet Armstrong had given me, about drugs disappearing from the evidence room during a prior administration. "Maybe it was checked out so the lab could test the powder in the bottle," I suggested.

"Maybe. Or maybe it was sold on the street," she said with a shrug. "Or went up somebody's nose around here." I read disgust in her voice and the curl of her lip.

"Do you think that happens with evidence sometimes?" I watched her face carefully, trying to gauge her feelings. "Sometimes?" She laughed. "Ma'am, you log in a pound of sugar as 'white powder' and it'll be gone out the back door before you get out the front."

"Does Internal Affairs know about this?" I asked. She laughed again; she found me very humorous. "Okay, then does Internal Affairs care about it?"

"Look, I don't have anything else to say. Tonight is my last night in this dump, and I don't give a shit anymore what they do." To demonstrate her anathema, she lit a cigarette and blew smoke at the No Smoking sign. "I got me a good job at a casino, working security. Plainclothes. Working *days*. Sleepin' *nights,* you know? I been here two years and never got the day shift. I'm not one of the *boys*, you know?"

I nodded sympathetically. I most certainly *did* know. "Well, thanks, Juanita, and good luck with your new job. I've got to run or I'll miss an appointment."

I made it to the Southwest Airlines ticket counter with only minutes to spare. I stopped about 30 seconds to buy a hot dog along the concourse, then sprinted to catch up with Mace halfway to the gate. While standing in line to board the plane, I devoured the hot dog, troubled by a premonition that the "meat and meat by-products" might not rest easy atop the canapés I'd eaten when the trays came back with a few mangled remains.

Mace was known to the flight attendants as a law enforcement officer carrying a gun, thanks to paperwork he'd filled out before I arrived. As such, he couldn't have any alcohol. I, however, enjoyed a glass of wine. "As they say in the best restaurants," I said, swirling the wine in its cheap plastic cup and sniffing its bouquet, "there's nothing like a fine Chardonnay to accent the flavor of an Oscar Meyer Wiener."

Airborne and relaxed just slightly by the wine, I pulled

my pocket notebook out of my purse and gave Mace a quick recap of my computer search of Ted Landers and Kim Kaylyn. "Did you talk to Alicia Cormer at the wake?" He grunted in the affirmative, adding, "Your name didn't come up." His voice showed his fatigue. "She probably forgot all about you the minute you veered from her line of sight."

"If she thought about me at all, she may have doubted I'd follow up on the job tip." I recognized my hope for what it was – unlikely – but held on to it anyway. "Now, tell me what Kim Kaylyn's agent said when you called him."

"Yeah, Barnard Cohen. He had her fax right on his desk, with the automatic printout of his fax machine saying what time Wednesday he received it, two minutes after seven p.m., Eastern time. And he was sure it came just a few minutes after their ten or fifteen minute conversation, because the fax confirmed the salient points of their conversation."

"Did it say it came from St. John's fax number?" I finished my peanuts and decided not to add the cheese crackers to the perfect storm in my stomach. *Whatever possessed me to eat that hotdog?*

"Uh-huh. And he had called her at St. John's house right before that."

I lowered my voice. "So she can prove she was at Charles St. John's house at four o'clock our time. Big deal. What about her gun?"

"I don't have the ballistic report yet, but I have reasons to doubt it was the gun that killed Margot."

We were interrupted by the pilot saying he'd turned off the seat belt sign and we were free to move about the cabin, but to please keep our belts on while we were in our seats. I changed the subject to our destination, Los Angeles. How, I asked, had he found out where to check Aronn Young's alibi? When he didn't answer I looked over at him, ready to repeat the question, but he'd dozed off.

I studied his face. In some ways, Mace looked older asleep, especially with his five o'clock shadow. But in other ways, he looked younger, as if the tousle-haired little boy he used to be was still there, wanting to play ball.

I reclined my seat the maximum amount, about one-degree off vertical, and tried to sleep myself, but too many things were banging about in my brain. My left brain. My methodical, analytical side wouldn't stop making lists and comparing alibis and reminding me of stones left unturned. Meanwhile, my right brain was trying to drag me down memory lane. At last I surrendered, and let memories of Mace Emerick and San Diego wash over me.

At the time, 12 years ago, I wasn't looking for love in all the wrong places. I wasn't looking for love anywhere. With two daughters to raise and a job I loved with the sheriff's department, plus night school to get my associate's degree in criminology, I had neither time nor energy for a relationship. But Mace just kept being there, changing my tire on the freeway, and driving me to the emergency room when I sliced my hand on a can lid, and patiently helping Valerie with her homework. Blame propinquity. It's as good as anything else I can think of.

Gradually, making love with Mace just seemed predestined. I'd had sex before, in three marriages and a couple of forgettable flings in my youth, but Mace was the first man who ever *made love to me*. It was more than "skill," although he had that. It was more like exquisite art, something that reached inside my body and mind and made me see myself and the world around me in a new, thrilling way.

When Mace broke my heart by marrying SueEllen, I swore off sex. Well, it wasn't a conscious B follows A decision. But I didn't want to risk that deep a wound again. And having experienced true sexual fulfillment with Mace,

I wouldn't settle for just "having sex" again.

Feeling his arm and his thigh next to mine in the narrow seats made me tingle just a little. "Oh, shit," I murmured, causing the older woman on my left to look over at me. I smiled and edited my remark. "Oh, shoot."

Oh shit, I said again, but this time in my mind. *Why did I ever agree to work with Mace again? Am I a masochist?* This time when I closed my eyes I, too, dropped off to sleep.

A sensation of slowing and gently falling forward woke me up. My head was on Mace's shoulder and my neck ached. "Ladies and gentlemen," the pilot said, "we are beginning our descent into Los Angeles."

"Are you ready?" Mace said softly, his mouth only inches from my ear.

I raised my head slowly and rubbed my stiff neck muscles. "I'm ready when you are."

*****

We parked the small rental car in East Los Angeles, on a street no wider than an alley. Loud Mexican music and ads for *cerveza* blared from radios in every apartment. The smell of rancid grease, onions, and a pervading odor of dog waste made the heat in the narrow street even more oppressive. At a shop on the corner, hardly more than a stall, two men in patched, faded jeans, dirty T-shirts and straw cowboy hats let the screen door bang shut behind them. Each had a plastic bag full of brown liquid held tight at the top around a straw, the best way to have a Coke without paying extra for the bottle. They stopped and watched us pass. Mace stepped into the street so I could stay on the crumbled concrete that passed for a sidewalk. We moved down the block to an unnumbered door we figured must be "1823." There was still enough light to make our way, but night would be really dark, with no streetlights.

A woman we thought might be Carmen Espiña or her sister opened the door just a crack. I smiled and spoke in a friendly tone. *"Hola, señora. Cómo ésta?"*

Beneath her face, another set of dark eyes looked back at us, a boy maybe eight or so years old. Tiny hands appeared, shoving the boy's face away and tugging at the door. Cautiously, the woman let the toddler pull it open another foot. Once the child got a good look at us, she buried her face against the woman's leg. The woman hoisted her up, forming a perch with her hip.

"Mi llama Señora Wright. Su llamar Señor Emerick. Cómo se llama, señora?"

She said nothing. The toddler peeked back at me, coyly.

"We are trying to find a *señora*, Carmen Espiña. Can you help us?" Mace spoke in English, slowly.

"Lo siento, pero no puedo complacere," she answered.

"She says she's sorry, she can't help us." Again I asked her name. *"Cómo se llama?"*

"Mi llama Maria." She gave a shrug of resignation and added, *"Carmen es mi hermana."*

"Your sister, *bien, gracias*, Maria." In Spanish, I asked her how we could find Carmen, to speak to her. She answered that Carmen would be home soon, but did not invite us in. The baby, who I noticed wore tiny pierced earrings, was soundlessly playing peek-a-boo with Mace.

Two children shrieked inside and Maria turned to see why. To us she said, *"La comida está servida. Con su permiso, por favor?"*

"Si, yes, your dinner is ready. We'll wait here for Carmen." I hoped fervently that the wait would not be long. Our presence in the barrio was a magnet to children. We smiled and said, *"Hola,"* to each of them.

We got lucky. About five minutes after Maria left the door, a woman turned the corner, saw us at Maria's door, and stopped suddenly. I called in as friendly a voice as I could. *"Señora Espiña?"*

She nodded. She was a beautiful woman, dressed in a clean beige skirt and blouse. She had a way of standing, shoulders square, chin angled up, that bespoke pride and confidence. We stated our names and I apologized in Spanish for intruding on her family at the dinner hour. She nodded again, then strode toward us with her hand outstretched.

"I speak English," she said. "Let me talk to my sister and we can go to a restaurant to talk."

When she emerged from the apartment, she wore a blue full skirt and an embroidered white blouse that showed her light bronze skin to advantage. Her hair lay in a tight black braid down her back. "It's not far," she said.

A ceiling fan cooled the cantina only slightly, and the cold Corona beer I ordered never tasted better. "You worked for Margot Farr in Las Vegas. Is that correct?" I asked.

Carmen waited for the waiter to set down a bowl of tortilla chips and told him in Spanish that we would not be ordering dinner. When he was out of hearing, she answered me. "Yes, I cleaned house for her. It was a good job, and I liked her very much. I heard about her murder on the television, and I'm very sorry."

"How long did you work for her?" Mace asked. "And why did you leave?"

"Two months more than a year. It was fine, everything was good. Until her daughter moved in." She studied her beer. "Esmé lied and said I stole something, a ring of great value. But I know I did not steal anything, ever, and Esmé lied all the time. She put the ring in my room. She wanted me to go away."

"Did Margot fire you?" I asked.

"Yes. She wouldn't listen to what I tried to tell her. Esmé

had her mother. . ." She made a motion with her fingers. "What do you call it?"

"Wrapped around her finger?" I asked.

She smiled. "Yes, wrapped around her finger very tight."

"What was your impression about Margot's husband, Aronn Young?" Mace asked.

Her smile evaporated instantly. "He is a *cucuracha*. He wanted to . . ." She paused. "This is not easy to say. He wanted to have the sex with me. I wanted to have nothing, no contact, with him. I know he had the sex with other women. He brought women to that house, Margot Farr's house, late at night after she went to sleep. He brought them to a room in the other end of the big house."

"Did you know who any of them were?" I asked.

"No. They all look the same, the blondes."

Mace frowned and I laughed. "I know exactly what you mean, Carmen."

She smiled, then grew serious. "Margot Farr had many enemies. People who she believed were her friends." She drained her beer and Mace signaled the waiter by holding up the empty bottle and two fingers.

"Please tell us about that," I urged. The waiter set dripping bottles and more chips in front of Carmen and me. Mace still had half a bottle.

"I heard the exercise man and the cook laughing and making fun of Margot when she couldn't hear them. They called her names like fatso and lard-ass."

"Did you ever take pictures – photographs – of Margot looking fat? For any reason?" Mace asked.

Carmen seemed surprised, even bewildered, by the question. "I don't have a camera."

"Do you know if anyone else did that?" Mace asked. "Any of these enemies, who maybe wanted to embarrass her, or get money for the pictures?"

She thought it over. "No, I don't know anybody who did

that. But I can tell you *Señora* Farr's worst enemy. It is Charles San Juan. I mean, Saint John. She had big fights, bad arguments, with him. But I'm sorry, I don't know what they argued about. As soon as they started to argue, I went fast the other way, to the market sometimes."

We asked about other people – Liam Kiley, Alicia Cormer, and others I'd seen mentioned in Margot's appointment book – but none of the names meant anything to Carmen. As we walked her back to her sister's apartment, she talked about her new job with a hotel. She liked the job, but she had a long commute on hot and crowded buses morning and evening. She took Mace's card and said she'd call if she thought of anything that might help us. He wrote his personal cell phone number on the back.

We went west to Highway 101, then went northwest to Santa Monica Boulevard. At the Beverly Wilshire Hotel we talked to the front desk manager and the bell captain. We weathered a long wait while the front desk manager called Mace's contact with the Los Angeles Police to check our *bona fides*. Mace got comfortable on a couch in the lobby, practicing his identification skills. When he had time on his hands he liked to observe people, then write down a description. He was much, much better at it than I was. I noticed too much what people were wearing instead of really seeing their features and other marks that wouldn't change. The process always renewed my doubt in what "eyewitnesses" swore they saw – in a few seconds and while under duress.

To kill time I went to the hotel gift shop to buy gum. The headline on the Los Angeles paper made me stare: *Vegas Police Evidence Missing*. I put the gum back in the rack and paid for the paper without looking up.

I left the gift shop and stepped into a wide, fast-moving stream of traffic headed toward a bank of elevators. A running toddler slammed into my leg and fell flat on his back. I dropped the heavy city paper, which hit the marble floor like a *piñata*, scattering dozens of sections and what appeared to be scores, if not hundreds, of advertising inserts across the corridor. The little boy scrambled to his feet, and the traffic of shoes, strollers, wheelchairs and wheeled luggage parted around me as I crawled around, snatching papers off the floor and clutching them to my chest.

I saw Mace step into my island of chaos and squat to help me. "You're supposed to read the news, not make the news," he said with a chuckle. He helped me carry the rat's nest over to a trash receptacle, where I dumped in every section but the front. I opened my mouth to tell him about the Las Vegas article on page one, but a bellman stopped to say the front desk manager could see him now.

I plopped down in the nearest chair and read the article quickly, then again, slowly. It was copyrighted by two Los Angeles reporters, and told of an internal audit of items in the evidence room. Scores of items listed on logs could not be found, while more than two hundred items, including eighty-some-odd firearms, were lying about, tagged but not logged in. *What a mess!*

Chief Harold Armstrong was quoted throughout the article, in a favorable light, but mention of missing narcotics was conspicuously absent. Capt. Avery Wacker, I noticed, was damned with faint praise by Hornet for his "initiative" in furthering the investigation. The custodian of the evidence room had been placed on administrative leave, effective immediately.

"Let's go," Mace said, startling me. "Aronn Young's alibi just went down the toilet."

*****

Ever since Mace asked me to go to Los Angeles with him, as we stood outside Charles St. John's house, I'd felt a low-voltage current of anticipation. I didn't know what to expect from him, but I was even less sure what to expect from myself. Sure, I moved to Las Vegas to have more "fun" in my life. But did that mean throwing my self-respect in front of a speeding train? *Mace Emerick is a jerk!* I told myself, but it came out sounding more like a wistful question than an exclamation.

Maybe it was my abortive brush with terminal illness, the bad news/good news from Dr. Bostwick that had spurred my sudden move. Maybe it was just maturity. Whatever the cause, I was discovering that staying angry took a lot of energy.

I realized I had been only half listening to Mace since we left the hotel. It was only 10:30 p.m., but I was exhausted from the hideous day. First Margot's funeral, then the wake, and I'd been on my feet throughout both events.

"How many people looked at the pictures?" I asked. Mace was saying something about having trouble getting in touch with the day shift personnel at the hotel.

"A bellman and a valet parking guy both remembered Aronn Young by name, said he'd been here Tuesday and Wednesday, like Aronn told us he was. But both identified a photo of Liam Kiley as the man they saw."

"I don't get it. I thought Aronn used fake ID with his picture and Liam Kiley's name. And Liam Kiley said that was true, that he let Aronn get a fake ID made, so Aronn could travel incognito. Isn't that right?"

"Half right," Mace said, sounding as tired as I felt. "But it now appears the fake ID business goes both ways, a little wrinkle Mr. Kiley failed to mention. Kiley was in Beverly Hills Tuesday and Wednesday using the name 'Aronn Young.' I still have to check the airline, of course, but it looks like Aronn either wasn't here at all, or was not here as long as he said he was."

I saw the advantage of two-way fake ID's right away. "So, if I had a fake driver's license with my picture and, say, 'Candace Mason' on it, and Candace had one with her picture and 'Olivia Wright' on it, we could use airline tickets in either name. So round-trip tickets on different dates would be interchangeable, and either of us could go and return at either time."

"It's not legal," Mace said.

I thought it over. "Well, I don't think it should be legal for an airline to say I can't let my daughter or my friend travel on the second half of a round trip ticket, just because it's in my name. What difference does it make whose butt is in the seat, as long as it's paid for and occupied?" He said nothing, just sighed, so I continued. "Do you think the Aronn Young-Liam Kiley charade stopped there?"

"Huh?"

"Maybe it's a whole fake ID business. A ring."

"It wouldn't be the first. And I wish you didn't sound so enthusiastic about it."

"Sorry," I said, sounding anything but. "I can see Aronn's advantage in convincing us that he was in California when Margot was murdered. That's a no-brainer, which is about all I'm capable of tonight. But why would Liam Kiley cover for Aronn?"

"All Kiley said was that he hadn't seen Aronn for several days, and that he didn't know anything about a trip to Los Angeles. Since we asked if he knew whether or not Aronn had gone to California, not about any trip by Kiley, he gave himself room to maneuver."

"Yeah, enough room to maneuver a tank." I fiddled with the car radio, seeking an oldie station, but turned it off when all I found were commercials. "What about the fax to Margot? The one that came in just as she was being shot?"

"It did come from the hotel. But it was Kiley who sent it to the front desk."

"Let's say it was just a favor for a friend, that Kiley knew, or thought he knew, that Aronn was involved in something, say an affair, and Kiley agreed to send Margot a fax to cover Aronn's ass. Now he discovers that his little prank is Aronn's alibi in a murder case. Wouldn't he want to put a firewall between himself and Aronn?"

"By doing what?"

I took a long drink of bottled water. "By telling us he was in LA and that he sent the fax to Margot."

"Think of it this way," he said, passing an RV the size of a railcar, "say he did an innocent boys-will-be-boys favor for his good buddy, Aronn. What the wifey doesn't know won't hurt her, that kind of thing. Then he discovers he holds the alibi. It's a marker."

"A marker?"

"Yeah. In gambling, you know. If I lend you money, you give me an I.O.U. in some form. A marker. As long as I hold your marker, you owe me. That gives me power, sometimes power out of proportion to the amount of money."

I thought about that and drank some more water. What he said was valid about human nature, but it might have no bearing on the Liam Kiley question. "So, we know nothing of Aronn Young's real whereabouts at the time of Margot's murder." I wondered silently if he had any clue that Margot had no money to leave him. "Wait a minute," I said aloud. "About Aronn. He may or may not have known that Margot didn't have any money to leave him, but he may have counted on her life insurance."

"Good point. I'll look into that tomorrow. Hey, let's forget murder for a while."

I figured we'd stay at a motel near the airport, but Mace turned west off the 405 onto Venice Boulevard. Unable to drop the topic of murder, I told him about the article in the paper, the Las Vegas police evidence exposé, and that the prescription bottle of white powder Mace had bagged at Margot Farr's house was apparently missing. He listened, but made no response.

"Where are we going?" I asked as we took a sharp left turn on Pacific Avenue. On our right I caught glimpses of the ocean in the moonlight.

"It's a surprise," was all he'd say. We entered Marina del Rey, an enclave of expensive waterfront homes with yachts close by. He parked in front of a seafood restaurant and said, "I'll be right back."

He returned with an envelope, which he placed on the dashboard. Before I could ask another question, he held his finger to his lips. "A surprise, remember?"

We parked near a dock, got out, and locked the car. From the trunk Mace took my carry-on bag and his small duffel. A brown fixture on the pier startled me by flapping its wings and lifting off into the darkness. I took my bag and followed Mace, overwhelmed by the perfume of salt air. Oh, how I had missed it!

Mace aimed his flashlight at the envelope he'd apparently picked up at the restaurant, then at numbers on pilings and the names of sailboats. "Here it is," he said softly, and steadied my arm as I slipped off my street shoes and clambered aboard the Manta Raye. She was a beautiful – no, make that a magnificent – sloop, 40 feet or so of hardwood and brass that cost more money than most people earned in a lifetime. Like J. P. Morgan said, if you have to ask how much a yacht costs, you can't afford it.

Mace opened the envelope and a set of keys slid out. He unlocked the door to the galley and disappeared for a moment. "Hand down your bag," he called.

I stood with my legs apart, feeling the swells of the marina shift the boat. A foghorn sounded out in the darkness, and gulls answered from buoys at the harbor entrance. I handed Mace my bag and my shoes, and went forward to sit down and soak up the sounds and scents I'd lived so long without.

I felt Mace's warm breath on my neck and turned my face to kiss him, quickly before I had too much time to think about it. Some things are best left unsaid. Or said without words.

"I poured you a glass of wine, in the galley," he said, kissing my lips softly as his arm stole around my waist and pulled me to his chest. "Do you want me to bring it out here?"

"No," I whispered as I kissed his ear, his jaw, and found his lips again with my own. When I caught my breath I tilted my face upward and smiled at the moon.

"Let's go below," he said. Or maybe that was my voice.

Chapter 17

I used to be able to make love most of the night (not every night, sure, but on – ahem – *special occasions*) and function at something like 80 percent efficiency the next day. Well, when I woke up that sun-splashed Sunday morning in a king-size bed, nestled beside Mace Emerick in the gently swaying belly of the Manta Raye, I knew the answer to one of life's little mysteries. I knew why people call 50 "over the hill."

Best sex I'd had in 11 years. Okay, the only sex I'd had in 11 years. And it had been great, sweet, magical and memorable – but I felt like I'd been keel-hauled. Aware of increasing daylight, I lay in a state of exquisite exhaustion and examined the inside of my eyelids until I felt Mace roll toward the edge of the bed.

"I'm awake," I lied.

"I feel like making passionate love again," he growled.

My eyes flew open in shocked disbelief and he laughed. "By golly, you are awake." He tugged at the sheet that I held tight against my breasts. I resisted his pull for a few seconds, then threw the sheet over his head and darted past him into the head. In the space whimsically called a "shower," I felt like Alice in Wonderland when she ate the side of the mushroom that made her too big to fit in a house. I laughed at the vivid image I conjured of Mace showering in that space.

Our hair was still wet as we sat cross-legged on the

deck and savored coffee and croissants. I felt worlds away from real life, with all the pressure of paychecks and rent, the niggling minutiae of loose buttons and burned out light bulbs, and the immense dark cloud of a murder investigation and missing evidence. No wonder I wanted to float away on a yacht, leaving no forwarding address. He poured more coffee in my mug and stretched out on the deck, his eyes closed and a sly smile on his face.

Like a morning glory, my face sought the sun. That gentle warmth and the fragrance of the Pacific combined with the rocking of the boat. I had no choice but to cry. It was one of those moments that distills time into the unforgettable perfect moment, the hour or even a whole day that you hold in your memory and savor – the time that you would choose to live over again exactly as you did the first time if you were given one brief chance to return to your life, like Emily in *Our Town*.

As we dressed and cleaned up the galley we tried to stay away from the topic of murder, but it proved to be insidious. "Aronn Young may have been a thousand miles away from Las Vegas when Margot was killed," Mace said, "or he may have been standing in her house with a smoking gun in his hand. Only thing I can say for certain is that I'm looking forward to our next chat with the merry widower."

"And don't forget Ted Landers' previous life in the Michigan pen. Oh, and what about Kim Kaylyn's quick trip to the kitchen where a videotape may or may not have been in the recorder." An hour later, I dropped Mace off in front of Southwest Airlines and headed for Beverly Hills to see an old friend.

It had been eight, maybe nine years, since I'd seen him, but Raul Mendez had surrendered nothing to Father Time, and he'd lost none of his flamboyance. In fact, since being gay had become so mainstream, he had to be even more overstated and extravagant to be considered *outré*.

I knew him "when," as the saying goes. When he was a hairdresser and I was a make-up artist in Hollywood. That was one of the short careers I dallied with in the years after I left law enforcement. A.M. – After Mace. Raul had introduced me to the two movie stars for whom I became a discreet and very well-paid ghostwriter. If Margot had lived, and if she checked references, she would have called Raul and the two stars.

"Olivia! Darling girl!" Raul called as I entered his ultra-modern home. The décor was chrome, slate and acres of glass. The furniture was soft leather, some in white and some in red. "Come here and let me look at you! Up here where the light is better, come here!"

I followed him from his hammered metal front door up a winding staircase to a loft. The light was, indeed, better, with a window the size of an A-frame cabin overlooking West Hollywood. Raul didn't do hair any more, having invested in an independent film company that grossed $100 million on a film that cost $3 million to shoot and produce.

"I'm so excited to see you! And just wait until you meet Virgil. Oh, my dear, he's to die for. Brilliant! I mean, Mr. Hollywood. Has more money than God. But then, so do I." He looked me over as if he were measuring me for a wig and tutu, then clasped his hands together. "You look wonderful, Olivia. Oh, I'm so glad you called! Now, why did you say you needed to see me? Needed to see me! Don't think I didn't notice that! When all I want is to be wanted. Like Connie Francis, or – who was it who sang that song?"

"Brenda Lee. I want to be wanted."

"Oh, yes. I love her, I love Brenda Lee. Always have, always will. Oh, look, here's Virgil now. I can't wait for you to meet him." We watched a tall man with a deep tan and silver hair extricate himself from a gunmetal gray Jaguar and disappear under the overhang from the second story.

Raul leaned over the chrome railing of the loft to call Virgil as the large front door opened. "I'm up here with a dear friend. We'll be down in a minute. Will you join us for a Bloody Mary?"

Virgil called in a deep bass, "Take your time, I've got to make one quick phone call."

"So, how's your love life?" Raul asked. I must have blushed, because he grinned knowingly. "That good, huh?"

I just shrugged and shook my head. "I'm not going to kiss and tell."

"Oh, you've always been like that! You're no fun!" His eye caught the immense television screen downstairs and he held up his hand for quiet. Together we watched Tiger Woods putt for eagle. "How does he do that? How, how, how? Ruins the game for mere mortals!" He headed for the stairs and slid down the center pole like a fireman. "Come on, I dare you."

It was a surprise to see him disappear like that, but it didn't look too hard, so I slid down the pole. "I am, too, fun!"

I had a Virgin Mary, no vodka, while Raul and Virgil each had a Bloody Mary in tall slender glasses. The two of them shared the house, Raul explained, their individual previous homes having "too many memories, you know, too much baggage." Virgil was an executive producer of movies, mostly made-for-TV, but right now he was working on a major film for theatrical distribution. They chatted amiably about stars who jockeyed for the leads in the film, and tidbits they knew about coming divorces. It took me a minute to understand they called any breakup of gay partners a divorce, too.

"I hate it when they want us to take sides," Raul said. He licked the tomato juice off his celery stalk and waved it for emphasis. "Just get over it, that's what I tell them. Straight or gay, it makes no difference. Just get over it!"

We were seated in armchairs made of white leather as

soft as crushed velvet. Raul and I had our legs curled under us, and Virgil rested his long legs and Birkenstock sandals on the mirrored coffee table between us. I looked around the room, admiring the abstract paintings and sculptures, especially a set of five dolphins in pink alabaster. A chair constructed of small sections of red leather arrayed on a chrome frame, and reclined like a dentist's chair, puzzled me – until I realized it was a piece of erotica. I quickly turned my attention back to the dolphins.

"But Olivia, you didn't come to dish the dirt about people you never even met, did you? So, come on, now. Why are you in California? Not that you need an excuse to come. You belong here, like we do."

"I'm working for the Las Vegas Police, but sort of undercover. And only on one investigation, the murder of Margot Farr."

They bit into their celery stalks simultaneously. *Crunch, snap.* "Yes," Virgil said, chewing slowly. "Go on."

I gave a concise outline of my involvement with the late Margot Farr as they nodded their understanding of how sad it all was. Both had known her, in a peripheral way, through mutual friends.

"And that brings me to the reason I'm here. Umm, let me ask you a question. What is your impression of how Margot looked in the period of time shortly before her death?"

"Our impression?" Virgil cocked his head. "I don't know what you mean."

"Just say whatever comes to your mind. I'm talking about her physical appearance."

"Well, she looked wonderful on the *Redbook* cover," Raul said. "Everybody says so. I know people who saw her when she was fat – that was, I don't know, two years ago? – and she had really gotten her figure back."

"Or at least it appeared that she had, in that picture," I said with a sigh.

"Spit it out, Olivia. What's wrong with the picture?" Raul said. He stuck his feet out on the coffee table.

"The picture was shot a year ago, and improved electronically. Painless plastic surgery by an expert."

"Liam Kiley?" Raul asked, his eyes wide with interest.

"The same. Margot's favorite, in fact her only, photographer. She had put on a lot of weight – a LOT of weight – since the photo was taken. She had become pretty much a recluse, therefore only a small number of people knew what she looked like. And as the saying goes, it's not pretty." I stood up and sat down again, curling my stiff legs in the other direction to get the circulation going again.

"So, at last, I come to why I'm here to see Raul. That I got to meet you, Virgil, is a bonus, because I'm pretty sure the two of you know a great deal about what goes around and comes around in Hollywood. My question is, what do stars and celebrities do to lose weight when money is absolutely no object? I know cocaine can keep you up for days on end, eating nothing. But I don't think she was on cocaine. There was no sign of it in the autopsy, although the toxin screen is not finished yet. But I'm sure we can rule out cocaine. I can't say I knew her like we were friends, but I did observe her closely for a while." I looked from Raul to Virgil and back again. Then they looked at each other.

"Zed," Virgil said. "Costs more than cocaine or heroin and it's way harder to find someone who can get it."

Raul nodded. "Oh, I've heard of Zed, but I've never known anyone who actually tried it. Except – wait a minute. That model, she was 17, the redhead." He tapped his fingers on his forehead, trying to think of details, of a name, then shook his head, unable to mine the information in his brain. "She got skinnier and skinnier, and she died. They said the cause of death was asthma or severe allergy, something about an inhaler. But everybody says she was anorexic. One of my former clients, however, worked for her doctor, and she told me the girl was on Zed. I didn't give it a lot of thought until now."

"Do you think you could find out more?" I asked. "I want to know if it leaves any telltale signs in the body. And how someone with a pile of money can get it."

"I can call my former client," Raul said. "And don't worry, the name of Margot Farr will not pass my lips." He rubbed his forehead again. "I think she said it looks like cocaine, very white and powdery, and that it comes from Mexico."

"I will be grateful if you try to find out more about it," I said.

"I can call her this afternoon. The three of us are the only people in California awake so far."

I said I'd call him from Las Vegas late in the afternoon, and gave him Mace's two cell phone numbers, just in case I missed him. "Which reminds me, I've got a plane to catch." I stood and placed my glass on a coaster. They both walked me to the door and assured me they'd be discreet and try to find out more about Zed.

"Maybe you should be careful whom you ask," Virgil said to me as he draped his arm across Raul's shoulders. "If you're on the right track, and who knows, not me, certainly, but if you are on the right track, you might end up knocking on a murderer's door."

The cold chill I felt had nothing to do with the light breeze I felt on my way to the car. On the way to the airport, I found myself looking in my rearview mirror again and again.

Chapter 18

I checked in at the Southwest Airlines gate and received a plastic card with a number higher than sixty. I'd be in the third batch of people to board the plane. To kill time, I meandered into a bookstore/newsstand and scanned titles. A list of New York Times Bestsellers was posted on a display of the latest books by John Grisham, Dean Koontz, Danielle Steel and a few others. Another section featured trade paperbacks of "Oprah's Picks."

The "Non-Fiction Bestsellers" list was heavy on diet books. Always was, I thought wryly, probably always will be. I was tired, both physically and emotionally. I snapped out of my mental holding pattern, however, when I heard the name "Margot Farr."

"I'm sure she had plastic surgery." A woman who by federal law should never wear shorts was leafing through *People* to my left. She must have weighed upwards of 250 pounds, and her legs were squeezed into pink walking shorts like Cheez-Whiz into two plastic tube dispensers.

"Well, duh!" her friend or relation said. "If I had her money, so would I." The second woman was heavier than the first. She wore a Mickey Mouse T-shirt in a size I didn't know existed, perhaps intended for players in the NFL, and flowered clamdiggers. Both wore sandals.

"She sure lost a lot of weight," the first woman said, holding the magazine open. "Look at her here, Barbie. Ooo-whee, and look at him! Ted Landers, lordy, what a hunk."

"Oh, yeah, she lost weight," Barbie answered with disdain. "She had her own exercise guy, her own gym, and her own cook to supervise her diet. No damn wonder she lost weight! It's not like she had to take care of three kids and a job, and a car that's got bald tires and bad brakes."

"I don't think she should have married that guy, Aronn Young." She put the magazine back on the rack and edged toward the open front of the store.

"Why not?" Barbie countered. "Men have trophy wives. Why shouldn't women do as they please? Have a boy toy if they want?"

"I'm not saying that. I just don't think she should have *married* him. I think he's a creep."

As they wandered out of the store, I picked up the magazine they'd been looking at. Margot's murder was the cover story. I paid for the magazine and a pack of gum and followed the herd at my gate down the chute and onto the plane.

The article was light on details of the murder investigation, having gone to press before the autopsy. Photos of Margot as a "starlet," a poster girl, and with four husbands in turn bordered the story. A display of magazine covers that spanned maybe forty years was arranged around the now-famous photo of Margot used on the cover of *Redbook* just a few weeks ago.

Ted Landers was quoted and featured in an extremely flattering photo. Kim Kaylyn was mentioned in passing, as was "Margot's only child, Esmé Mott, 38." Her father, the article said, was Margot's second husband. I guessed that Esmé was probably seething at the printed report of her age.

On my steno pad I wrote: Esmé. Under her name I wrote three questions: Having affair with Charles St. John? Getting life insurance money? and Alibi – shopping, where?

I managed to doze for fifteen minutes before we

prepared to land, a nap that made me groggier than I'd been before. I reclaimed my car at the lot and drove straight to Candace's apartment, glad to see I'd arrived before she got home from her outing to a ranch. I took a long shower and slept about an hour. The door to Letitia's room had been closed when I lay down. The fact that it was open when I got up told me she'd left. Feeling refreshed at last and ready to reenter the fray, I called Mace. Inside of ten seconds, I was sorry I had.

"Where the hell have you been?" were his first words to me. Since I was still basking in the memory of love-on-a-yacht, I was shocked by his tone. I figured now I knew how amorous dogs felt when hit with cold spray from a garden hose.

I returned his snarl. "In California, working. And just who the hell do you think you are?"

He sighed. "Sorry. I guess I need an attitude adjustment."

"Either that or a face rearrangement to get your nose back in joint." I didn't know who I was angrier with, him for being an ass, or myself for building up our intimacy in my mind.

"I said I'm sorry. Wacker's been chewing my ass so hard I'm ready to slug the first person who crosses my path."

"Well, I won't be the one to make that mistake." I paused. "Want to talk about it? At a safe distance, I mean."

"Yes and no. I want to talk, but not at a distance." He paused; I said nothing to fill the silence. "Have you told Candace yet? That you're seeing me again?"

We'd discussed that on the boat. I convinced him I had to tell her I was working with him, and that I was "seeing" him, as he so casually put it. Not that I wanted to call our dangerous liaison what it was, either. *Candace, dear, you remember Mace Emerick, the man I loathe and detest and abhor? Well, funny thing – this will crack you up! – I ran into him last Wednesday, and by Saturday night we were sleeping together.* Even that was a euphemism. We were, in the unvarnished vernacular, fucking our brains out.

"She's not home from her weekend on a ranch yet. I'm working up my nerve. But why is Wacker gnawing on you?"

"Oh, that story in the LA Times, about missing evidence. He's livid, not about the missing evidence, but about somebody leaking it to the press. Naturally, since he hates my guts anyway, I'm the first one he suspects."

"Naturally." I knew the leak didn't come from Mace. He hadn't been in the Vegas PD long enough to have inside information and, furthermore, he had a deep distrust, if not paranoia, about the media.

"But enough about me. Hornet says he's got to talk to you. Do you have his cell phone number?"

"Yes, it's in my billfold. Did he say what it's about?"

"No, but I can guess. Something about the missing evidence."

"Okay, I'll call him right now." I wanted Mace to say something, well, romantic. He'd never been one to verbalize his feelings, and I told myself he wasn't likely to start now.

As if he were reading my mind, he said, "I miss you. I wish we were back on the boat, sails up and heading out of the harbor."

"Yeah, me too. Well, I'll see you in the morning. I'd better call Hornet now."

"Call me later, okay? After you talk to Candace? Maybe I could stop over, say hello to her."

"Sure. Later." Softly I added, "'Bye."

* * *

I scrambled eggs with potatoes and ham for supper while I waited for Candace to return and Hornet Armstrong to call me back. When he did, at 7:00 p.m., it was to ask me to meet him at the marina again. I dressed in slacks, a cotton pullover and a windbreaker and gave my face the four-minute makeup treatment.

Candace still wasn't home when I left, so I left her an intentionally vague note regarding my plans for the evening.

Clouds had blown in from the southwest and kicked up a dust storm on the desert. The dirt swirled in the orange glow of sodium vapor lamps along the highway, making the tall lights look like fuzzy orange topiary trees. As I left the lights of Las Vegas behind, there was no sign of the moon through the clouds to mitigate the darkness. I was glad I'd driven that route once before at dusk. Driving back in the dark Friday night hadn't bothered me. I puzzled about that for a moment, until the obvious explanation surfaced. Going home from the lake I'd been driving toward the glow in the sky, casino lights shooting into the universe from millions of bulbs.

I felt cheered by the thought that my second trip back from Lake Mead would be even easier. With light bouncing from the clouds, I'd be driving toward a rose-colored Oz.

Hornet was in the galley of the Vega Star when I arrived at his slip at the marina. He answered my hail and said to come aboard. I accepted a wine cooler and he opened a beer for himself. I couldn't help but think "beer belly" about his midriff. His T-shirt, which extolled beautiful Mission Bay in San Diego, looked to be under a strain.

"Let's get out on the lake," he said as he lit a cigarette. "I'm getting squirrelly tied up to the dock all the time." He shook loose the knots that tethered the boat to the dock, coiled the two ropes, and stored them under a seat. The motor turned over and we putt-putted away from the dock. The lights of the marina seemed to retreat as we headed for the dark lake. When we got to the edge of the No Wake area, Hornet shoved the throttle toward the front and the boat hurtled forward.

"How big is the engine?" I called.

"Two-fifty horsepower, inboard-outboard. Pulls two skiers up easier and smoother than any boat at the marina." We rode at what I presumed was top speed for three or four minutes, then he abruptly cut the motor. "Here, take the wheel."

We changed seats and he lit another cigarette. "This here," he said, pointing to white plastic switches on the right hand side of the wheel, "is the trim tabs. When you shove the throttle forward, the back of the boat drops down. Right away you adjust the trim to get the front of the boat down on the surface of the water, which gets the boat into the plane you want, right on top of the water."

A voice crackled through static on a radio. "Is that for you?"

"Nah. I keep the marine band CB on 16, the common channel. That was some guy looking for his buddy. When the other guy answers they'll talk on some other channel."

I located the microphone, hooked to the dashboard below the steering wheel and the trim tabs. "Am I supposed to press up or down on these tabs?" I asked. He gave me a thumbs-down signal. I looked over the gauges for temperature, rpm, and the compass. We were facing south. I looked back toward the shore and saw the marina at our six o'clock position. It seemed far away. Maybe Hornet felt caged at the dock, but I felt caged by the blackness around us. As we banged over oncoming waves, I asked him where Hoover Dam was. He answered by pulling a laminated and rolled nautical map from beneath the driving console. I held one end of the roll and he held the other while directing a flashlight onto Boulder Basin.

"You see that red light to the port? That's the alpha buoy showing the entrance to Calville Bay. It's blinking A in Morse code. Farther away to our port, see that green light?" He pointed with the flashlight. "It's flashing at four second intervals." Again he threw light on the map. "See there? Says Beacon Island. That's the entrance to The Narrows. Scary son of a bitch in the daytime. You get a stiff neck from looking up at the cliffs on both sides. At night the only way to navigate is by beacon lights. Look here at the map. On the north of the canyon is a flashing green, four seconds. See the 'Q R' on the south side? That's what they call a quick red. Flashes at one-second intervals, give or take."

I read the words Boulder Canyon in the narrow waterway between Boulder Basin and Virgin Basin and asked Hornet about its significance.

He released his end of the map and it rolled shut. "Boulder Canyon was the first choice for the site of Hoover Dam. The Black Canyon turned out to be more geologically stable, though. Building the dam downstream like that created this big basin. Now, turn west by southwest and we'll go around Fortification Hill so you can see the dam."

"What's that?" I pointed at a bright light that appeared to be moving on the water.

"What? Oh, that's the Desert Princess, a paddlewheel tourist boat. Goes out of a dock near Lake Mead Marina." He placed the map back in its net holder under the console and lit another cigarette.

I looked over our stern; Calville Bay was out of sight. When I looked east, there seemed to be no shore ahead, no place to use for reference.

He must have sensed my uneasiness. "We can't get lost. Right there on the dashboard is a GPS."

"Global positioning tells me where I am, but it doesn't tell me where the shore is."

"You're doing fine. Okay, let's pick it up. Now, when you throttle forward, press down on the white tabs. Ready? Okay, hit it!"

It took three stops and flying starts, each time almost swamping the back end of the boat, before I mastered a smooth takeoff at maximum speed. After a while Hornet took the wheel again, bringing the boat around to due south. We seemed to be racing the Desert Princess toward a black pinnacle, as if to see who could disintegrate first.

"Dead ahead is Promontory Point," he said. "We'll be slipping through a narrow opening to its east." I watched the tour boat maneuver around the point. "Up there are mountain sheep," Hornet said. "Big herd. You hardly ever see them, though. Too shy."

As we came abreast of the Black Canyon we were slammed by wind from the south. We banged across the tops of waves that met us head on. I had thought the wind was bad on the open lake, but the canyon was a funnel. Hornet gave me the wheel again and I lowered the speed.

"How deep is it here?" I asked with an involuntary shiver. I looked over the rope marking the closest point of approach and stared in awe at the stone towers and the spillways.

"A little over 400 feet."

I cut the motor way down and we bobbed like a cork in the pitch black water.

"Let's get out of the canyon before the paddle-wheeler," he said. I noticed he was massaging his left arm.

With him giving me directions, I left the canyon and headed toward the middle of Boulder Basin. The farther out on the lake we went, the more we were buffeted by the wind that now came from the south-southeast. I cut the motor and let the boat bob and drift. To the southwest we could see the red alpha buoy for Boulder Harbor. To the northwest, toward Las Vegas Bay, one flashing green and one flashing red lights were so close together I hoped I'd never have to navigate between them.

"See that?" Hornet pointed almost due north, maybe

slightly northeast. "Flashing green, seven seconds. That's Battleship Rock." He sat down and opened the ice chest. "That's enough navigation for one night."

I declined another wine cooler, more for the "cooler" than the "wine." As chilly as it was getting, I would have said yes to anything hot.

Hornet went below and came back with a blanket. "Here," he said, tossing it to me. He sat back in the passenger seat and lit yet another cigarette.

I tucked the blanket around my legs and zipped my windbreaker. "You gonna tell me what's on your mind?"

"I'm feeling old and beat up. Feel like Atlas with the weight of the world on my shoulders. This is my last gig. After this, the Wackers of the world can have it." He smoked quietly, the flare of his cigarette showing that his eyes focused somewhere far out in the dark. He dipped the stub of his cigarette in the lake and the fire went out. He put the butt in an ashtray with the remains of more than a pack. The moon finally appeared between the clouds, and our eyes met in the faint light.

"You don't throw butts in the lake," I said.

"It's against the law to litter." He spit out the words, then sighed. "I'm just a sentimental old fart, not wanting to put garbage in the fishies' bellies." He sighed again. "Okay, enough of that already. I am pretty sure Wacker is on the take. No, make that I *am* sure. Here's the shorthand version: the previous chief, my predecessor, was caught, red-handed, with the marked bills used to buy heroin from cops. The FBI, with uncharacteristic skill and unprecedented secrecy, set up the heroin in the evidence room with a radioactive marker. It was that heroin the cops sold to the Feebies. The chief, Pratt, was allowed to retire and four detectives in narcotics resigned. No scandal. End of story? Nah. The problem with evaporating evidence continues. Although Internal Affairs bought Wacker's righteous indignation, I had my doubts. I came here not trusting anyone, and so far my confidence has proven to be well placed."

He lit another cigarette and coughed hard, about six times. I noticed then that he'd been rubbing his left shoulder and bicep with his right hand since we stopped. No, earlier. He was massaging his bicep when he came up from the galley, back at the marina.

"You probably saw the *LA Times* story. That was just the scoop of vanilla in this banana split. Next to break, the scandal *du jour*, is missing guns. For years the department has accepted guns from citizens, you know – say a guy dies, car wreck or something, and his widow doesn't want guns in the house. So she takes them to the police, who say the guns will be destroyed. But they're not destroyed. They go down the funnel to the street." He opened another beer. "Are you sure you don't want something?" I shook my head and he continued.

"The *Times* is going to run a story Tuesday or Wednesday about a gun used in a robbery/murder in Los Angeles that was easily traced – by a social security number engraved on the barrel, no joke – to a man who died of cancer two years ago in Las Vegas. His widow has the receipt for the gun from the Vegas P.D. And that's just the introduction to the story. They've got a shitload of evidence of corruption here."

"Do you know of any evidence missing in the Margot Farr murder?"

His head jerked up in surprise. "What have you found?"

"It's not what I found, it's what I noticed is missing. Police took a prescription bottle for Zoloft from Margot's bathroom, noting that it had something else in it, a 'white powder.' Apparently it grew legs and walked out of the evidence locker."

Hornet gave a snort of disgust. "Grew legs, huh? Lot of

that going around. Well, I think I know whose desk the legs are under. Look, I have no way of knowing if Margot's white powder is connected with her murder, or if it's connected with other drug mysteries, but Wacker is hiding something. Some hot new drug, rare and expensive as hell, is coming in, and I've heard a rumor that it's being packaged for distribution near Las Vegas. I'm not prepared to say any more."

He drank some beer and lit another cigarette. "The bottom line is, things are going to get ugly, and I don't want you in the crossfire. Never mind what I said about looking for problems in the evidence room. I've got the goods on Wacker now, in my safe at home, and I'm going to turn it all over to the state attorney general." He swore softly and rubbed his arm. "Maybe we'd better head back. I feel shitty." This time he threw the lit cigarette in the lake and said, "You drive."

I turned the key in the ignition and tried to get my bearings. I started to ask Hornet for help but he stumbled to his feet and said, "I'm going below. Gotta lie down." There was a loud thump when his feet hit the floor of the galley, then a crash. I looked down the hatch and saw the door to the head swing open.

I sat down in the driver's seat, just letting the engine idle in neutral, while I tugged the plastic map from its holder under the dashboard. With the flashlight, I tried quickly to make sense of the map. As I noted north and south on the map, I consulted the compass on top of the dashboard. We were drifting slowly north as I'd guessed. Calville Bay was northeast, but I wouldn't see it until I got east of a butte that sheltered the bay.

I aimed the bow north by northeast and gradually picked up the power. I didn't want to throw Hornet to the floor with a racing start. When I'd gotten up to about thirty miles per hour, fast but not maximum speed, I called, "Hornet, are you all right?"

There was no answer, so I powered back, left the throttle in neutral, and went below with the flashlight. The door to the head swung toward me, then slammed shut. I stepped off the stairs and held onto the edge of the sink for stability. I heard a moan; turning toward the stern, I shone my flashlight onto the double bed behind the stairs.

Hornet lay there on his back, his eyes closed. I turned on the light over the sink and a reading light over the bed. "Hornet, what's wrong? Are you sick?"

His eyes flew open with a look of shock and he moaned. Again he rubbed his left arm and shoulder. His face was pale and sweat stood out on his upper lip and forehead. My first thought was "heart attack." My second was "angina," which is painful, but treatable.

"Hornet! Do you take nitroglycerin?" He moaned and tried to roll toward the front of the bed, the only side not bordered by the body of the boat. "Hornet! Answer me. Do you take nitroglycerin?"

This time he clearly shook his head and moaned, "No."

"Are you having chest pains?" I asked as I grabbed his wrist. His pulse seemed irregular, but I didn't feel confident that I was the best judge of that. My own was racing out of my control.

"Yes," he said, the sound wheezing from his throat. "Chest hurts."

"Okay, lie still. It's going to be all right." I felt his pockets for his cell phone. Nothing there.

He gripped my right forearm, making me wince with pain. "Listen! You've got to listen. Tell Betty I'm sorry. Promise me!"

"I promise. I'll tell Betty." I nodded vigorously as I tried to pry his fingers off my arm.

"I made a mistake," he went on. "I shouldn't have married her."

"Betty?" I said stupidly.

"No, Vanitsa. I . . . shouldn't have . . . Oh, Betty," he moaned. Tears dripped over the bridge of his nose and dropped onto the bed. "Tell her," he said softly. I scooted backward off the bed, bumping my head hard on the cabinet over the sink. It felt like the corner dented my forehead, but I didn't detect any blood. I looked around the galley and saw a canvas backpack on the bench seat behind the table. I opened the top and dumped the contents on the seat. His phone slid onto the floor and I scrambled under the table to grab it. The power was already on, and an "R" indicated we were out of the service area and would have to "roam."

I dialed "911" and pressed Talk. The message Internal Battery Low displaced the numbers I'd tried to dial. I tried again, but the battery message didn't budge. I looked back at Hornet. He was now drenched in sweat and tugging at the collar of his T-shirt.

I'd been certified in CPR four times over the years, five if you count when I was a teenager working at a swimming pool, but I hadn't taken a refresher course in eight or nine years. I felt that loss now, as I had to wrack my brain to think what to do. "He's breathing," I said aloud, "so that's okay. He's got a pulse." I needed help, and the phone was useless.

I flew back up the stairs and grabbed the microphone to the marine band CB. Pressing Transmit, I shouted, "I need help! I'm on Lake Mead with a possible heart attack victim and I need help! Boat is the Vega Star. Can anybody hear me?"

I released the Transmit button and listened, first to static, then to a jumble of voices, then to a clear, calm voice. "This is Lake Mead Dispatch. Please describe your emergency."

"I'm on the lake, uh, northwest of Boulder Harbor,

heading toward Callville Bay. The man who is ill is about 55 years old, and he's having severe chest pains. They've only been severe for ten minutes or so, but I think he had some pain for the past hour."

"Is he conscious and breathing?"

"Yes. I think so. He was a minute ago – I can't see him from here." I tried to keep my voice calm, but hysteria was creeping in. As I spoke I shone the flashlight on the dashboard, found a toggle switch for lights, and flipped it. I could see to read the GPS and gave our position to the woman at Dispatch. "I'm at 36 degrees, 6.3 minutes north, and 114 degrees, 44.4 minutes west. I'm going to check on him."

I jumped from the deck to the galley, landing hard and banging my left hand sharply on the edge of the sink. I spun around to face the ladder and ducked behind it. Hornet's eyes showed the severity of his pain. They showed panic as well. Trying to hide my own fear, I leaned over him. He made a keening sound, lifted his head off the bed, then went rigid — then fell back, his eyes closed and his mouth slack.

"Hornet!" I shrieked. "Answer me!" I felt his wrist, couldn't find a pulse, and felt instead on the side of his neck for his carotid artery. There was a rapid, thready pulse, but he was motionless. An alarm went off in my head, a residue of all the cardiopulmonary resuscitation classes I'd attended with half my attention on my kids' squabbles and my money worries. *He's not breathing!* I wished I had rubber arms so I could reach the microphone without leaving his side, but I wanted more than anything to see him breathe.

I adjusted his head to make a clear air passage, took a deep breath, and pressed my mouth wide over his lips. I exhaled, watched his chest rise, did it again, three times, then made a fist, straddled him for leverage, and pressed my fist into his chest with the weight of my torso.

His chest didn't rise. The best thing I could do for him was get real help fast.

I leaped back to the deck and grabbed the microphone. "Hello? Are you there? He's not breathing."

"Vega Star, we know where you are. We have a rescue boat in the water, headed toward you," the woman said, her voice not quite as calm as before. "We need you to go at your top speed on a course that will meet the boat more quickly. Look at your compass. Go due east until I tell you to change direction. Do it now!"

Without a word I brought the bow around to the east and hit the throttle all the way forward. Dropping the microphone and letting it dangle from its holder, I pressed down on the trim tabs. The boat shot across the water as if from a catapult and I hooked one finger on the microphone cord and pulled it to my mouth. "We're on our way!"

"All right, hold steady," she said, then asked my name and the name and age of the victim.

I blurted them out, adding, "He's the chief of police in Las Vegas."

"Okay, Ma'am, make a turn to the north. Watch your compass," she said.

As soon as I made the turn and regained max speed, a man's voice broke in on the CB. "I see her! We're closing. Keep her coming, Ma'am."

What looked like a motorcycle headlight ten miles away quickly grew to a spotlight in my eyes as we closed at the equivalent of a hundred miles an hour. Behind the white spotlight I saw rotating red and blue lights to tell one and all to get the hell out of the way.

I cut the engine and the boat settled into the water like a fat duck, coming to a stop just as my feet hit the floor of the galley. "Hornet!" I tried to scream, but no sound made it past an obstruction in my throat, which I think was my heart.

I began CPR with the strength of someone twice my size. My body knew exactly what to do, as if I'd been certified an hour ago. I vaulted over him, positioned myself on my knees beside his chest, and found the notch at the lower edge of his breastbone with the fingers of my right hand. I placed the heel of my left hand on that spot, covered it with my right hand, twined my fingers to keep them above him, and pressed down hard with the weight of my upper body.

"One and two and three and four and . . ." I pressed down on each number, trying to compress his chest two inches, and let his chest rise on each "and."

In ten or twelve seconds I had completed the cycle of compressions. "Fifteen. Come on, Hornet, come on, damn it!" I pressed my mouth on his and exhaled once, took in another breath myself and forced the air into his lungs. I watched his chest rise, then instantly resumed the position beside his chest and gave him fifteen more quick compressions. One breath, two breaths.

Compressions again. I kept count; I'd given four sets of compressions and breaths when I felt heavy feet jumping onto the deck above. The galley was suddenly filled to overflowing with humans and what looked like red suitcases. I backed away into the dark part of the sleeping space as I gave them a rapid-fire rundown of his condition and what first aid I'd tried.

A large man in a bulky uniform crawled over Hornet to the place I'd been occupying and pulled Hornet's T-shirt up over his head. As he began CPR, another paramedic placed two electrodes on Hornet's chest. I craned my neck to watch and saw him press a button on a portable console.

"Ventricular fibrillation," the second man called. "Clear!" The paramedic on the bed giving CPR stopped and backed up, pressing me against the wall. We watched Hornet's chest jump, then the eyes of all three of us were riveted on the screen of the console. The wild gyrations continued.

"Come on, buddy," the big man shouted at Hornet. "Work with us, come on!"

"Try again. Clear!" the man squatting on the floor said.

Again Hornet's chest jumped. His skin now had a bluish cast and his lips were purple. We stared again at the console.

In an instant the erratic lines snapped to attention and we saw heartbeats marching across the screen, one after another, like good little soldiers. It was a miracle. I stared at the console, willing the little spikes and lines to keep marching, afraid if I looked away that the good news would turn bad. I don't know why I kept staring at the screen, though. After a half-minute or so I couldn't see anything through my tears.

I wiped my eyes on the sleeve of my windbreaker and took a good look at Hornet. His eyes were closed, but his skin was pink, and he was breathing on his own.

The big paramedic said, "Excuse me, Ma'am" as he crawled carefully over Hornet and tried to find a spot on the patch of floor for his big feet. He had to settle for one foot on the floor, a pivot, and he was up the ladder.

The EMT-III on the floor, whose nametag said he was Deke DeSantee, said, "So far, so good. But we've got to get him to a hospital."

Immediately, the other man, whose nametag said Gomer Riggs, was down the ladder again. "It'll be faster if I carry him," he said.

Deke nodded, removed the electrodes, and closed up the console. Gomer lifted the console up out of the galley and Deke placed his hands gently under Hornet's neck and head. Gomer put his big arms under Hornet's body and lifted him.

One grunt from Gomer was the only indication that lifting this dead-weight man was a tough job. He stepped on the ladder, steadied from below by Deke, and handed Hornet to waiting hands above. I followed Deke up the ladder into the blinding glare of the spotlight. I was just in time to see Hornet being strapped to a board and handed from the Vega Star over to the larger boat. On the side was the word RESCUE, and under that, in block letters, Lake Mead National Recreation Area.

"Ma'am," a man's voice said behind me, "could you move to your left, please?"

I did as he asked, then turned to see who had spoken. A skinny man in a Mae West had a video camera to his face, obviously filming the transfer of "the victim" to the rescue boat. I didn't think much of it until I saw the bright blue call letters of a Las Vegas TV station on the side of the camera.

Without warning, he turned his lens toward me. I turned my back to him, but not fast enough. From behind the camera he called, "Ma'am, can you tell us what happened on the boat, what the victim's symptoms were? How long was it from the time you saw he was ill until you called for help?"

Gomer stepped between us as he retrieved the portable defibrillator unit and I reached out and clung to his arm. "Can you make him stop filming me, please? I have a right to privacy."

"Yes, Ma'am, sorry." Instead of wasting words while the camera continued to roll film, he placed his body directly in front of the camera lens. "Sir, the lady does not wish to be photographed. We let you accompany us on the condition that you would respect privacy." As he talked (and simultaneously blocked the lens), he herded the photographer toward the edge of the boat. "Step over onto our boat, sir, thank you, watch your step, sir."

Gomer turned back to me. "Are you all right, Ma'am? Do you need someone to drive the boat back to the marina?"

"No, I'm fine. I'll take the boat back. I'm fine. You just take care of Chief Armstrong." I was shivering, but I clutched my arms close to me and clenched my teeth to hide my shaking. "I'm fine," I said again. "Fine."

"Okay, then, Ma'am. We're on our way. A helicopter will meet us at the shore."

"Thank you. Thank you very much, for – saving his life." I slid into the driver's seat and pulled the blanket around me. At the same time, I kept my face averted from the rescue boat in case the bozo with the camera was not minding his manners.

I watched the rescue boat turn around and speed northeast across the black water, lights and sirens blazing. Instead of making another flying start in its wake, I proceeded at a speed about one-third what the Vega Star could do.

I had a sick, cold feeling in the pit of my stomach, the feeling that I'd soon see my face on TV, privacy be damned.

Chapter 19

As soon as I came abreast of the alpha buoy to Callville Bay, I saw lights, lights, lights. In the distance was the amber glow of Las Vegas against the clouds, punctuated at intervals by the powerful beam from the Luxor's pyramid. I wondered if Vegas is visible from the moon on a clear night. In the distance I saw blips of light, planes lined up and homing in on McCarran International. And in the foreground, above the glaring illumination of the marina, were the lights of the medical chopper. I watched as it settled to the ground, then rose again about two minutes later, swung in a circle, and blinked away toward the hospital.

I had a sensation I was hovering on the water, not getting closer to the shore, but the lights of the marina continued to grow brighter and shapes more distinct. The inevitable could not be postponed any longer. I pulled the collar of my windbreaker up and aimed the Vega Star toward its slip. As I came alongside the dock a dozen people jockeyed for my attention. I locked the galley and stuck the key ring deep in the pocket of my slacks, uncoiled the two lengths of rope, and secured the stern to a cleat. Someone reached out for the other rope and secured the front.

I looked up as I stepped onto the wooden dock – right into the light of a camera. I knew instantly it was the same photographer who had intruded out on the lake. No one was around now to help him spell the word "privacy." All I could do was hunch my neck down into my chest and barge ahead toward the parking lot. Unfortunately, the only route was across a network of wooden walkways, paths crowded with onlookers. I had to bob and weave all the way to land. Then I made a run uphill to my car.

I pulled out of the lot and headed toward Vegas. The state of New Mexico never sounded so good to me as it did at that moment. Ditto California.

My anonymity might still be intact, I told myself as I turned on the heat in my car. The outside temperature, now that I was off the water, was balmy, and the wind had died down to nothing, but I was still shivering. *Yeah, and my virginity.*

I left off hoping the TV station would not use my name and put my wishing-energy into hoping Candace was sound asleep. I could tell her in the morning. About Mace, and Hornet, and Margot Farr.

I parked in back of the apartment complex. Although it was past midnight, the light in her bedroom was unmistakably on. I didn't waste any time hoping she was up reading a thriller.

I'd hardly opened the door a crack when she started working me over. Candace always did have a lash for a tongue. I understood as I never had before how the boy in her second grade class felt when he made the mistake of calling her Candy-ass.

"Mother! What in the name of holy hell have you been up to? Why, WHY, were you out boating in the middle of the night with a married man?"

"I can explain . . ."

"Great, I can't wait to hear it, and while you're at it you can explain why Mace Emerick called here for you." She was waving her arms like a wild Italian in a pasta commercial.

"Let's sit down . . ."

"I don't feel like sitting down!"

"Well, I do." I reached up on the top shelf of the cabinet over the stove and got down the brandy and two small snifters and set them on the coffee table. I poured two fingers in each, then tipped another dollop in one and handed her the other one. I settled on the couch much as a cat would settle on a cactus, took a hearty swallow of brandy, and said imperiously, "When you sit down and shut up, I will explain what I've been 'up to,' as you put it."

She plopped down in the armchair that matched the couch. "The sooner the better!"

"I worked with Hornet Armstrong and Mace Emerick in California. They both work here now. I ran into Mace under difficult circumstances, and, since I needed a job and I do have a degree in criminal justice, I took a temporary job with the police department. I was doing some work specifically at the direction of Hornet, who is the new chief of police. He happens to think well of me, whether you can stretch your imagination that far or not."

"What difficult circumstances?" She spit the words out without unclenching her teeth.

I took a deep breath and let a swallow of brandy trickle down my throat. As I poured another two fingers (as measured on a fat truck driver) I spoke. "On Wednesday, when I got here, I went to a job interview at a hotel. It was a job in publicity. I'd been in touch with the people in that department before I came. However, they filled it right before I got there, and the woman who was hired gave me a tip about a job opening. I went to help a movie star with her memoirs."

"So, that's what you've been doing when you pretended to be doing transcription?" She kicked her shoes off and they landed clear across the room. "Who's the lucky woman?"

"Nobody lucky, I'm afraid. It was Margot Farr." Before she interrupted I gave a quick rendition of my interview and hiring, the gunshots, and coming face to face with Mace Emerick.

"Mace had a crazy idea, well – it's not completely crazy – for me to work for the police, sort of undercover, as it were. And Hornet wanted me to help, so I did. I'm on the payroll of the Vegas P.D."

"So, under the guise of consulting with you, the chief of police had you on a boat, on Lake Mead, in the middle of the night. Where he suffered a heart attack." She sounded like an attorney for the prosecution, making a scathing statement to a jury.

"Was there something about it on TV?"

"Something?" she bleated. "Something? Yes, there was dramatic footage, probably already sold to *Inside Edition*, of an overweight white male, age 55, being transferred to a rescue boat. I couldn't see his face, as he had an oxygen mask over it, but I could see yours. And, also, I had the helpful voiceover telling me, and everyone else in Las Vegas, the names of the two individuals alone on a boat when he fell ill." She said "alone" in an ominous tone.

I rotated my head gently on my aching neck and concentrated on sensing the brandy warming my neck, chest and arms. The silence was anything but companionable. "Did they say if he's going to be all right?"

"They said his condition is stable. Oh – do you want to know how his WIFE is taking it?"

My most sincere guess was that Vanitsa was probably examining his life insurance policy and calculating her proceeds, but I said, with appropriate concern, "Of course I do."

"She was at the hospital when the helicopter arrived."

"On second thought, don't tell me, let me guess. She's devastated with fear for his life. She's near collapse." I took a large swallow of brandy, widening my eyes as it burned in my throat. "Well, Candace, forgive me if I doubt the depth of her on-camera concern. It might interest you that Hornet begged me to tell his first wife, Betty, his wife of almost thirty years, that he made a terrible mistake by leaving her. I'll bet she's more concerned about his health than Miss Photogenic." I drained my snifter just as the doorbell rang. "Why do I feel like I'm on stage in a melodrama that placed last in a script contest?"

"I'll get it," she said.

"I'll get it, she said nastily," I muttered. The brandy seemed to be creeping up the back of my neck and warming my brain. I leaned over to the coffee table and switched my empty glass for the snifter Candace had scarcely touched and said, "Surprise!" I took a tiny sip and added, "Surprise, she chortled amiably."

I heard the door open, and close, without a word from Candace. I added mood music, the theme from *Dragnet*. "Dum da dum dum."

"Olivia . . ." Mace said from behind me.

In my best directorial voice I said, "Say it again, with dripping emotion. Say "Olivia!' then cross to the fireplace and draw your sword."

"You never could hold your liquor," he said as he deftly lifted the snifter out of my hand and drank it himself.

I opened my mouth to mimic him in the cackle of a witch, then thought better of it. I sat back in the corner of the couch and tucked my feet under me. The brandy hadn't warmed them at all, so I rubbed my toes to improve circulation. Mace sat in the armchair and Candace took the other end of the couch, as far from me as she could get and still be in the living room.

I focused my eyes on Mace with difficulty that I ascribed to being bone-tired. "Have you been at the hospital?"

"Yes. You did a hell of a job out there. He'd be dead — or at least brain-dead – if you hadn't acted so quickly."

Tears sprang to my eyes and gushed down my cheeks.

"I was scared. It seemed like too many minutes from when he stopped breathing until they used the fibber, the fibberil – oh, you know what I'm talking about." Defibrillator was hard to say sober, and was way beyond me at that point. "Is he conscious?"

"Yes. He regained consciousness in the helicopter. He can't remember how he got there, but other than that he's lucid. He knew me, and he knew Vanitsa."

"Is he going to be all right, then? He's okay?" My voice broke like a boy soprano on his last day in the choir.

"Well, he's a very sick dog, according to the vet, and they're running lots of heart tests. Best guess is, he needs angioplasty. Possibly a bypass. Or two or three. They'll know more tomorrow afternoon." He looked at his watch. "This afternoon."

I yawned. "I don' wanna talk anymore."

"Why don't you go on to bed," Mace said. "Candace and I have some things to talk about."

"I think I'll go to bed, she said, exiting stage right." I unfolded my feet, which had preceded me to sleep and now had needles and pins. I rose and walked painfully toward the bathroom, then turned to Candace. "But you're sitting on my bed."

"You go sleep in my bed tonight, Mother. I'll sleep out here."

I brushed my teeth, washed my face, and crawled into bed in a T-shirt. I had a warm feeling I recognized as the afterglow of brandy coupled with relief that Hornet had survived. Sure, it was the pits that Candace was mad at me, but Mace could explain everything.

Everything will be fine, I thought sleepily.

Everything will be fine, she thought stupidly. Exit stage right to the ringing of a gong.

Chapter 20

Monday, Monday. *First the good news*, I told myself. *I suffered no after effects of the brandy.* Truth be told, I hadn't drunk a lot, I just drank it in a short span of time. I woke far from refreshed, however, after two nights of scant sleep. I allowed myself one minute to relish the memory of Saturday night and Sunday morning aboard the *Manta Raye*.

Okay, your minute is up, love puppy. *Time to deal with Sunday night – and Monday morning.*

I continued to tabulate my good news and bad news. In the plus column, I hadn't signed a lease for an apartment. I could leave Las Vegas and make a fresh start somewhere else. Such as Homer, Alaska. Or Bar Harbor, Maine. Maybe I'd just throw a dart at a map.

In the minus column, however, was the damage to my reputation. I wanted to clear my name. I wasn't doing anything wrong on Hornet's boat. It was just like Candace to believe the worst.

Lying in bed, I recalled Hornet's heart attack, the rescue boat and paramedics, and that damn TV cameraman. May he roast in hell. On camera. At that precise moment, as if by sheer perversity, Candace turned on the television in the living room. And I was certain as sin she wasn't watching cartoons.

I took my time in the bathroom, then traipsed into the living room and said, "Good morning." It didn't take long to recognize silent treatment as the order of the day. I shuffled into the kitchen and made a small pot of hazelnut coffee. Golf was the focus of the TV news people, a too-brief blessing, like a pause while a guy in a black hood wipes gunk off the blade in the guillotine. As I feared, just ten minutes after I emerged from the bathroom I had to see my guilty-looking face on board the Vega Star, then the transfer of Hornet, first to the rescue boat and then to the helicopter, followed by my arrival at the marina. And now, for our viewing pleasure, good old Mindy Ransom was standing by a sign that said Emergency Entrance. The word LIVE was posted on screen.

"Norman, Chief of Police Harold Armstrong is in stable condition at Valley Medical Center. We've been told by a spokesperson for the hospital that tests are being run this morning to determine how much damage was done to his heart. The spokesperson said angioplasty is one possible route for the doctors to take. Another route is a multiple heart bypass."

Norman thanked Mindy in a voice dripping with concern and went to the station's medical expert, who pointed to a diagram of the heart as he gave a quick, colorful look at balloons in veins and how surgeons bypass arteries. It was less nauseating than a diagram of colorectal examination, but not by much.

Back at the news desk, Norman added that since the chief of police was incapacitated, the mayor had appointed Capt. Avery Wacker as acting chief of police, and that Wacker would be holding a press conference at 10:00 a.m.

The phone rang and Candace ignored it. It drives me crazy to let a phone ring and go to an answering machine, but I steadied my resolve and disregarded the phone until Mace's voice boomed, "Pick up the damn phone, Olivia."

Candace snatched the receiver off the cradle and thrust it at my face. She still wasn't speaking to me, a form of punishment not really painful from my perspective.

"Hi. I'm up watching the news," I said. "Is that the latest on Hornet? It doesn't sound like they know more than what they said last night."

"I talked to Vanitsa half an hour ago. She's upbeat. The doctors are very optimistic that he didn't suffer irreparable damage to his heart. That's due to your quick thinking and fast driving, but Vanitsa won't admit that. She says she thinks you two were 'involved.' He's been acting strange lately, she thinks, like he's all wrapped up in something." Mace sounded like he was recounting the plot of a soap opera for a friend who'd missed two episodes. *Today: Olivia shocks Vanitsa, claiming she's pregnant with Hornet's baby. Vanitsa pushes her out a fifth story window. Tomorrow: Olivia lies in a coma while doctors struggle to save her baby.*

Highly incensed at Mace's tone, I snapped, "Well, I hope you set her straight!"

"Now, Olivia, you know I'm limited in what I can say at this point . . ."

"Listen to me, you weasel, you're limited to the truth, nothing more, nothing less. I don't want Hornet's wife thinking I'm a home wrecker."

"Calm down, Olivia, we have enough problems without clawing each other."

We have problems. We. It seemed to me at that moment that problems were all we had in common. It was time for fight or flight, and I made up my mind in favor of flight. *Bar Harbor, here I come.*

"Capt. Wacker is the General Haig of the Las Vegas Police Department." Mace went on in broad imitation of Haig, "'I am in charge at the White House!' Wacker's mad with power, and he's going to hold a press conference at 10:00."

"Yeah?" I said, in a *so what?* tone. All I had to do to terminate my tenuous connection to Capt. Wacker was drop off a fare-thee-well note, along with my keys and my photo ID badge, downstairs at police headquarters. I could leave my engine running.

"I don't think you . . . You're not . . . What this means..." He paused and sighed. I pictured him rubbing the back of his neck raw and tugging on his earlobe. "I'm coming over there." He hung up before I could argue.

That's just great. Candace can vent her spleen on him. Then it occurred to me that the two of them had plenty of time to vent after I crawled into her bed. I wondered what had transpired, but didn't have much hope of finding out.

"Mace is coming over here," I said. "I'm going to take a shower and start packing."

Thirty minutes later I looked a lot better, but I didn't feel any better. And even though I've never been what anyone would call "psychic," I had a strong sense that I was destined to feel a lot worse.

"I had to take the phone off the hook," Candace said. Since she was glaring at me when she said it, I eliminated telemarketers as the cause of her wrath. I didn't buy in with a request to explain why the phone was quiet, certain she'd continue her rant if I waited.

"It might interest you to know that your location has been ascertained by the fourth estate, by what nefarious means I don't pretend to know. They are sharpening their knives in the parking lot and probably preparing to throw ladders against the battlements."

Nefarious? I had never noticed before how much Candace sounds like me. Ah, motherhood. One never knows what will stick, does one?

The sharp knock on the door was accompanied by Mace's voice. "It's me, Olivia."

Candace opened the door and "greeted" him with, "I hope you're satisfied!"

He strode to the television and turned it on. Mindy

Ransom was LIVE again, this time in the lobby of Valley Medical Center. A lectern had been set up with a modest bank of microphones protruding above the great seal of the state of Nevada and its motto, Battle Born.

Candace closed the door and all three of us sat on the couch, intent on the sight of Capt. Wacker unfolding a sheet of paper. "He looks pretty good in makeup," I said. "Almost lifelike."

"I have a brief statement to read, and then Dr. Samuel Lilly, the hospital's chief of staff, will answer some of the questions you have already posed." He put on his glasses and adjusted the position of the paper. "Chief of Police Harold Armstrong suffered a massive heart attack last night while on his boat on Lake Mead. His companion used a marine citizens band radio to summon help. Thanks to fast reaction by the rescue personnel at Lake Mead National Recreation Area and by the emergency room staff here at Valley Medical Center, he survived the heart attack and is now resting comfortably."

The camera shot widened a little and I saw a striking woman about two feet to Wacker's left. Her golden tresses looked a bit jumbled. "That's Vanitsa," Mace said.

Hornet's new wife was tall and tan and young and lovely, just as Mace had said. Well, not *that* young, I meowed to myself.

Wacker introduced her as Vanitsa Noble Armstrong, adding that doctors had just informed "Mrs. Armstrong and myself" that surgeons would do a triple heart bypass on Chief Armstrong within the next few days.

"It might even have to be a quadruple bypass," Wacker continued. "Doctors have ordered total isolation and rest for the chief, and they say he will be incapacitated for at least five weeks. In fact, they recommend a longer period of rest. As you know, the mayor has appointed me to carry out the responsibilities of chief of police for the foreseeable future, and I am doing so."

He folded the sheet of paper methodically and removed his glasses, playing for the cameras. Looking deep into the eyes of Mr. and Mrs. Las Vegas, he said, "I've had a lot of questions from the media regarding the female companion with Chief Armstrong last night."

A strangled sob of disbelief escaped from my throat. Candace looked stricken. "Oh, no!" she gasped, covering her mouth with her fingers. Only Mace remained silent, staring at the screen.

"Olivia Wright, age 50, is said to be a friend of the chief's from his time at the San Diego Police Department. Although she has little experience in police work, the chief insisted she be hired on a temporary basis to work with detectives on the investigation of the murder of actress Margot Farr. Ms. Wright was, in fact, at the scene of that murder before the fatal shots were fired. Although she is not at this time a suspect in the murder, I have determined that it is in the best interest of that investigation that her employment by the Las Vegas Police Department be terminated, effective this morning."

Wacker introduced the hospital's chief surgeon, who answered questions about Armstrong's condition and the anticipated heart surgery.

My own heart was having problems, all my blood having pooled somewhere below my diaphragm. "Oh, my God," was all I could say. "Oh, my God."

Mace pulled me to his chest in a smothering hug. "This is all my fault."

"You've got that right, Bucko," I said into his chest. Twisting my head sideways to be heard, I added, "If you're hoping for absolution, see a priest."

"That slimy son of a bitch!" Candace rasped. "That stinking, rat-faced, slimy son of a bitch."

"You go, girl," I cheered. I didn't know whether to laugh

or cry, so I did both.

"You haven't heard the BAD news yet," Mace said. The look on his face required a thesaurus to describe: gloomy, dismal, dejected, depressed, despondent, grave.

"There's more?" Candace and I asked in a duet of disbelief.

"He's saving his gold nugget for the evening news, but he's already informed me by phone. Not directly, but by voice mail. He has placed me on administrative leave pending investigation into the missing evidence scandal. He's got to feed something tasty to the LA Times, and I'm it."

"You don't have anything to do with missing evidence, and he knows it!" I shouted hoarsely.

"What are we going to do about this shit?" Candace stood and paced the room.

We? I feared my hearing was faulty. Did she say We?

Mace stood and crossed to the sliding glass door. "First step," he said to Candace, "is what we talked about last night."

"How many reporters are out front?" she asked.

"Only six or seven now, plus cameramen. It will get worse. We'd better make our move now."

"What are you talking about?" I interjected.

They went on as if I weren't there. "I've got two cell phones," Mace said. "My personal phone and the one I'm supposed to turn in to the police department today." He pulled a business card from his pocket, scribbled something on the back, and handed it to her.

"I have one," she said. "You have the number." She turned to me. "We're going to Kenneth's apartment. Just take one bag. I'll be ready in five minutes."

There's something about action as an antidote to shock. I wasted no time with questions, just retrieved essential items from my suitcase and stuffed them in a canvas bookbag. Candace was as good as her word, emerging from the bathroom in khaki shorts and silk blouse. She set her metal overnight bag on the couch, darted into the bedroom to grab some clothes in a gym bag, a couple dresses still in plastic from the dry cleaners, and a pair of high heels, which she handed to Mace. He stuck them toe down in his jacket pockets.

"Okay," he said, "We'll go down the middle stairs, cross the pool area, and leave by the back gate to the parking lot. Olivia and I will follow you in my car."

Candace took a large bottle of water from the refrigerator, put the phone back on the hook, and stuck her cell phone recharger in her purse. In unison, we took deep breaths, then headed for the stairs. I went out last, making sure the door was locked.

It was a quick trip to our destination. I had time, though, to ask Mace why Candace had jumped on board my sinking ship. "We had a talk last night," he said, "after you went to bed."

"Yes, go on."

"She's mad, mostly because she thinks I treated you like shit in San Diego. So, yeah, she's mad at me, has been for years, but now she's even more angry at you for not having enough pride to tell me to get lost when we met again. If it were just the three of us she'd stay mad at you and me. But as soon as someone outside attacked you, she was ready to defend you. And, too, I explained how much you'd done to save Hornet's life."

At the gate, Candace told the guard we were with her and he waved us through. Kenneth's apartment was a townhouse, with a private ground-floor entrance off a common walkway bordered with lush blue-green grass.

Candace had apparently been on the phone to Kenneth en route, because he welcomed us emotionally. "Olivia, you poor thing," he said as he held me tight to his chest.

Candace introduced Mace, and Kenneth shook his hand vigorously and clapped him on the shoulder.

"Like I told you, we're in a shitload of trouble," Candace said. I was still finding it hard to believe she said "we."

"I didn't see the press conference," Kenneth said. "I guess there's more to come?"

"Yeah, Acting Chief Wacker will drop the other shoe on the evening news." Mace shook his head. "If Hornet Armstrong hears what Wacker is up to, he'll rise up and roar."

I nodded. "Especially since he's sure Wacker is on the take and was close to exposing his thieving ass."

They all looked at me as if I'd dropped in through a trap door in the ceiling. Mace spoke slowly. "What did you say?"

"Hornet told me last night, on the boat, that he was ready to turn over evidence about Wacker to the state attorney general. The *LA Times* is about to print another Vegas police scandal story, with juicy details about guns that reappear where they shouldn't. He also said some hot new drug, something 'rare and expensive as hell,' is coming in to the city." I thought back to Hornet's face, and the intensity of his voice. "He said he's heard a rumor that the drug is being packaged for distribution near Las Vegas."

"Where?" Mace barked. "What else did he say?"

"He didn't tell me anything else. He said he was taking me off the Margot Farr case because he didn't want me caught in the crossfire when things get ugly." I tried again to retrace my conversation with Hornet. "I told him about the missing white powder, the prescription bottle found at Margot's house, and how the evidence room officer couldn't find it. I don't remember if I told him this or not, but I remember the officer told me, on Saturday right before you and I went to Los Angeles, that drugs 'go missing' all the time from the evidence room. She seemed pretty disgusted. In fact, it was her last night on the job. She was definitely disgusted."

One of Mace's phones rang. He removed the one in his inside jacket pocket. "Detective Emerick." He listened. "Yes, I did leave a message for you. Thanks for calling me back, Mr. Lazar." He pulled a small notebook and pen from the other side of his jacket and sat on a stool beside Kenneth's breakfast bar. "How do you spell your first name?" He scribbled something in his notebook. "So Mr. Lazar, I spoke with the owner of AquaMate, Mr. Diaz. Is he correct that you were working on the pool at Number Three Manzanillo last Wednesday?"

I moved a stool to his line of sight and sat down. He nodded to tell me the man said yes and continued. "How long were you there? From noon to about 3:30? Okay. Did you notice any cars near Number Four when you arrived?"

I leaned over to try and read his notes, but Mace's handwriting had always been inscrutable. I had to content myself with listening.

"A silver BMW in front of the closed garage, okay. And all the garage doors were closed? Did you see or hear anything going on at Number Four while you were there?" He shook his head. "Oh, I see, you had a compressor running part of the time. Well, was the BMW still there when you left? It was?"

Kenneth held up a carafe of coffee and Mace nodded that he'd like a cup. "Mr. Lazar, I understand from Mr. Diaz that the pool cleaning and pump repair was done while the owners of that home were out of state. How did you arrange to get in to work?" He nodded his thanks for the coffee to Kenneth.

"We'll be in Kenneth's office working on contracts," Candace whispered. I nodded and tuned my ear back to Mace's conversation.

"So the guard was expecting you? I see. So you arrived at noon and the guard left the guard shack to let you into the back yard of Number Three. And he disarmed the security system? Sure, I understand. What about when you left?" Mace gave me a wide-eyed look, as if to say, "Aha!"

"So you called the guard, told him you were finished, and he again left the guard shack and met you at Number Three. In the back yard? And as far as you know, he was still there when you left, because he said he had to turn the security system back on. That's fine, thanks very much. But, one thing – is there any way you can say when you were finished, that is when you called the guard?" He shook his head no, then yes, then no. "Yeah, you wrote down 3:30, but you think you called him a few minutes before you were finished, to give him time to come over. Makes sense. Thanks a lot for your time, Mr. Lazar. And please thank Mr. Diaz again for me."

"The time element makes sense," I said. "I know I drove through the gate right at 3:30, and there was no guard in sight. He must have been at Number Three. The pool truck probably left right after I went inside."

"I have to confirm that with the guard, but yeah, it looks reasonable."

"When is the guard supposed to get back to you?" I asked as I poured a cup of coffee for myself. Kenneth was a perfect host, setting out cream and sugar in bone china.

Mace flipped back the pages on his pocket notebook. "Guy's name is Boyd Daniel. Or maybe it's Boyd, comma, Daniel. He worked eight days straight, ending last Wednesday, and went to Lake Havasu. He's due back on the job today."

I took my steno pad from my bookbag and turned it every which way, trying to recall where each of the players in Margot's life – and therefore potential players in her death – were when she was shot. Correction: where each of them *claimed* they were.

Meanwhile, Mace called the company in charge of manning the gate at Margot's exclusive enclave of houses. "They'll call him on the radio and have him call my cell. And Boyd is his last name." He smiled at Kenneth, sitting at the dining room table with Candace. "Good coffee, thanks. And thanks for letting us come over. Nice place," he added, looking up at the high ceiling shared by the living room, dining room and kitchen.

His phone interrupted his query about how long the townhouses had been there. "Detective Emerick. Yes, Mr. Boyd, thanks for calling me back." I listened as he asked the guard about his hours of work on Wednesday, April 11, what cars he'd observed coming in and out, and any activity that had taken him away from the guard shack. I could tell from Mace's end of the conversation that Boyd confirmed what the pool guy said.

"Mr. Lazar told me he saw a silver BMW parked in front of one of the five garage doors at Ms. Farr's house when he arrived at noon and also when he left, shortly after 3:30. It was not there when police arrived in response to a 911 call. Did you see it leave the compound before your shift ended at 5:00?"

He listened intently, jotting notes in his pad. "So, that was how soon after you returned to the guard shack after securing Number Three? About ten minutes, and he drove back out, alone, three or four minutes later? What time did Ms. Mott drive out the gate? Oh, I see. So of course you're sure about that time. And you're certain no one else came in or out until the first police unit arrived at 4:55?" He thanked the guard and pressed "End."

To me he said, "What did Ted Landers say he was doing Wednesday afternoon?"

I flipped the pages over on my notepad. "Ummm. Oh, yeah – he said he had a late lunch with Esmé at Spago's, dropped her at her home so she could pick up her car, and then he went to Sinbad's to work in his office and play racquetball."

Mace thought it over. "What did Esmé say she was doing all afternoon?"

Again I flipped pages. "She had a long, late lunch with Ted Landers. Then she spent the afternoon shopping, checked her voice mail around 5:45, and met a police officer at Sinbad's right before six. She found out about Margot and ran in to tell Ted." I looked up. "She didn't mention that Ted drove her back to Margot's house."

"The guard was helpful about that. Ted drove in with Esmé about ten minutes after the guard returned to the shack. That puts it at approximately 3:50. Ted was in the compound only long enough to drop Esmé off. Then Esmé drove out in her silver BMW. The guard is sure of the time because she stopped to chat with him and made a point of asking him the time. It was 4:10."

"Sounds like someone establishing an alibi to me," I said. "Sinister."

"She didn't go back in," Mace said. "Nobody drove through the gate until the police arrived."

"Maybe she crawled over the fence."

"Maybe. So we have to check her 'shopping' alibi," Mace said. "My neck is killing me."

"Go sit on the couch," I said.

He winced as he rose from the stool and moved to the couch. He removed his jacket and shoulder holster, took off his tie and unbuttoned his white shirt. "I think my neck is going to hell before the rest of me," he grumped.

I stood behind him. "Take off your shirt."

He tugged it forward over his head. I slathered lotion on my hands from a plastic bottle I keep in my purse. As I kneaded the muscles in his neck and shoulders I concentrated on relaxing my own painful neck and jaw muscles. "You're as tight as razor wire," I groaned, leaning into the task. "Relax the muscle between your ears and we might get somewhere."

"The tissue between my ears is not muscle, thank you very much. The only way to relax my brain is with drugs, which I don't do, and alcohol, which it's too early for. Ouch!"

"Don't be a wienie." I continued to apply pressure to the knots along his upper spine. As I worked I drew a matrix in my mind. Time down one side, people with a motive to kill Margot along the top. Three was the maximum I could plot without paper and pen so I gave it up for the time being. The process did remind me, though, of the mysterious Liam Kiley, who said he "didn't know anything" about a trip to Los Angeles by Aronn Young using fake ID.

I shared my musings with Mace; he said nothing for a time. "The ticket was in Kiley's name, the reservation at the hotel was in Young's name. We don't know with absolute certainty who flew on the ticket. On either end, to or from L.A. Either of them could claim to be Liam Kiley and show a photo ID. We know from the hotel staff that the 'Aronn Young' who stayed there April 10 was actually Liam Kiley."

Kenneth and Candace returned and got comfortable, Kenneth on a loveseat and Candace on a recliner. I gave them a recap of the Liam Kiley-Aronn Young conundrum, ending with, "so the bottom line is, we know Liam Kiley was in Los Angeles at the time of the murder, but we don't know where Aronn Young was."

Candace cleared her throat. "I know where he was."

Mace lifted his head. Simultaneously he said, "Where?" and I said, "What?"

"He was at an orgy at the palatial home of an extremely wealthy movie producer, here in Las Vegas. At the time of the murder, Aronn Young was passed out cold in the producer's screening room. Just prior to that, he was engaging in wild, lascivious sexual acts with multiple partners, and sniffing cocaine."

My heart rate and respiration increased, but I remained outwardly calm. More or less. She could be joking, I told myself, so don't be too quick to bite this hook. "An orgy. Good. Great alibi, plenty of witnesses. May I ask, I mean, surely I may ask - uh, what *you* were doing there? At the aforementioned orgy?"

"Even deviants have to eat," Kenneth interjected.

My eyebrows must have disappeared under my hairline. "Are you saying you *catered* an *orgy?*" They both nodded.

"Of course, on the contract it doesn't say 'o-r-g-y.' It was just a 'private party,'" Kenneth added. "In this business, especially here or in southern California, discretion is the better part of profit."

"I don't happen to agree with Mormon theology," Candace threw in like a curve ball from outer space, "but I cater their events." Her tone was combative, daring me to argue.

Determined not to be dragged into a catfight with Candace, I stopped massaging Mace and plopped myself down beside him on the couch. "An interesting counterpoint," I said, nodding my head. "You do orgies, and Episcopalians. You do orgies, and Republicans. An equal opportunity catering company. Kind of makes me proud."

"We cater weddings," Candace said with a huff, "and what's that besides an elaborate prelude to sex?"

"Speaking in generalities," I intoned, "and not knowing much about wedding customs in Las Vegas, sex is usually not performed by all the guests, at least not at the reception."

"I don't care who has sex or where," Mace blurted. "Or whether they do it with fruit platters, or layer cakes! I just want to know, with certainty, where Margot's husband was when some person or persons unknown to me - unknown to me, the *detective* – were in Margot Farr's house, shooting her." For good measure he added, "Fatally!"

"What on earth were you *wearing*?" I asked Candace.

"Olivia!" Mace snapped. "She's over 21!"

"So?" I snapped back. "What's your point? She's still my daughter."

"Mother," she said as if weary of dealing with my tender sensibilities, "I wore what I usually wear to a job. A black skirt and white blouse. Which I kept on! Kenneth and I handled the job without hiring wait staff. At the time Mace says you called 911, at 4:40 p.m. Wednesday, Aronn Young was draped across a chair in the producer's screening room, stark naked and sound asleep. And no, I don't want to testify in open court, but I will if I have to."

I smiled for the first time. "Think of the lineup down at headquarters."

"Now," Candace said, "are there any other suspects we can help eliminate?"

"You might want to rephrase that," Mace said with a sly grin. "But if you find a way to eliminate Acting Chief Avery Wacker, I will ask no questions."

Chapter 21

Time had a jerky rhythm that afternoon, like watching a pro football game, where the two-minute-warning signals 20 minutes until the end of the game – if you're lucky.

Mace and I wanted to jump in his car and drive all over town, pinning down the whereabouts, on the afternoon of April 11, of all our present suspects in Margot's murder. But we had to lie low or the press would be on us like fat on a fanny. I say our "present suspects" because there could be someone completely unknown involved in Margot's murder.

Because we had so much ground to cover, and so little time to cover it, the day passed quickly. But each hour dragged us closer to the local evening news when we knew Capt. Wacker would announce – in the most prejudicial way he possibly could – that Mace Emerick was on administrative leave.

"I can already see tomorrow morning's headline," Mace said. "Emerick Axed by Wacker."

"It could be even shorter," I suggested. "Emerick Whacked."

Candace and Kenneth had gone to the Royale Catering office to plan a high school 20-year reunion with four of the class representatives.

"Probably another 'clothes optional' event," I sniffed to Mace after they left.

"Are you kidding?" he laughed. "After 20 years there are probably only three people who still look good naked."

Royale had an event scheduled for that evening, a wine

tasting for symphony benefactors, but Kenneth said he could handle it, so Candace said she'd see Mace and me late in the afternoon. The words "in time to watch the evening news" were unspoken, but hung in the air all the same.

Mace put his police cell phone on a recharger. "I'm not going to answer it the rest of the day anyway. I'll just check voice mail later." He brought in his toilet kit and a change of clothes from the trunk of his car.

While he shaved and showered, I drew the matrix I had in mind. Across the top I wrote: Esmé, C. St. John, Kim K., Ted, and Aronn. I tapped the end of the ball point pen against my teeth for a minute, then added Philly and Alicia C. I had room to add two or three more if I thought of anybody suspicious.

The time frame was very narrow. The fax that came into Margot's office arrived at the same time I heard the gunshots. The fax, from the Beverly Wilshire, said, in printed letters, "Margot – I'm finished here. Be home tonight around 8. Love ya, Aronn." According to the information on the top of the page, it arrived at 4:38. The police checked the fax machine, and its time was correct.

My call to 911 was recorded at 4:40. And I had looked at my watch when the person sitting on Margot's bed stood up and left. That was 4:55.

As for when Margot stormed out of her bedroom, on the heels of her outburst on the phone, the best I could estimate was 4:25.

"Are you ready to make an arrest?" Mace asked. He wore blue jeans and a faded denim shirt. I recognized his belt buckle of the Golden Gate Bridge as one of two I'd given him about 12 years before. When he looked over my shoulder I could smell his aftershave. Polo Sport, my favorite.

"I think Aronn had the strongest motive, to sidestep a

divorce that would enforce what her lawyer told you is a draconian prenuptial agreement. But if he was engaged in acts between consenting adults 10 miles from Margot's house when she was shot, he had to hire someone to do it, and that will be hard to uncover."

"What about Liam Kiley?"

"We have determined that he was in Beverly Hills."

"True," he said, "but he also could have hired someone. Same reasoning as with Aronn. No motive I can see, but he deserves a place on your list."

"True. 'No motive we can see' is not the same as 'no motive.'" I jotted Liam on the top right of the matrix. "Ted Landers says he was at Sinbad's from a few minutes after four until Esmé told him Margot was dead, about six p.m. Do you think his employees can be believed, that they saw him there all that time?"

"I do. But if I ever arrange for a hit, I'll make sure I'm seen by a dozen people elsewhere at the time of the murder."

"So, you think Ted is another possible murderer by remote control?"

He shrugged. "Possible, but not probable. The strongest motive award goes to Charles St. John. Which reminds me, I've got to talk to Margot's lawyer again."

"Reid Champion," I muttered. "Now there's a name I'd choose. What are the odds he was born with it? If Vanitsa married him, she'd be Vanitsa Noble Champion. Sounds like a bitch in the Westminster Dog Show."

I could tell Mace was only half listening to me. His attention was on my grid. Without a word he picked up the kitchen phone and stabbed a series of numbers. "Yes, good afternoon. This is Detective Emerick. Is Mr. Champion available? Not until five? Umm. Which court would that be? And the judge? Yes, I know where that is. Thank you."

His personal cell phone rang. "Emerick. Yes, this is

Detective Emerick. Who? I'm sorry, could you repeat that? Oh, yes. Ms. Espiña. Are you in Los Angeles? You are, okay. What can I do for you?" He signaled to me to get him his notepad from his jacket on the couch. He sat down on a stool beside me. "No, you did the right thing to call me, Ms. Espiña. If you observed something you think was, uh, suspicious, you're right to tell me. I'll look into it, without jumping to any conclusions."

He listened, saying, "um-hum" from time to time and "sure, sure."

"As far as 'making you testify,' as you put it, I can't predict what will happen way down the road, when someone is charged with Ms. Farr's murder and brought to trial. But that isn't something you need to worry about. I'll just use your information like you said, just look into it. And I'd be glad to call you back . . ." He paused. "Okay, Ms. Espiña, I understand. But will you call me if you think of anything else? Good. Feel free to call anytime. This number, the one you used, that's the best number. Thanks very much, Ma'am. You too. Have a good evening."

He smiled broadly at me. "Well, if God didn't make little green aliens!"

"Yes? What's up?"

"Well, as you could tell, that was Margot Farr's former live-in maid. She started working for Margot at roughly the same time Kim Kaylyn moved to Las Vegas and started supervising Margot's diet, about fourteen months ago. Margot was very fat then. Well, Kim fixed attractive but tiny meals, and Carmen heard Margot rave about how Kim knew exactly how to combine foods so she was full after a few bites. She went on and on about how her craving for sweets and potato chips was totally gone. And sure enough, she lost all the excess weight. She looked great."

"That all sounds . . ."

"That's right. Too good to be true. Carmen saw Kim

acting very sneaky one day, setting Margot's plate down on the counter while she got a vial out of her purse. She looked around but didn't see Carmen, and sprinkled a white powder in Margot's diet soda. She put the vial back in her purse, and served the soda and the meal to Margot. The first time Carmen saw Kim do it, it was a random chance that she was in position to see without being seen. But at least a dozen more times she watched Kim do the same thing."

"A drug that makes you lose your appetite? Speed maybe? Or cocaine?"

"Based on this, I can't rule those out. But maybe it's a new drug whose purpose is just to kill your appetite, not as a side effect of a mind-altering substance."

"Well, speaking as a woman – no, speaking as a member of the human race – that would be a miracle much to be desired."

Mace set his cell phone down and used Kenneth's phone. "Come on, be there, be there," he said softly. "Dr. Rodgers? This is Detective Emerick. I was wonder . . ." He listened and leaned his forehead on his hand. "So, you've heard. Yes, I have to turn in my toys and take a long time out." He listened, chuckled, and looked at me, a surprised look on his face. "No Ma'am, Doctor. I don't think that colorful expression would be too crude to use in describing Capt. Wacker. I've used it myself in exactly that, uh, anatomical context." He chuckled again. "Well, here's what I'm thinking. You remember Olivia Wright, I introduced you at Margot Farr's house? Yes, that Olivia Wright, the woman on the boat."

I winced and lay my head down on my forearms.

"Chief Armstrong wouldn't be alive if it weren't for Olivia. She was there because she was helping him with a very sensitive investigation." He brought their conversation around to the Margot Farr murder investigation and told Dr.

Rodgers he wanted me on the phone as well, so I went into Kenneth's bedroom and lifted the extension.

Mace told the medical examiner what Carmen Espiña said she'd seen Kim Kaylyn do to Margot's soda, and how Margot lost her appetite completely and slimmed down.

"That sounds like the Holy Grail of weight loss," Rodgers said thoughtfully.

"Doctor, have you ever heard of a drug called Zed?" I blurted out. "Two friends of mine in Beverly Hills told me that's what they hear the very rich are using."

"I've never heard it called Zed, but I've read of drug tests on a compound that very effectively kills appetite in mice, rats and rabbits. It's years away from human trials and years more than that until it's approved for sale – if it ever is. For all we know now, it kills your appetite right before it kills your liver, lungs and heart."

"But if someone could get hold of some and sold it on the black market, there would surely be buyers," I said.

"To say 'buyers' would be an understatement," Mace said. "It would be worth a fortune." He asked the doctor about the results of Margot's toxin screen.

"I always say it might be four weeks 'til a toxin report is back," she sighed. "Sometimes it's faster, but usually it's pretty slow. I'll check on it and call you back. Can't promise it'll be today, but I'll try."

"Thanks, Doctor," Mace said. "We had a chemical to test, but it disappeared from the evidence room." He filled in a few details and she clucked her tongue.

"Well, the more things don't change, the more things don't change," she said.

Mace gave her the number of his personal cell phone and said good-bye. "Come on, hurry," he called to me. We've got one chance to talk to Reid Champion, before he goes into a civil trial."

I put my sandals on in the car to save time. At the

courthouse Mace jumped out at a red light, leaving me to run around to the driver's side and circle the block six times. I spotted him hurrying down the concrete steps and beeped the horn. He pointed to a bus stop off to my right and I zoomed up to the curb to make a certified getaway-car pick up.

"Me Bonnie, you Clyde," I said as I took the next corner on two wheels. "Anybody on our tail?" Mace rolled his eyes and shook his head.

"Come on, what happened in there?" I said as I slowed down and blended with the traffic. "You know how I hate to miss the fun."

"I got lucky . . ."

"Excuse me? YOU got lucky? Who is driving this car and making it possible for you to chase ambulance chasers?"

"All right! WE got lucky. I caught Reid Champion outside the courtroom with four minutes to talk to me . . ."

"Oh my God! That's 50 dollars at his hourly rate!"

"Do you want to hear this?"

"Sorry. Yes, I want to hear it." I looked over my shoulder, honked, and darted – late – into the turn lane I needed to be in. A very large truck driver in a very large truck made a very rude gesture in my direction.

"Never mind, I don't think I'll live long enough to tell you."

"Oh, for pity's sake. We made the turn, didn't we?"

"I don't know. My eyes are closed!"

"What did Reid Champion say? I presume you wanted to know about the life insurance?" I sped up to 80 on the interstate for three miles and slowed to 70 to exit.

"He said Margot had a million dollars in life insurance, payable to Esmé – information I'm glad to have, and there's a bonus. Champion told me Esmé knew Margot was preparing to sue Charles St. John for the $5 million he allegedly embezzled, and she ratted on her mother. She told St. John so he'd be ready to fight Margot."

"We seem to have a plethora of suspects," I said as I pulled into Kenneth's driveway. "Motives galore."

Back in Kenneth's kitchen, I made a half-pot of strong coffee. "I wish I could get back in to the police department to talk to people in the evidence room."

"Well, you might as well forget about it, 'cause it's not gonna happen."

"I might be able to get in the back door." Before he said what a stupid idea that was, I added, "I am speaking, of course, of the back door to the computer system."

"I hate to state the obvious," he sighed, "but what about passwords?"

"I think I know someone who can help with that," I said with a smile.

*****

It was Candace who tracked down Juanita Peron by the most convenient means. She let her fingers do the walking. I had already narrowed the search by calling the police department evidence room and asking for her in Spanish. The man who answered couldn't speak or understand Spanish and my repeated questions annoyed him. If I'd asked in English he would have said, "Call the human resources office," and they would have refused to give me any information. But to get rid of me he finally said, "She works at one of the Hiltons. Call the Hilton Hotel." Then he swore in English and hung up.

Candace called both Hiltons to confirm employment by Juanita Peron, whom she said had applied for part-time work on banquets with Royale. The Flamingo Hilton said, no, she wasn't on their computer, but the Las Vegas Hilton found her name right away. Candace knew better than ask for her phone number or address, since if Juanita had really applied to Royale, Candace should have that right in front of her.

"Now, Juanita said she was starting at the Hilton today," she said, "but I don't have anything down here about what shift she starts on, so I can't work her into anything soon. I guess I can call her and hope I don't wake her up . . ."

The lady had no problem with the shift question, and said Juanita would be working days, getting off at four o'clock, "starting today, but her days off will rotate."

Candace gave me the thumbs up and thanked the lady. To me she said, "Juanita Peron should be walking out the employee exit right after four today."

Candace drove one of Royale's small vans, I rode shotgun, and Mace sat on the floor in the back, leaning against an icebox that said "Cold Beer." Hopefully, he lifted the lid, but it was empty. "Something is terribly wrong here," he muttered.

"Are you sure you'll recognize her?" Candace asked when she'd parked in a loading zone way behind the hotel.

"If she walks out, I'm sure. If she drives out with her window open, I'm sure. If she rides with someone else, I'm not sure," I said, glibly overstating my certainty.

But I got lucky. Juanita Peron walked through the gate by herself, either looking for a lift from a friend or family member, or for the bus. I jumped out of the van and approached her as she stopped to light a cigarette. "Juanita Peron?"

"That is me. And who may you be?" She looked directly at me and aimed her lips sideways to blow smoke downwind.

I refreshed her memory, by which time Mace joined us and introduced himself. "Olivia tells me she met you in the evidence room?" he said smoothly.

"Yeah, that's right. I'd like to see your badge, Detective. No offense intended."

"None taken, Ma'am." He opened the badge holder and

she examined it cautiously.

"Y'all gonna tell me what you want? My feet hurt, you know? New shoes."

"Ms. Peron," Mace said, "could we buy you a beer and talk somewhere cool? I got sweat running down my back and I'm thirsty as hell. You look hot and thirsty, too."

"Y'all got that right. You call me Juanita, none of this Miz Peron shit, and you can buy me a beer. Hell, you can buy me two beers!"

I gave her the passenger's bucket seat and I joined Mace at the icebox. En route to Kenneth's apartment, Mace and I gave her an overview of Chief Armstrong's suspicions about the missing evidence. We were vague about who he suspected, figuring the less said about Wacker the better. We had to come clean about our pariah status, though. "Capt. Wacker will be announcing my forced leave on the news," Mace said, "in about an hour."

"He already 'outed' me as a brazen hussy caught with another woman's husband. That was the morning news."

"Capt. Wacker's got shit for brains," she said. "I'd be glad to help y'all if I can."

Juanita was right about her thirst. She was on her third beer by the time I broke though the firewall into the police computer. "Now it gets easy," she said. "I'll tell you the passwords. They never change 'em."

By the time she unscrewed the cap on her fourth bottle, I was downloading and printing everything I needed.

Mace was reading a list of missing evidence, a list intended for use only by Internal Affairs and the FBI, when his phone rang. "Emerick," he said, distracted by the next sheet coming out of the printer. "Yes, Dr. Rodgers!" He handed the sheet to me and gave his attention to the call, moving to a quieter location. I continued to monitor the printer and assemble the pages.

He returned with a triumphant look on his face.

"Preliminary results of the toxin screen on Margot show a heavy concentration of a chemical that closely resembles the drug now being used on mice, the one we talked about that completely wipes out their appetite."

"Mom, Mace," Candace called. "Show time!" She carried a tray with a big bowl of popcorn and four open bottles of beer to the coffee table in Kenneth's living room.

Juanita was already in front of the TV with her feet up on a leather ottoman. She exchanged her fourth empty bottle for a fresh beer just as Wacker's ugly face filled the screen.

Mace took a good swallow and patted the couch beside him, inviting me to sit down. "Detective work is a lot like picking up change out of the gutter," he said with a grin. "A penny here, a nickel there, pretty soon you've got enough for a six pack. Or – in the case of detective work – an indictment by a grand jury."

Chapter 22

"I come to bury Mace Emerick, not to praise him," I intoned, staring at Capt. Wacker on the TV screen. Juanita was the only one to look at me, and she didn't get it.

"Marc Antony's speech in *Julius Caesar,*" Candace murmured out of habit. When she was a little girl I gave her M&Ms for correctly identifying Shakespearean quotes and classical music. Pavlov would be proud.

Mace and Candace also stared at the screen. Wacker stood at a lectern again, this time in the conference room of the police department. His skin had a slightly greenish cast, which could probably be fixed by adjusting the set, but I thought it improved his looks. His hooked nose and the bony protrusion of his forehead cast shadows on his face from a too-bright overhead light. Another improvement.

"I have a statement to read, and then I'll try to answer your questions." He placed a single sheet of paper on the lectern and put on his reading glasses. "As I said this morning, Mayor Engle has asked me take over the day to day management of the police department during Chief Harold Armstrong's heart surgery and his lengthy recovery, and I have taken on that task. I'm receiving 100 percent cooperation from the department heads and the rank and file, as well as from the mayor's office. The men and women of the Las Vegas Police Department are all outstanding professionals, and it is a privilege to work with them."

"All but one," Mace said bitterly.

"However, I do have some concerns with missing evidence, a matter which was brought to the public's attention in a recent article in the *Los Angeles Times*. Although I would prefer to work on this internal problem with less, uh," he paused and tried to look coy, "less 'oversight,' I have already made some changes and begun a rigorous investigation into the matter. I regret to say I found it necessary to put one officer on paid administrative leave pending the outcome of that investigation."

He cleared his throat and removed his glasses. "I know you are eager for news of Chief Armstrong's condition. As you are all aware, the chief suffered a massive heart attack late last night aboard his boat on Lake Mead. He has been undergoing a battery of tests at Valley Medical Center since he was transported to the hospital by medical helicopter. Doctors say he is resting comfortably, but all of us who know him well," here he paused for a little theatrical chuckle, as if he and Armstrong were close friends, "know the doctors have their hands full to get him to rest."

He gave his uniformed minions and the reporters time to share his chuckle, then pasted a somber look on his visage. "Unfortunately, Chief Armstrong's heart will not heal with rest alone. Surgeons have determined that he must undergo surgery to bypass at least three arteries. I was informed some fifteen minutes ago that the surgery is scheduled for tomorrow morning."

"Ah, shit," Mace said. The somber look on *his* visage didn't have to be pasted on.

Wacker took a question about more allegations of mismanagement rumored to be coming out. "I've heard something about that, too. I invite reporters to call me before they run stories, and maybe we'll root out problems more effectively – that is, if there really are problems. Not every story in every paper is 100 percent true."

"Are you disputing the story that ran in the *Los Angeles Times* two days ago?" someone in the audience shouted.

Wacker held up his hands like a referee. "No, that is not what I'm saying. I just want reporters to know I'm available for questions before they print stories, as well as after they print stories."

The question we were expecting was the next one shouted.

Wacker did a pretty good imitation of a man forced to disclose information he would prefer to retain. "I asked Detective William Emerick to stand down for the time being. Since the investigation is just in its initial phase, I have no further comment."

"Was he the detective in charge of the Margot Farr murder investigation?" a strident female voice called. "And what about the woman on Chief Armstrong's boat?"

"*Cherchez la femme*," I sighed. It was an old plot device, but still popular. *Look for the woman.*

Wacker turned to confer with a man in a dark sportcoat. Mace said he was a lawyer from Internal Affairs.

"Yes, in answer to your question, Detective Armstrong was working on that murder investigation. Another officer has taken over that work and the investigation is moving along very well." To a barrage of questions about Margot Farr, he held up his hands again. "I cannot say anything further at this time. I don't want to jeopardize the investigation."

The strident woman got her hands on a microphone so her question stood out like a pimple on a prom queen. "Capt. Wacker, I attended your press conference this morning at Valley Medical Center. I believe you said the woman on Chief Armstrong's boat, Olivia Wright, was inside Margot Farr's home shortly before the murder. Has the new detective in that investigation interviewed Ms. Wright about anything she may have seen or heard?"

Wacker bent his ear to the lawyer again and nodded to him. "The answer to your question is 'No.' Frankly, I expected to hear from Ms. Wright by now, but there is no answer at her residence."

Again with the microphone. I had to suspect Wacker had arranged for her to have it. "Is Olivia Wright a suspect in the murder of Margot Farr?"

He hesitated, long enough for me to snarl, "The word you're looking for, asshole, is 'No.'"

"Ms. Wright is wanted for questioning as a material witness. The sooner she calls us the better. I'm sorry, but legal counsel advises me I can't go any further in my statement."

He picked up his sheet of paper and glanced around the room. "Ladies and gentlemen, thank you for attending. I have piles of work waiting for me, and I've got to go."

"Well," I said brightly, "let's take a vote. How many of you think I should turn myself in?"

Candace and Mace raised their hands and Juanita's eyes got big. "They're kidding," I told her. "Next question, who's the best lawyer in town?"

"Criminal?" Candace asked, thinking it over.

"Candace dear, how many years have you known me? Don't I use a criminal lawyer *every* time I'm arrested?" I suddenly recalled I had a dozen sheets of paper on the coffee table, information I'd hacked into police computers to. . . lift. Lift is a nicer word than steal.

Actually, my criminal mind was racing ahead to more plans for stealth. "Candace, could I speak to you in the kitchen?" I gathered empty beer bottles on my way. "Please drive Juanita home or wherever she needs to go. I can't involve her any further in my trouble."

"What are you going to do?" she asked, as if dreading the answer.

I also didn't want to involve my daughter any more than

I already had, but I had to. "Just take Juanita. I've got to talk to Mace, and I've got to call a lawyer. By the time you get back here I should have a better handle on this." Impulsively, I hugged her.

While they were gone, I let my fingers do the walking through Capt. Wacker's bank transactions and credit card billings. I did some fact-shopping for Mace, too. He wanted to know who had taken over Margot's murder case.

"Curly Falwell?" he bellowed when I read the name Detective Curtis Falwell. I knew that Falwell thought his nickname was a good-natured jibe at the flat-top haircut he'd gotten by force in the Marine Corps and kept by choice. But Mace said he'd really been nicknamed Curly because Larry and Moe were already taken. "He's so dumb he thinks that's Shinola on his nose."

With more injured muttering, he extended the antennae on his ringing phone and answered. "Emerick here. Yes, Dr. Rodgers." He smiled. "Yeah, I'm here with 'the woman on the boat.' She's looking through the Yellow Pages for a good criminal lawyer. Do you think she should go for someone near the front alphabetically, or the ones with the biggest ads?" He laughed, paused, and laughed again. "Let me call you back so Olivia can be on the other line, okay?" He wrote down her number and called on the phone in the living room while I moved again to the bedroom.

She wasted no time getting to the point. There had been a suspicious anomaly in Margot's blood and other tested tissue. My idea to look at a drug called "Zed" had been a good lead, Rodgers said. She had called two experts in forensic pathology, got them thinking about it, then called the pharmaceutical company that is testing a potential cancer-fighting drug on mice. The drug didn't work as hoped on tumors, but one of the side effects was an almost total cessation of appetite. Before the mice died of cancer, they got very skinny.

"Did the researcher think there was any way some of that drug could have gotten out for sale?" I asked. The question seemed like a no-brainer, as no researcher would likely admit carelessness and invite liability.

"Oh, yes," she said readily. "Steps leading up to its formulation are in the scientific literature. Someone with a lot of expertise in chemistry and biology could create Zed with some trial and error and a lot of dead mice. Or, someone could skip the delay by stealing the formula."

"And the researcher thinks that happened?" Mace asked.

"He knows someone hacked into the research records of a university where his best consultant works. He said he's been waiting for a call just like mine for more than a year now. He was just starting to breathe easy when I called."

"Does he have any idea where Zed is manufactured?" Mace asked. "And any clue who stole the formula?"

"The answers are yes and yes. But he says he could be wrong and wrong. From what he's been able to get from the FBI, he thinks the hacker was in Berkeley, California, and that he or she got the information to accomplices in Mazatlan, Mexico. Whether it's being manufactured somewhere in Mexico and imported, or possibly being manufactured here in the U.S., he has no guess. Hackers are expert at routing their calls around in a maze. The inquiry might come from Russia, when the hacker is down the street at Hewlett-Packard." She sighed. "Hackers can be anywhere."

I was glad she couldn't see my red face at that moment.

"Anyway," she went on, "I called my forensic pathologist friends back and we batted ideas around on a conference call. One of them ran a computer check while we talked, and she found something very interesting. Two female cadavers in the Los Angeles area show the same toxin screen results as Margot Farr. Both were in their forties, and they died eight months and six months ago."

"What was listed as the cause of death?" Mace's question mirrored my own.

"One said complications of chronic alcoholism, although the liver wasn't so bad as all that, and the other said acute asthma. They do not seem in any way to be related except . . ." She paused and I heard paper shuffling noise. "Except they had both been morbidly obese and lost a lot of weight in the months before they died. One lost 85 pounds and the other lost 90."

"What's that 'morbidly obese' about?" Mace asked.

"It means at least 100 pounds over one's recommended weight. It's called morbid obesity because it can kill you." She went on to say both women had tried every legal diet drug they could get their doctors to give them, and every over-the-counter diet drug in the stores. "So there was a lot in their medical history, way more than the average person has. Both of them had undergone liposuction, one of them two times, one three times."

"Didn't Margot have liposuction?" I answered, recalling scars on her abdomen.

"Oh, yes. Both thighs and the abdomen."

"Sounds like they had something else in common," Mace tossed in. "Lots and lots of money. Enough to pay whatever someone asked for a miraculous appetite suppressant."

We thanked her for calling, and for wishing us good luck with our respective problems.

Candace returned a few minutes later. "Juanita said to wish you luck, Mom. She added, of course, that she's glad she's not in your shoes." She looked in Kenneth's freezer compartment and said, "Oh, good! I'm hungry." A little rattling of plates and pinging of the microwave oven as she set it, and the kitchen filled with a delicious aroma.

"Medallions of veal," she said as she set plates on linen placemats.

"Want me to toss a salad?" I asked, glad of something to get my mind off the Attorneys, Criminal Law section of the phone book.

Over the veal, egg noodles, steamed broccoli and a Caesar salad, we told Candace what we'd learned about Zed.

"It's pointless to wish, I know," Mace said sadly, "but I wish we could talk to Hornet about this."

"I know what you mean. He wants to expose Wacker, get his evidence to the state attorney general. And instead, he's facing the knife in the morning."

"And you and I face the knife in the hand of Avery Wacker," Mace said. Then, looking puzzled, he added, "What evidence?"

"Well, of course I don't know that. Hornet told me he had it, in a safe at his home, but he had the heart attack before he said any more."

"In a safe at his home?" Mace said.

"No, please!" Candace inserted. "I can see where you're going, and it's a terrible idea."

"I'm just thinking creatively," Mace protested.

"The same way Mom thinks creatively as she hacks into the police computers!"

"You know," I said, "for someone who caters orgies, you certainly have a fine sense of legality and morality."

"Oh, we're back to that, are we?" she said haughtily.

Mace jumped in to deflect the claws he could see coming out. "We need to think of how to get into Hornet's safe. He lives in a gated community, and he probably has a security system directly hooked up to the police department. I know I would if I were him."

We ate in silence, Candace stewing and Mace and I plotting.

"I've got an idea," I said slowly, still forming it in my mind as I spoke. "I need to get into the hospital and talk to Hornet, just for a minute or two."

"Mother, the poor man is facing open heart surgery in the morning. Do you want to upset him further tonight? Besides which, nobody is going to let you anywhere near him."

"I believe if he knows we will take his evidence to the attorney general that he'll actually rest easier." I wasn't sure of that at all, but it had a certain logic I could justify.

"How can we get you in?" Mace obviously liked the idea, a fact that made me nervous.

"How about the old janitor ruse?" I said tentatively. "Or a nurse's aide, but a janitor has the better job and is noticed less."

"What would you wear?" Mace wondered aloud.

"I don't know . . ."

"A uniform, of course," Candace said with a heavy sigh. "Help me clean up these dishes and we'll go to the uniform store. It's open all night."

Ten minutes later, as I put liquid detergent in the dishwasher, I noticed the TV in the kitchen. Candace had left it on the Weather Channel. White letters against a blue background scrolled as I watched. "A cold front is moving into southern Nevada from southern California. Winds will increase after midnight. Tomorrow: rain and a possibility of high winds and sleet."

Chapter 23

If the three of us ever turn our hands to serious crime, stand back and clear the dance floor!

Instead of renting a janitorial uniform in the style required for Valley Medical Center, I bought one off the second-hand rack, telling Mace, "The way things are going, I may be applying for that job for real. This could be a tax-deductible expense."

I wondered if the retainer I would have to give P. Fenton Mitchell, Esquire, the next day was deductible under any arcane section of the U.S. tax code. Mitchell agreed in our phone conversation to call Detective Curtis Falwell on my behalf and assure him I'd come in to see him at 9:00 a.m. Tuesday.

In the catering van, en route to the hospital, I folded the uniform in a tight bundle and shoved it in Candace's purse, having removed about three pounds of cosmetics in zippered bags, a city map, hairbrush, and one pair of thong panties I didn't care to know more about.

We wandered in the main entrance shortly before 11:00 p.m. Mace and I loitered by the directory while Candace inquired at the information desk about where she could find her sister.

"It's spelled N-o-b-l-e." As the woman searched the computer, Candace added, "Oh, I'm so sorry. I don't know what I'm thinking! You need the *patient's* name, that's her husband – Harold Armstrong."

The woman at the information desk was a rare example

of the right person in the right job. She showed no annoyance at Candace's scatterbrain act, just keyed in the patient's name, then spoke in a kindly voice. "I'm sorry, but Mr. Armstrong can't have any visitors."

"Oh, I know," Candace said. "He's going to have heart surgery in the morning. But I need to be with my sister, she's here with him, of course. So if you tell me his room number, I'll go see her, try to get her to rest."

The woman complied and murmured some words of encouragement to the visitor in her obvious distress. Candace stepped away from the desk, then repeated the room number to the woman, just to confirm her understanding, and loud enough that we could hear it.

We followed her to an elevator and rode up in silence with four other people. On the fifth floor we stepped off and Candace and I meandered down the hall toward a restroom. Still saying nothing to her, I stepped into the restroom. In a stall I changed into the uniform, tucking my hair under a disposable paper cap with elastic border.

I emerged and set her purse, now containing my street clothes, beside the sink. I washed and dried my hands, adjusted my cap, and waited.

When Candace came in I told her we were alone and she told me the layout of the floor, including where an unlocked cleaning supply closet was located. Mace would approach Vanitsa as soon as he saw me with a mop and talk her into joining him for a cup of coffee – in the cafeteria if possible, otherwise in the visitor's lounge. Later, Candace would tap on Hornet's door to let me know Vanitsa was on her way back.

I preceded her out of the restroom and walked directly to the supply closet. I ran water into the metal tub from a tap inside the closet, added disinfectant, and tugged the tub on its rollers out in the hall. I doused the mop in the water and wrung it out in the metal wringer suspended above the water. Whistling tunelessly, the only way I *can* whistle, I mopped my way toward Hornet's room. Out of the corner of my eye, I saw Mace talking to a statuesque blonde. He gave her a brotherly hug and listened intently to what she whispered. I heard him say, "It's going to be a long day tomorrow, and you're not doing him any good by exhausting yourself. Let's go get a sandwich, or at least a cup of coffee."

She seemed to be saying no, then yes, then no. He prevailed, and they walked past me toward the elevator. As soon as they turned the corner, I shoved the washtub to the wall opposite Hornet's room. With my mop clutched to my chest, I slipped quietly into the room.

"Vannie?" he called softly. "Did I hear Mace out there?"

"Hornet, it's Olivia. I've got to talk to you, and we only have a few minutes." I approached the bed. "Mace took Vanitsa to get a cup of coffee."

He looked like hell, but better than he had the last time I'd seen him. "I never had a chance to thank you," he said, motioning me to come closer.

"No need for that. Listen, Mace and I are working on your theory that Wacker is on the take. We need to get your evidence out of your safe – the evidence you told me about on the boat."

He looked puzzled, confused. I waited, not wanting to press him in any way and stress his heart. He was hooked up to machines on both sides of him and above the head of his bed. Everything was beeping along nicely.

"In my safe? Oh, yeah, Wacker. I remember."

"How can we get it out of your safe?" The beep beep of the machines reminded me the clock was ticking, too. "How can we get in, and what is the combination?"

He thought for 10 or 15 seconds, but it seemed like longer to me. My nerves were beginning to fray. He gestured toward the table beside him. "Dry. Can't talk."

I held a cup of water beneath his chin and directed the flexible straw into his lips. "Ah, thanks," he said. "Okay, now listen. The combination for the gate is 2479. My house is number 79. My keys are in Vanitsa's purse, over there."

On the window wedged between two enormous flower arrangements I saw a beige purse the size of a hardback book. I lifted the flap and peered in. I took out a knot of keys and hurried back to the bedside. Hornet took them from my hand and quickly sorted them. He handed me one bunch, saying, "That's her set." Deftly, he twisted a ring on the larger clot of keys and handed me a single key. "Front door."

He lay back, resting, as I stuffed the keys in the purse and squeezed it back between the arrangements. My pulse was racing then, as I was certain my time was nearly up. Maybe Candace wouldn't see them in time to give me a warning tap.

"Is there an alarm system?" I whispered. "In your house – an alarm system?"

He nodded slightly. "You have to key in 9811 in less than 30 seconds or else a silent alarm goes off."

I repeated the number. "What about the safe?"

"It's a little wall safe in my bedroom closet. Combination is 35-55-12."

I mumbled the number, then spotted a black grease pencil on one of the portable monitors beside his bed. On the inside of my arm I wrote 35-55-12-9811-2479. "I've got to go. Good luck tomorrow."

"Good luck to you and Mace. Don't get caught."

"We won't. But don't you give us another thought. Just concentrate on healing."

"We'll go sailing," he said sleepily. "When I'm well. Sailing."

"Yes," I said softly, already taking big but quiet steps toward the door. I couldn't afford to waste a moment. I opened his door and backed out, my attention on the mop and the floor. No sooner had I placed the mop in the big bucket than I heard Mace's voice. I released the lock on the tub's wheels and whistled back down the hall, passing them as I headed for the cleaning supply closet.

In the restroom closest to the elevator on the next floor down I threw away my "shower cap" and tried to enliven my matted hair with my fingers. Candace walked in, making no sign of recognizing me until I said, "There's nobody else here."

She handed over her purse and I took it in a stall. In three minutes I had changed back to navy blue slacks, light blue blouse, and pale yellow jacket trimmed in navy. I wadded up the uniform and stuffed it in the purse. As I changed clothes Candace explained why she couldn't knock on Hornet's door to warn me. A nurse had challenged her by the nurse's station, and she didn't want to draw undue (or, in this case, due) attention to herself, so she "discovered" she was on the wrong floor and left.

By the time we got to the van, Mace was leaning against it. Like hunters returning to the cave, we exchanged sagas of our adventures. Back at Kenneth's apartment, Mace and I told Candace she was off duty. "The less you know about this, the better," I insisted.

Not that she resisted. "I'm going home to bed. I'm going to leave the phone off the hook, so if you have to call, use my cell number. Oh, and if it's regarding bail, don't bother to call until the banks open."

We took Mace's car, with him grumbling that he'd better turn it in first thing in the morning. "I wouldn't put it past Wacker to charge me with grand theft, auto."

He'd retrieved his police cell phone and charger at Kenneth's and listened to his voice mail messages, punctuated with oaths and deprecations on his end. "Curly Falwell is getting ugly," he said with a grimace of disgust.

"What about Wacker?"

"He was born ugly."

"I mean, any messages from him?" I dreaded the answer.

"Hell, yes. Just what you'd expect. He's so mad I think he's going to have a seizure. He's bringing me up on charges of insubordination."

We rode in a heavy silence to Hornet's exclusive subdivision. It was close enough to midnight that thoughts of glass slippers and pumpkins flashed through my mind. Mace pulled in beside the darkened guard shack and rolled down his window. I gave him Hornet's gate code, he pressed four numbers, and the red metal arm shot up.

He knew right where the house was, having been there a dozen times, but he parked a block away. Before he opened his door, he thumbed the overhead light switch to Off. He didn't have to tell me to be quiet. As stealthy as we were, we still set off three dog alarms on our way, but I wasn't too worried. My experience with barking dogs is that the owners sleep through it every time. Same with car alarms.

Mace said they didn't have a motion-triggered light, so we walked at a fast clip across the dark part of the big yard, then stepped up to the front door. A Victorian motif porch light was on, as was a light in the entryway, visible through leaded glass panels beside the door. Mace turned the key in the lock and I called out the numbers to disarm the security system.

"We made it with 15 seconds to spare," I said, my heart pounding. "Where's his bedroom?"

Mace turned on his flashlight. "Upstairs. Let's go."

I kept thinking of scary movies where the audience shouts, "Don't go up the stairs!" as the idiot ingenue does just that. At the top of the staircase I put my hand on the back of Mace's belt. We weren't actually breaking and entering, I reminded myself. We had the permission of the owner – or one of the two owners – to come in and get something. If the other owner caught us there, however, or a neighbor or the police, our invitation would be hard to prove.

Mace had never been upstairs in Mace and Vanitsa's home, but he made a good guess on locating the master bedroom and I guessed the right closet. The safe was at eye level, behind suits, sportcoats and pants, all on wooden hangers and lined up on the rack with military precision.

I shoved the sportcoats one way and the pants the other. Mace aimed the flashlight on the combination lock. "I don't know which way to turn it first," I said as I checked the black numbers on my arm in the light.

I tried clockwise; no luck. Aloud I said, "Counter-clockwise to 35, clockwise to 55, back to 12." I felt the tumblers surrender. With my shoulder I shoved harder on the suits and sport coats that encroached on the safe. "Hold the flashlight closer."

As fast as I could, I sorted through jewelry, coins, and envelopes labeled Deed, Divorce papers, and Will. Two more envelopes were labeled "Important, evidence." I handed them to Mace and felt all the way to the back of the safe. "That's it. Let's lock and go."

Seven minutes later we were in the car, having reset the house alarm system.

Seven minutes after that we were seated in the back booth of the closed section of a Denny's Restaurant on the Boulder Highway, near Sam's Town Casino, with a carafe of coffee between us. I handed him one envelope and I began reading the papers in the other one.

At last our eyes met over the tops of the pages. "No wonder Hornet wants this in the hands of the state attorney general," Mace said. "Does this map make any sense to you?" He smoothed it out and turned it one way, then the other. "Which way is north?"

"This way, I think. Yes, this line marked H.D. is Hoover Dam. That's at the south end of Lake Mead. The marina where Hornet keeps his boat is here, almost due north of the dam across Boulder Basin. This is a rough drawing, or maybe a tracing of a map of the lake."

He set it to one side and looked at another map, turning it so we could both see it. "There's Temple Bar, on the Arizona side," I said, "and Echo Bay, on the Nevada side of the Overton Arm. I don't know what this is up here, marked C.P."

"If I read this correctly," he said, tapping the corner of the papers in his hands, "it's Claw Point."

"And the significance would be?"

"The location where a drug is delivered and prepared for distribution, with the blessing and protection of Avery Wacker."

"What drug?" I asked.

"Zed. What Dr. Rodgers called the Holy Grail of weight loss. Hornet found proof of calls from Wacker to one Vicente Amis in Mazatlan, Mexico."

"The card I found stuck in a book in Margot's office!" I crowed.

"Yeah, and Hornet says here that Amis is well-known to the DEA as a major black tar heroin supplier. This drug, Zed, is something new in his closet."

"What are the odds there will be a shred of physical evidence of that at Claw Point by the time the attorney general investigates?" I said bitterly. "And who's going to look around? Wacker's bowling buddies?" I poured us each a second cup of coffee and laced mine generously with cream.

Mace poured a scant teaspoon of cream in his and stirred it slowly, then looked at his watch and sighed. "I've got to turn in my car, badge and gun in seven hours."

"And I've got to meet my lawyer at police headquarters in eight hours." We looked at each other over our coffee cups, looked back at the map, and at each other again.

"Where were you when Hornet had his heart attack?" he asked.

I pointed on the map. "In the middle of Boulder Basin."

"How long did it take you to get that far?"

"Hard to say. He was giving me lessons in driving the boat, how to work the throttle and stuff. In a straight line at continuous top speed it wouldn't take terribly long to get from Calville Bay, through the west part of the Virgin Basin and north this far into the Overton Arm. The problem is getting through Boulder Canyon. They don't call it The Narrows for nothing."

He folded the papers, all but the map, and put them back in one envelope. I did the same with the other envelope. He tossed a five-dollar bill and two ones beside the carafe and cups. "Do you still have the key to the marina, and the key to Hornet's boat?"

I grinned. "I sure do. You want to go for a ride?"

"Yeah. I've got seven hours to kill."

I didn't like the sound of that phrase, "to kill," but I chose to ignore it.

Bad choice.

Chapter 24

We covered the distance from the highway to the marina in half the time it had taken me. But then, my car had been slowed by all that contact between the tires and the asphalt.

There were just a dozen cars and trucks in the lot where I'd seen about a hundred on Sunday. Mace parked a good 30 yards from the outermost mercury vapor lamp and opened his trunk. The only light was from his flashlight. "Hold this." He handed me the flashlight and the envelope he'd examined at Denny's.

He took off his sportcoat, folded it back at the shoulders, and laid it on the back seat, leaving the door open. He removed his shoulder holster, checked the ammunition in his service revolver, and transferred it to a black leather holster on a webbed nylon belt. He pulled out two black windbreakers with POLICE stenciled in white reflective letters on the back, turned them inside out, and handed me one. "That's warmer than it looks," he said. "You're going to need it out on the lake." He put on his jacket and the webbed belt.

I tucked the envelope in an inside pocket of my blazer with its mate. Then I put the black jacket on over the blazer and waved my arms. The extra ten inches of sleeve below each wrist flapped in the breeze.

"You look like Dopey," he grumbled as he grabbed a sleeve, rolled it up in four turns, and did the same to the other.

"You sound like Grumpy," I grumbled back.

He unzipped a leather case about 10 inches by 8 inches, examined the pistol inside for ammunition, and zipped it closed. "Hold this," he said again. He put spare magazines of ammunition into pouches on his belt. From his jacket on the backseat he took his two cell phones and snapped them into the outside pockets of his windbreaker, pockets that were now inside.

He closed the trunk and locked all the doors. "Let's go," he said grimly.

I had to jog to keep up with his long strides until we got to the wooden walkway. He slowed, admitted in a whisper that he'd never been to Hornet's boat before, and followed me on the circuitous route I now knew by heart.

The marina key was on my key chain. We closed the wire mesh gate silently behind us, listening for the click of the lock. The boat keys were on Hornet's Budweiser key ring. I'd used the second one Sunday night to secure the door to his galley; I used it again to open it up and make a quick inspection. Everything appeared undisturbed. Back on deck I lifted the cover on a seat and took out two life vests. We strapped them on while I checked the fuel. The Vega Star had a big tank, and I was pretty sure we had more than we would need.

Mace untied the ropes from metal cleats on the dock and dropped them back on the deck. As he gingerly stepped back on board, I started the engine. "Purrs like a well-fed cat," I whispered, and gently put the throttle in reverse. We edged away from the dock and continued in reverse until we were well away from the other boats where people could be sleeping, then I brought the boat around in a lazy circle and turned on the lights. I held the throttle slightly forward of neutral and we continued slowly and quietly out to the No Wake demarcation line.

Mace sprawled against the port side, his butt on a white

vinyl cushion and his long legs crossed at the ankles near my driver's seat. I was planted firmly, my back against the seat, my hand on the throttle.

"Damn," he said, "this may get dangerous. I shouldn't have brought you."

"Brought me?" I said. "YOU shouldn't have brought ME?" I shoved the throttle full forward and snapped the trim tabs down. The Vega Star shot forward as if from a cannon, and Mace shot backward, an equal and opposite reaction. Unable to get his ankles unwound and his feet under him fast enough, he arced through the air and landed against the stern, hands first, perhaps a millisecond before his face would have made contact.

I was prepared for the stream of invective I knew would follow. In fact, I rather enjoyed it.

We came out of the bay banging violently over choppy waves. On the open lake the wind was fierce. I tuned to channel 16 and asked for a weather report. Winds increasing after midnight out of the southwest to a steady 35 knots, gusting to 45. Barometer was 29.6 and falling rapidly. Cold front moving in from the west, and remnants of tropical storm Amberly moving north from Baja California. By six a.m. winds were expected to come around to the northwest, with winds gusting to 50 knots in squall lines. Small craft warnings were up on Lake Mead, Lake Mohave, and Lake Powell.

"The good news," I shouted, "is that the wind is from the south and we're heading north."

"The other good news," he shouted back, "is that we're not in a sailboat."

Actually, we had a long way to travel east before we turned north. We bisected whitecaps across the northern part of Boulder Basin and slowed to traverse the Narrows. I spread the plastic-coated map out on the deck, beneath the console, and held it steady with both feet. If I lifted either foot, a mistake I made twice in the first couple minutes, the map snapped shut in a tight roll.

I hugged a heavy military flashlight between my knees, lowering my head to lap level and turning on the light every time I needed to consult the map. I had a hunch my method didn't belong in a video on Boating Safety.

Mace went down on one knee and used his flashlight on the map. "I get the numbers in the water, 403, 168 and all – that's gotta be the depth of the lake at each point. But what are the numbers along the raggedy edge of the lake?"

"Feet above sea level. Surface of the lake is about 1200 feet. Get a load of the numbers on the brown part of the map, beside the Narrows. It's a topo map."

He swore softly. "Arch Mountain on one side of the canyon, 3300 feet, Guardian Peak on the other, 2800 feet."

"Help me watch for the navigation lights. We should see a quick red, number 12, on our starboard." The navigation rule of "red on right" meant keep a red light buoy, flashing at four-second intervals, to your right as you enter a harbor, but a red light flashing each second, a "quick red," meant watch out for a hazard such as a rock. According to the map, the number 12 quick red light was due east of Flamingo Reef and due south of an unnamed reef and of the green light on Bearing Point. We had to stay in the extremely narrow channel between the reefs.

The silence in the sheer canyon made me think of the eye of a hurricane. Even the engine noise from the Vega Star seemed muffled, as if in awe of the canyon. Time crept by like the black water under the hull.

"Flashing green on the port, number 13, quick red on the starboard," Mace said softly. When we reached a point between those two lights, he spotted the next beacon, a red light flashing at four-second intervals, on the starboard, and from that bend we both spotted a flashing green way ahead on the port. At that point I put the motor in neutral, came to a stop, and got on my hands and knees over the map. With both flashlights we studied the beacons that would lead us through the narrowest stretch of Boulder Canyon.

We turned off the flashlights and sat in the darkness, only our boat's headlight ahead. The light was almost useless. It told us the canyon walls were a few feet from us, but we already knew that.

"I should be able to see the number 17 flashing green directly behind us all the way through this stretch of the canyon, and another flashing green straight ahead." I licked my dry lips, but I had no spit to wet them with. "There's the quick red beacon we need to see; number 18. We have to keep it close on our starboard." I continued to slice the Vega Star's white hull through the black water, slow and steady, repeating aloud what I was watching for and what I saw. I sounded like a psychologist talking a woman off a bridge, saying, "Don't look down," but in this case I was talking to myself and saying, "Don't look up."

When we emerged from the canyon into Virgin Basin, Mace expelled a great lung-full of air. With a weak laugh he said, "Olivia, I take back every snide remark I ever made about your driving."

To our left and right were the tops of the Black Mountains and far beneath us, deep under water, was the original cleft of the Colorado River. Calling them the Black Mountains that night was redundant. Everything was black.

The wind and waves instantly battered us, but getting out of the canyon made me giddy. "Resume warp speed," I called an instant before I jammed the throttle forward. Mace had learned his lesson and was solidly placed like a tripod, facing backward, his butt on the seat to my left, feet firm on the deck, and one hand clamped tight on the rail.

We continued on a compass heading of east until we were clear of the Black Mountains on our port. Then we turned due north into the Overton Arm.

The wind was not directly out of the south, but the southwest, putting the whitecaps at an angle to our progress, and since waves had so much farther to travel (and build) in the long north-south arm of the lake, the whitecaps were high and nasty. Besides giving our stomachs a ride like a HumVee up a dry riverbed, the visual feedback of being off-kilter made me queasy. The tailwind, though not perfect, was definitely adding to our speed.

"Take the wheel," I called. "I've got to look at the map, out of the wind."

In the galley I squeezed my torso, swathed in the bulky life vest, behind the dinette table. I braced myself by planting one foot against the oven and the other against the wood veneer of the outside wall of the head. In good light from overhead, I examined the official map and compared it to Hornet's hand-drawn map. To my immense relief, I could tell the latter was traced from the former. The scale could be trusted.

I darted back up the passageway and read the Global Positioning System, then bumped like a drunk from the sink to the head to the oven on my way back to my seat. There was a spit of land to our northwest, maybe 15 minutes at top speed. It had no name on the official map, but it hooked a little, and if I were inclined to name it, I'd call it a claw or a hook. An unnamed desert wash, just a dotted line on the map, ran from the mountains to a jagged cove beside the claw. North of the unnamed wash I saw Cleopatra Wash, and south of it, Manganese Wash.

We couldn't go at top speed all the way to Claw Point, of course. The land around Lake Mead, and especially dry land that stuck into it like a pointing finger, was all that was left of high desert mesas and cliffs that once jutted majestically above the Colorado River. One foot below Claw Point might be solid land extending out 200 yards or more. The map seemed to indicate shallow spots in that area, but it was hard to read such tiny numbers under good conditions, and with them dancing before my constantly moving eyes, it was a mariner's crapshoot.

I turned off the overhead light and went topside again. The night was darker than a sensory deprivation tank, but my senses weren't being deprived. They were being overburdened with wind, waves, the boat's speed, and a chill factor that made me wonder if my nose and hands were suffering frostbite. It was 2:30 a.m.

"If there's no light at Claw Point," I called, "there's no way we can find it. We'll be in danger of running aground."

Just then lightning split the sky and seemed to hover like a flare for four or five seconds. My retina had not given up the ghost of the hot pink light before thunder rolled back to us from wherever the lightning had gouged the atmosphere. "You wanted light?" Mace said cheerfully.

I stood close enough to be heard without yelling and told him about the maps. He handed off the wheel and 10 minutes later I cut our speed in half and doused our lights.

"What's that?" I pointed toward the west. I thought I'd seen a light, but I wouldn't bet on it. If I closed my eyes I still saw the lightning. "There. Yes! It's headlights."

Mace whipped his binoculars from a pouch on his belt and confirmed my sighting, then asked me for our compass setting. He stared into the binoculars for about fifteen seconds. "He was coming almost due east when you spotted him, close to right angles to our path. Then he veered north. I see his taillights. Hold on, he's got a shadow, or more likely a buddy. Coming east, coming east. Turning north."

We proceeded north at half speed until Mace said, "He's turned east again. I see a faint light, I think, no." He took the binoculars away from his eyes and stared; used the binoculars again, then stared into the darkness. I, too, stared in the direction he kept looking, and scanned the area from our nine o'clock position to straight ahead, but I couldn't see any spot of light.

Mace scanned the same quadrant with binoculars. "I don't see the vehicles, but I still see a faint stationary light at our eleven o'clock."

Lightning lit up the scene and we got a snapshot of the land and the lake. There was shoreline along our port side, about 500 yards away and pretty much parallel to our trajectory. To the northeast was a spit of land jutting into the lake, high on the west end and flattening out toward the lake, then one last smaller hump before the water, like a humpback whale facing the western horizon, with its tail above the water.

"The vehicles must have gone behind that butte." He spread his legs to parade rest position for stability and raised the binoculars slowly. "I've lost the stationary light, too. Oh, yeah, I see it now. It's a light on a pole. Seems to be banging around in the wind. Whoops, gone again. Can you come back to port a little, and slow it down?"

"How's this?"

"Good, more to port. Yes! I can see the light again between the two humps. If we go slightly to starboard it's hidden by the mound nearest the water. Let's angle in and go ashore."

I wasn't afraid of beaching the boat, as long as I did it slowly, as she had a very shallow draft. But if a solid boulder lurked offshore, we could put a jagged hole in the hull. In daylight I could at least have seen any boulders or former mesa tops that poked above the water. In the dark I lacked even that comfort.

Having no lights on the boat improved my night vision somewhat, and I proceeded slowly in a direct line to the south side of the spit of land. As we closed on the solid landmass to our west, the mountains shielded us from the

wind and we didn't have to battle whitecaps any more.
I stayed close to the shore and motored north at further
reduced speed. "Hang on," I said, "we're coming into the
armpit." I moved the throttle to neutral, waited ten seconds,
and cut the power. We glided silently, waiting tensely for
the sound of the boat scraping against sand and gravel, if
we were lucky, or against a jagged hunk of rock that used
to be a bad-ass pinnacle above a bad-ass river, if we
weren't so lucky.

Silence, silence, then Flash-Boom. The landscape lit up
like a fireworks factory explosion, followed maybe four
seconds later by a clap of thunder I swear I could feel
rolling through my chest cavity. In the ensuing darkness I
could smell ozone and something else. Fear? I submerged
that thought and concentrated on the boat.

"We're here," I said, a little giddy at the realization that
while the thunder reverberated in our ears, the boat slid
ashore as smooth as a canoe on sifted sand.

Mace crept forward to the bow and leaped onto dry
land. With his feet dug in for leverage, he pulled the boat in
as far as he could. Pull, rest, pull, and rest. Once more and
the boat was tight on the shore. He hoisted himself back in
over the gunwales and we checked our location by GPS,
took off our life vests, and ran over our gear again. I went
below to get the extra flashlight held by a flange above the
bed, and spare batteries from the kitchen drawer. I put the
pistol, still in its leather pouch, and Hornet's two evidence
envelopes in the refrigerator, then locked the door to the
galley. I didn't trust the pockets in my slacks or the inside-
outside pockets of the police jacket, which fit me like a
tractor cover, so I tucked the Budweiser key ring into the
net map holder under the dashboard and made sure Mace
saw where I put it.

"In case you get aboard before me and we're in a hurry
to leave," I said. I left unsaid, "in case I'm injured, or

worse." The thought crossed my mind, too, that he'd better know where I hid the keys in case I fell into such a state of panic I forgot where I put them.

Lightning and thunder struck again, this time with no measurable break between them. I couldn't remember if a boat offered any safety from lightning, like a car does, but I was pretty sure the car depended on rubber tires. "Let's go!" we said, as simultaneous as the lightning and thunder, and jumped clear of the boat.

"Remember," he said, "if you feel your hair stand on end, lie down flat, flat, flat. Spread your contact with the ground as much as possible."

Feeling my hair stand on end got less likely at just that moment. The squall line that had probably been chasing us in the dark caught up and tried to obliterate us. I'd never before gotten so wet so fast. I was already cold, so I only got colder by comparison.

Lightning flared again, but we were comforted by the six or seven seconds of silence that preceded the thunder. In the light we saw that we were at the base of the big butte, a sandstone bump on the desert between the Black Mountains and the lake. The land flattened like a cactus-studded sandbar east of the butte, then rose once more in a smaller hill before surrendering sovereignty to the water. Somewhere north of us in the Overton Arm, I recalled, was the underwater ghost town of St. Thomas, whose last residents had plenty of time to relocate once the dam was complete and the Colorado backed up, gradually losing its identity as a river in the murky lake.

I followed Mace toward the sandstone ledges of the larger butte, rings worn around it by wind and sand and the occasional downpour so that it looked like a fat table leg thinned at intervals on a lathe. The squall lessened in intensity or, rather, it moved farther north, looking for targets worthy of its power, leaving us in its lee. Lightning, now a pale imitation of the bolts we'd weathered, let us assess our position and dart forward to the spine of Claw Point and drop noiselessly to the other side.

We saw the light on a pole, a bulb inside a metal cup shaped like a megaphone. Part of its mooring must have twisted loose in the wind, and it banged against the pole. The light aimed toward the base of the pole, then outward as if directed by a berserk lighthouse keeper, then down at the pole again. The dark windows of an old Winnebago reflected the capricious moonlight. The RV formed a triangle with the pole and the small butte that hid it from our view during most of our trip due north by boat.

Within the triangle were two vehicles, a dark blue Land Rover and a gray Jeep Cherokee. Probably nothing but a truck or tough car with four-wheel drive could have made it out to the lake. The map showed no roads between the distant North Shore Road and the Overton Arm until the turnoff to Echo Bay, many miles farther north. The only paths were the washes, the natural culverts that sat dry as burned toast 99 percent of the time, waiting for the one percent, the hour of rain in the distant mountains that gave desert arroyos their 15 minutes of fame. The sand and rocks that offered no impediment to water were no friends to vehicles, though.

When the light swung out, it displayed a sleek racing motorboat tied to a metal stake.

"Stay here," Mace whispered. I found a flat but sharply tilted rock and propped myself on it by digging in my heels in the soft ground in front of it. Mace moved toward the Winnebago, light on his feet. I lost sight of him behind it, figuring he was probably trying to see inside. A metallic crash from the RV made me jump and lose my footing. My backside slid down the flat stone and made contact with a beavertail cactus growing snug against the rock. I shot upright without emitting the shriek that made it past my throat and into my mouth. Immediately I saw the origin of the explosive noise. Someone inside the RV had opened the side door and the wind slammed the flimsy metal wide open against the side. As I watched, the wind fell back, letting the door swing outward, then *Bam!* Another bone-jarring slam against the side, as if the door were a giant's fly swatter.

Carefully, I put my hand inside my pants and palpated my right buttock. As best I could tell, the nasty needles had gone in and back out, leaving no splinter, just puncture wounds. The pain was so intense I wondered if beavertail spines left some kind of poison behind.

In the sporadic light, I saw two people emerge from the RV. A short person in a hooded coat jumped to the ground and turned to tug one end of a case or trunk out the door. The second person was tall enough, and strong enough, to step down easily from the doorway to the ground while holding the cargo steady. I could tell then they were both men. They walked toward the speedboat, carrying the trunk between them, each with one hand through a handle. I could tell by their stance it was either empty or the cargo was light.

They covered the distance to the boat in quick strides. The taller man got in the boat and handed a stack of something out to the other man, then did so a second and third time. The man beside the boat put each armload into the chest, then closed it slowly and latched it.

The tall man stepped out of the boat, they took up their handles, and walked away from the shore but not toward the Winnebago. They only took about six steps forward until I lost sight of them in the darkness outside the swinging light. They'd gone directly toward the mound between the lake and me. Since I'd come ashore I could see that both the butte to the west and the mound to the east were larger than I'd guessed from the water. Or maybe I was just smaller than I pictured myself. Either way, I didn't like the lay of the land. I shivered, only half from the cold.

A black bear emerged from the Winnebago into the puddle of light by the open door. Or so it appeared at first glance. After two blinks I recognized Esmé in a hooded coat that placed her in clear opposition to People for Ethical Treatment of Animals. She grabbed at the door, which was still flapping hard against the side of the RV, and forced it closed. I lost sight of her for about half a minute, then heard her laugh. The sound came from the general direction the two people had gone with the box.

I crouched and duck-walked forward. My butt felt like I had stuffed a burning briquette in my back right pocket. The sand between my tennis shoes and the smooth volcanic rock was thin, and in patches it worked like a lubricant. While creeping forward, favoring my right foot to protect my painful right rump, I felt my left foot shoot off the rock and pitch me backward on my left hip and the back of my head. My hands might have softened the blow, if it hadn't happened so fast that I was down flat on a count of One, but I probably would have broken a wrist or a forearm, or both. I lay in the dark, probing the back of my head with my fingers, and tried to count my blessings. I got to Two and paused.

Blessing number Three, that the rain had stopped, drowned in my throat as lightning again ripped open the clouds and tried to give the desert one-third of its annual rainfall in half an hour.

Esmé shrieked and sprinted for the Winnebago. Close on her heels were the load bearers, now empty-handed. In the light of the open door I could see them clearly: Avery Wacker and Charles St. John. A more unlikely pairing I couldn't conjure. Not only is there no honor among thieves, there's no taste.

Cupping my hands over my eyes to divert water, I searched for Mace and spotted him running from the back of the Land Rover right toward my sandy saddle. He had enough momentum to mount it in six or seven mighty strides and fell in a soggy heap beside me.

"Let's go down to see what's in the cave, now while it's raining." He was back on his feet, pulling me up as he stood. "Follow me. There's a better way down about a hundred yards closer to the water."

We scrambled along the spine of the rocky protrusion and I paused, unwilling to follow his leap into what looked to be a black hole. I was even less willing to stand on the rock alone, just waiting for the moon to spotlight me through a break in the clouds, so I slid down the rock, further torturing my poor butt.

"Over here," Mace hissed from a shadow even deeper than the shadows surrounding it. "I'll watch for them while you go in. Hurry! Use the flashlight."

He didn't have to tell me twice to hurry. Hunched to keep my head from hitting the rocks, I darted into the cave. I could tell it was shallow, since I could hear my own panting. I held the flashlight close to my body, shielding the light on both sides with the black jacket. The chest I'd seen Wacker and St. John carry to the cave was a metal footlocker. I tugged it open and saw it was full of orange life vests. "Give me your knife," I called.

"What is it?" Mace asked as he laid the knife handle in my hand like a surgical instrument.

"Life vests. Maybe a dozen of them." I knelt beside the locker and sliced open one vest with a quick, long incision. I was only half surprised when the knife also sliced through four or five plastic bags, and within the bags, into bags the size of teabags. I removed one, still intact, shaking off the white powder that had fallen on it from the sliced bag above. With one hand I stuffed the small bag into my bra, while with the other hand I dragged a second and third vest over the one I'd damaged and slammed the top of the locker. "Let's go!"

The rain had stopped in the scant minutes I was in the cave. Mace hugged me tight against him and said into my ear, "Head for Hornet's boat, no matter what happens." He pointed toward the RV, the cars, and a path I could use to get up and over the saddle of rock to the beached boat.

I ran double-time ahead of Mace toward the far side of the RV just as Wacker opened the door. The moon picked a shitty time to shine, glinting off Mace's forehead. I made it under the Jeep just as Wacker yelled, "There's somebody out here!"

A gunshot hit the light on the pole and exploded the bulb. Knowing Mace had made the shot, I took off in the unexpected darkness and confusion and raced up the rocks. I dropped over the other side, an adrenaline rush so strong I was quaking in my shoes.

The total silence was more frightening than the gunshot and yelling had been. I inched back up the rocks and peered over to the north side of the point. The moon was here and gone, here and gone, as clouds raced across the sky. A flash of lightning showed me Wacker crouched beside the RV, but it also showed Mace to him. Three swift steps and he had his gun at the back of Mace's head.

Wacker had surprise on his side, but not for long. Mace drove an elbow into Wacker's gut and whirled to kick him with his stiff leg. Wacker fired, but the sound of an exploding windshield told me he'd missed Mace by a mile. The Jeep was the handgun victim this time, but how long would Mace's luck hold?

I saw the RV door open and Esmé peered out, until the gunshot hit the Jeep, and she pulled her head back in.

Wacker and Mace were rolling on the ground, fighting for control of Wacker's gun. The RV door opened again, and Charles St. John ran out, clenching a small handgun in both his hands. With sheer dumb luck, he approached them as Wacker rolled to the top and gave Mace a vicious blow to the head. "Hold it! Don't move! I'll shoot!" St. John said, sounding terrified, but holding the gun steady and aiming at Mace's forehead.

"I've got the son of a bitch," Wacker barked, forcing Mace over and kneeing him in the back while he handcuffed him. Wiping something from his own face (blood, I hoped) Wacker stood and yelled at Mace to get up.

While Mace continued to lie in the sand, motionless, his hands cuffed behind him, I heard a low rumble, like thunder, but not thunder. Wacker figured it out at the same instant I did.

"Leave him!" he shouted. "Get the footlocker in the Land Rover and get it the hell out of this arroyo." Limping, but moving fast, he headed for the cave.

St. John stopped at the Winnebago to yell to Esmé to get out. "Move the Jeep out of the arroyo! Hurry!"

Wacker screamed at St. John. "Shut the fuck up and get the footlocker!" He stumbled into the cave and dragged it out by himself. Esmé, St. John and a third person ran toward him. "Get it into the Land Rover and drive it up there." He pointed toward my sanctuary on high ground.

I could see the third person now. Kim Kaylyn was helping Esmé and St. John run with the trunk. As they got close to the Land Rover she ran ahead and opened the back door. They stuffed it in, slammed the door, and St. John jumped into the driver's seat. In the sudden glare of his headlights, I saw the first fingers of roiling, muddy water heading for the lakeshore.

With them heading right for my hiding place, I couldn't get to Mace. Wacker was leaving him there to drown. Meanwhile, Wacker was running for the speedboat.

"Mace!" I called, my shout drowned out by the water and the spinning wheels and straining gears of the Land Rover. I saw Mace struggle to his feet, shake the water off his face, and head for the Jeep, which was starting to bob in the rising water. Right before I pulled my head back, I saw him vault onto the hood of the Jeep and lie prone, riding it toward the lake.

I slid down the incline and slogged across rushing water on the other side of the point toward Hornet's boat, which was straining against the rope Mace had used to tie it to a boulder. I gauged the power of the water and aimed for a point west of the boat, and therefore upstream. When the water pulled me under, I fought the current, flailing my arms and grabbing at the taut rope when one forearm whipped across it. The rope went slack in my hands. It must have slipped off the boulder. Dropping the flashlight I'd tried to keep, I twisted the rope around one arm and held on tight with both hands, moving hand over hand closer to the boat. The boat was moving away from me, stern first, and I feared the rope would pull me under the surface, but the stern hit something and stopped, letting the front of the boat swing around.

I mustered what strength I had left in my legs to touch bottom once and shove myself up high enough to throw one arm, then the other, over the lowest point of the boat's side. I wiggled my torso up and over the side until I fell on the deck, soaked and exhausted, but alive. I stripped off the sodden jacket, strapped on a life vest, and snatched the keys from under the console. The motor – God bless it! - started without a cough and I gained some measure of control over the flood that forced us out into the lake. I expected at any moment to come bow to bow with Wacker's fast boat. Quick as I could, I jumped down the galley stairs, grabbed Mace's spare gun from the refrigerator, unzipped the leather pouch and stuffed the gun in the waist of my pants. Back on deck I felt frantically for the extra flashlight I'd noticed near the inboard motor. With my hands and feet I kicked at the panel that covered the motor, grabbed the flashlight, and sat down hard to reseat the motor cover.

Before I could use the flashlight to read the GPS, I saw the light of the sleek cigarette boat about 300 yards west of me. Instead of heading out toward deeper and calmer water, he was coming about, heading back toward the other beach. He didn't see me yet, but he had a searchlight mounted on his windshield, and he was shining it toward the beach.

I cut my motor abruptly and floated silently in the semi-dark. It wouldn't take much for him to see me, but his attention was directed away from my boat, at least for the time being.

I saw the Jeep at the same instant Wacker did. Mace was a moving target, but the Jeep was sinking rapidly as water lapped up to the missing windshield. With my hand over my flashlight, I turned it on and let enough light through my fingers to read the GPS. I turned it off and slid the microphone out of its holder.

Keying the mike to transmit, and holding it close to my mouth, I said, "Mayday, mayday, emergency, off Claw Point, an injured man floating in a vehicle." I gave our coordinates and repeated "Mayday" again and again.

To my relief, a voice answered. "Lake Mead Dispatch. What is your emergency? Identify yourself."

"This is the Vega Star. Mayday, mayday." I repeated my coordinates and dropped the microphone. Wacker had drawn his gun and was waiting for the perfect shot to finish off Mace. The Jeep bobbed like a sitting duck, illuminated by Wacker's spotlight. My gun was useless with Wacker's boat moving, my boat moving, and Mace beyond Wacker in my line of fire. Instead I hit the throttle and raced toward the stern of the speedboat. Wacker only had time to turn and take one wild shot before I rammed him. As he was holding on to nothing, his face hit the deck about one second before his gun hit the water. I shoved the Vega Star into reverse enough to pull my bow free of his boat, and then shot forward.

Mace had worked his way to the roof of the Jeep, which was now completely submerged. He appeared to be sitting on the water, but he was sinking fast, unable to use his hands to keep his head above water. I pulled up close, but he couldn't propel himself to the boat. I put the motor in neutral and leaned out as far as I could, grabbing for his jacket, his ear, anything I could touch.

Suddenly, he sank from sight. "No!" I screamed. Keeping my eye on the spot, I took off my life vest, set the gun on the passenger seat, and stepped over the side. I couldn't feel anything with my feet, and kept going down, but as I had when looking for the boat's tiedown rope, I flailed my arms in front of me.

I felt something, maybe an arm, and hauled myself closer. I felt like I was moving in slow motion while the air in my lungs was on fast forward. Feeling like my lungs would burst, I kicked toward what I hoped was Mace. Yes! It was definitely an arm. I jerked it upward and grabbed the handcuffs, then tugged upward with all the strength I owned and some I borrowed from the universe. If he'd been dead weight, I think we both would have drowned, but he used his strong legs to propel both of us upward.

We broke the surface and I sucked great gulps of air into my tortured lungs. I had about five seconds to enjoy being alive and to feel relief that Hornet's boat was still close before I saw Wacker turn his boat toward us.

"Oh, shit!" I said. Only one of us had a prayer of getting in the boat before Wacker ran us over, and there was no question who it had to be. Mace would certainly drown if he went under again; the handcuffs locking his arms behind him were as deadly as a stone around his neck.

Together we kicked toward the stern of the Vega Star. I grabbed the wood of the stern to the side of the engine and grabbed Mace's belt in a deathgrip. "On three!" I gasped, "one, two, three!" Mace hurled himself up like a walrus at the same time I lifted his hips an extra foot above the water. It was enough. He was in.

There was no time for me to get in. If I'd lifted my arms up, Wacker could ram into me, crushing me between the two boats. Instead I kicked off the side of the boat and stroked hard for the shore. "The gun!" I called back to Mace. "On the seat!"

I could swim faster by lowering my head, so I didn't know if Mace heard me or not. The flash flood was over, and I felt the current from the arroyo drop to nil. Soon I banged my knee hard on the lake bottom and felt ground beneath my feet. I dragged my chest out of the water and turned to see what was happening behind me. Mace was racing north, leading Wacker away from me by steering with his knee and his chin. Wacker's boat should have overtaken the Vega Star easily, but was barely keeping up. I figured I must have caused him some grief when I rammed him.

I crawled onto the rocks of Claw Point and pulled my knees to my chest. I was shivering uncontrollably. A few minutes later, maybe 10, maybe 15, I saw the searchlight from the helicopter before I heard the beating of the rotors. "Over here," I called as I wobbled to my feet and staggered farther up the beach. "Over here." My knees buckled and I collapsed in a heap.

I watched the chopper rock back and forth as the pilot settled it on the sandy beach, and realized he'd spotted the lights of the Land Rover, which was stuck, high-centered on the saddle of Claw Point. A roar from behind me drew my attention to the water. Mace was heading directly for the beach. He cut the motor, drove the bow into the sand, and leaped out.

Wacker gave up his murderous pursuit of Mace and went streaking away to the south.

"He won't get far," Mace said. I tried to stand but my legs were like gelatin. Instead, I lay on the cold sand and flapped my arms like gills. He sank down beside me on his knees, his hands still cuffed behind him. Using his jacket for handholds, I pulled myself to my knees and put my arms around his chest.

My tears didn't make me any wetter, but they felt warm on my cheeks. And Mace's lips, cold as a Popsicle at first, grew warmer against mine. Or maybe it was the other way around.

Chapter 25

"I just don't get it," Candace said.

"I c-c-c-can't s-s-s-see you." I lay cocooned in a warming blanket in the emergency room. My body featured at least a dozen points of pain all crying for my attention, but my tongue hurt the most. I'd tenderized it with my severe teeth chattering. I thought my shaking would stop when my body temperature stabilized, but the doctor said I was having a reaction to adrenaline overload in my system. "Sh-sh-sh-shit," I managed to say, then laughed in a high-pitched voice. My laugh segued to a spasm of coughing. I didn't know until then how much my abdomen muscles had been strained by my frantic swimming, first to the surface with Mace, and then to the shore directly across five- or six-foot waves.

Candace leaned over the rail of the bed so I could see her. "M-m-m-" I said.

"Mace is all right. He's bouncing back from the hypothermia a lot faster than you are." She patted the bulky blanket to see where my hands were and squeezed one. "He won't shut up, raving about how you saved his life."

I wanted to wipe my eyes, but I had to settle for blinking hard so the tears could flow down the sides of my face. "What t-time is it?"

She looked at the wall above my head. "A little after seven a.m. They took X-rays and nothing is broken. As soon as you warm up enough, I can take you home." She read the question in my eyes. "Mace has some cuts. He said he got cut on the glass all over the Jeep. He has to get stitched up before he can go home." Again she said, "I just don't get it. What in the hell were you doing out on Lake Mead in the middle of the night? Again!"

"Wa-Wa-Wacker," I stuttered.

"How are you feeling, Ms. Wright?" A woman in a white coat over a chartreuse blouse displaced Candace in my field of vision. "I'm Dr. Eckhard." She put a plastic probe under my tongue. When it beeped she removed the probe and smiled. "We need this bed for sick people. I'm kicking you out of here."

The doctor rotated out of view and Candace leaned close to my ear. "What she means is that they need the bed for sick people with insurance."

"How is Hornet?"

"He's in surgery now. All anyone around here will say is his heart surgeon is the best and he'll probably be in the operating room about five hours."

A nurse appeared to turn off my intravenous drip, unzip my cocoon to expose my arms and remove the needle from the back of my left wrist. Distracted, she continued talking to someone in the next curtained area about vowels. Something about moving. It didn't make sense until I listened more carefully. Bowels. She wheeled the IV stand out of the space and closed the curtain behind her.

"I brought you some clothes," Candace said. She held her arm out perpendicular to the bed and stiffened it so I could pull myself to a sitting position. I put my bra on and awkwardly wriggled into panties inside the blanket. The white curtain gave me no sense of privacy, especially with the bowel discussion continuing unabated four feet over.

Candace helped me get her soft lavender sweatshirt over my head. The matching pants would be warm, but baggy in length. I figured I'd just be wearing them long enough to get to her apartment. My hair was matted and stiff with lake mud. I tried unsuccessfully to run my fingers through it. I needed a bath. No, I needed to go through a car wash, on a bicycle.

"The state attorney general wants to talk to you and Mace as soon as you're ambulatory." She was absorbed in examining her cuticles. "I called your lawyer about it. Fenton Mitchell. He's coming over."

"Here?" I asked. "Why here?"

"Because the attorney general is here. And they want to make sure you say nothing to the press."

I thought about that. "Does the press know about this yet? The . . .lake?" I waved my arm vaguely as if trying to conjure an image. I couldn't think what to call it. Olivia and Mace's less-than-excellent adventure? I wasn't sure I even remembered everything I'd seen, heard and done. I got a brief but vivid image of Wacker aiming a gun at me, and then me ramming his boat.

"Only a skeleton crew of the media is here, but reinforcements are on the way."

I recalled what Wacker had called them. *ABC, NBC and every other damn C.* "If they don't want me to talk to the press, then I know for certain what I want to do. Hold a press conference."

"I was afraid of that," she sighed. "Will you at least talk to your lawyer and to Mace before you face any microphones?"

"Okay, okay. Where's Mace?"

Before she could answer the nurse leaned in and asked Candace to come talk to a gentleman in the hall outside the emergency room. While she was gone I put fuzzy bedroom slippers on my still-cold feet and slid off the bed, a motion that further strained my sore abdomen.

"Fenton Mitchell is here," Candace said. She bent to pull a plastic garbage bag from beneath my bed. Water dripped from the bottom. "Your clothes," she said. "I don't know whether to take them home to salvage what we can, or drop the whole mess in a Dumpster."

"Salvage first, then the Dumpster," I said with a shrug.

"The plastic surgeon who stitched Mace's face said we can use his office down the hall to meet privately. Fenton Mitchell got the key and went down there already." She looped her purse strap over her shoulder and took my arm. "We have to leave the ER. I think they charge by the hour."

"Sounds like a motel I used to frequent." Seeing Candace's glare, I quickly added, "Just kidding."

"Do me a favor if you hold a press conference. Don't do any kidding. There's nothing even mildly amusing about this catastrophe. You could have been killed, damn it!"

There was a lot of truth in what she said, I admitted to myself. In the surgeon's waiting room, empty until office hours, I met my lawyer face to face for the first time. He had a kindly face and alert blue eyes, which worried me. I rather hoped he'd have the beady eyes and fierce brow of a take-no-shit and don't-you-dare-touch-my-client lawyer. Like most people, I dislike and distrust lawyers, but if I have to have one on my side, I want a hotshot with a killer instinct. Fenton Mitchell looked like he collected butterflies. And let them go.

"Have you talked to the police at all?" I asked as we sat down. Candace found a can of Folger's and a package of filters in a cabinet under the Mr. Coffee machine and got a pot brewing.

"I won't talk to anyone until you give the go-ahead," he said firmly. "You're my client, and you're the boss. All I do is give advice."

"How long have you been an attorney?" I asked. He looked to be about 40, but with so many "mature" people going to law school, I wondered if I might be his first client. No, at least he was in the Yellow Pages. That meant he'd probably been in the profession for a year or so.

He laughed good-naturedly, which worried me even more. I don't want an attorney with a good nature. I want an attorney with *attitude,* someone like the mother of an only child. An *ugly* only child.

"I was admitted to the Nevada and California bars 18 years ago. I charge a fortune, if that makes you feel any better about having me on your side."

It was my turn to laugh. "Okay, you have a client. And since you charge so much, and I don't have much money, let's talk fast." I gave a very quick summary of my seven days in Las Vegas, concentrating on the post-midnight adventure that had landed me in the hospital. "Candace says the state attorney general is here and wants to talk to Mace and me."

"He doesn't want them to talk to the press," Candace added.

"Oh, doesn't he?" Mitchell nodded as he thought that over. "Candace, would you please find out where Attorney General Usher is and if he can see me in a few minutes? Also, could you find out when Detective Emerick will be ready to talk to your mother and me?"

"Sure. I'll go right away." Before she opened the door to leave, there was a knock. She opened it to find Mace, his cheeks and chin a patchwork of bandages. His forehead showed a line of stitches that looked a lot like cartoons of Frankenstein's monster. His sideburns had been shaved and one ear was swathed in gauze and adhesive tape.

"I look worse than I feel," he said, giving me a crooked smile. One corner of his mouth had a butterfly bandage holding it closed.

"I feel worse than I look," I said, holding out my hand to him.

"Spoken by a woman who has not looked in a mirror," Candace added. Mace took my hand and put his other arm around Candace's shoulders. She leaned her head against his chest and made snuffling noises. When she looked back at me, her face was red and her nose was runny. "I'm so mad at both of you!" She grabbed a box of tissues off the counter and pulled out a fistful. I held out my hand for the box and used a few to wipe my eyes as well. "Do you still want me to go find the attorney general?" she asked Mitchell.

"Hold on a few minutes. I want to talk to Detective Emerick." He introduced himself and they shook hands. "Olivia is inclined to hold a full-bore press conference here and now. I understand her anger at the police, especially Capt. Wacker, for using the press to blacken her name, and yours, but I think we should hear what the attorney general has to say first."

"That's okay by me," Mace said. "Talk is free."

"Spoken by a man who did not retain Fenton Mitchell, Esquire," I said. Mace sat close beside me while Candace handed each of us a plastic cup of coffee. Mace tried to sip it in one side of his mouth, had to wipe it off his chin, and gave up. I, too, gave up when I burned the chewed surface of my tongue.

"What is it you - we - hope to achieve this morning?" Mitchell said. "We need to be clear on that before we open the door to any negotiations. Or to making irreversible public statements."

I wanted to scream and rant and rave into a TV camera, to draw and quarter Avery Wacker, and Charles St. John, and Esmé Mott, and Kim Kaylyn. At least figuratively. Hell hath no fury like I'd felt when Capt. Wacker aimed his gun at Mace, and then at me, and a few hours to warm up my body had not cooled my temper. But I had to bow in respect to the calm intelligence of Mitchell. As the saying goes, that's why he earns the big bucks.

"All right," I said with a sigh, "if you won't let me tear out

Wacker's liver on CNN, I'll settle for getting my reputation back, Mace's job and reputation back, a full investigation by the attorney general into criminal misconduct by Wacker and others in the Las Vegas Police Department. Also, a massive investigation into Margot Farr's murder. And into possible embezzlement by Charles St. John."

Mitchell smiled. "Is that all you want?"

I thought for a moment. "And world peace."

Mitchell rose and poured himself another cup of coffee. "How about compensation? Medical bills, lost wages while you recover . . ."

"Attorney's fees?" I added enthusiastically.

"I don't see why not." He held his coffee aloft in a toast. "Shall I go visit with Mr. Usher?"

Intellectually I could see the advantage of turning the matter over to Mitchell, but emotionally I wanted to wade in myself and hurl mud in every direction to see where it would stick. Candace helped me decide by taking my arm and walking me to a full-length mirror beside the receptionist's desk. For once, I was speechless.

"Now do you want to be on television?" she said, crossing her arms.

"You've made your point." I looked at Mitchell and gave as much of a smile as I could muster under the circumstances. "Counselor, I'll wait here."

Mace gave a crooked smile that could pass for a grimace and added, "Curly Falwell is here, too, asking ever so politely to talk to you and me about Margot's murder. Shall I bring him back with me?"

I shrugged. "Yeah. If we don't help him sort through the mess he'll probably screw up the case." Something occurred to me, and I added, "Please tell me they nabbed the footlocker with the tainted life vests. And that they didn't put it in the evidence room downtown."

"Don't worry. It's under lock and key with the FBI.

Whatever that's worth."

When the door closed behind Fenton Mitchell and Mace Emerick, I took another look in the mirror. "I hope they hurry back," I said to Candace. "I don't want to risk the plastic surgeon coming here to start his office hours and saying, 'If only you hadn't waited so long!'"

*****

With help from Mace and me, Detective Curly Falwell was connecting the dots between Esmé, Charles St. John, and Kim Kaylyn, especially the motive: good old reliable greed. But I have to give Curly all the credit for thinking more about the vine-shrouded back gate to Margot's yard. It was locked from the inside when Margot's body was found, but Curly found a road surveyor who saw it ajar that afternoon.

"We know Esmé went back to Margot's house to pick up her car," I'd said as the three of us sat in the doctor's private office. The receptionist moved us from the waiting room when she arrived, partly for our privacy and partly not to scare away patients. "We know that from the time Ted Landers dropped Esmé off until she left - making a point of establishing the time with the guard - was only a few minutes. It was enough time for her to go out beyond the pool area and unlock the gate."

"And the gate opens onto a sidewalk beside a two-lane road that heads nowhere, but is scheduled for widening and, eventually, access to the freeway. Hence the road guy traipsing by," Curly added with a smug grin. "And now for the best part."

Excited by what Curly had revealed, Mace jumped ahead of him. "You found a witness who saw someone go in or out that gate?"

"In the gate. Yes. Description matches Charles St. John and Kim Kaylyn. Time matches the murder time."

Mace made a fist and pumped it in the air. "Yes!"

*****

At her apartment, Candace hooked up her electric blanket while I took a long, hot shower. Wearing the lavender sweatshirt and a towel around my hair, I crawled between the sheets to sleep all day with it set on High. When she woke me up, at four p.m., I showered again, and dried and curled my hair. Thanks to the sleep, plus the miracle of Mary Kay, my face looked pretty good. Candace had gone shopping in the afternoon, and the rose-colored linen suit she'd laid on the bed fit me perfectly.

We were to meet Mace and Fenton Mitchell at his law office next door to the courthouse. I would get my wish to hold a press conference, but it would be an opportunity for the attorney general to announce the arrest of Avery Wacker for attempted murder. He would also say that a grand jury was hearing evidence in the Margot Farr murder investigation, and that he expected indictments to be handed down before the end of the week.

Something he did not say was anything about the drug Zed. As Mace explained it to me, if he said a drug existed that kills your appetite, that's all people would hear. No amount of warning that it's not been proven safe would matter. Better to let that sleeping dog lie for the time being.

The AG praised Detective Mace Emerick and praised me and apologized profusely for the indignity and physical injuries we had suffered. He announced that Chief Harold Armstrong's heart bypass surgery had been successful, and that the chief asked him to convey his appreciation as well to Detective Emerick and Olivia Wright.

"Chief Armstrong and his wife, Vanitsa Noble Armstrong, particularly asked me to convey their thanks publicly to Ms. Wright for her action on Lake Mead last Sunday night, quick action that saved the chief's life."

In front of the bank of microphones, I cleared my throat and thanked the attorney general and the chief of police for their remarks. For someone who wanted to speak to the media, I was surprisingly at a loss for words. Out of the corner of my eye I saw a man hand an envelope to Candace. She looked at the front and handed it to me. I stepped away from the podium and opened it.

The number beside the dollar sign caught my eye at once. A publisher and production company offered one-point-five million dollars for my version of the life and death of Margot Farr.

"Olivia?" I was aware of an expectant silence. Mace was standing at the microphones. Again he said, "Olivia?"

Had he said something important, and I'd missed it? I mumbled, "Sorry, uh, what?"

"I want to say, in front of God and everybody, that I'm alive today only because you risked your life to save me." He folded me into his arms and there was a round of applause and people saying, "Awww."

Blushing, I kissed the side of his mouth not covered by a bandage. We gave a final wave to the TV cameras, shook the hand of the attorney general again, and shouldered our way out of the tight circle around the podium. I kissed his cheek and placed my mouth close to his ear. "I've decided to stay in Las Vegas after all. I just got a job offer. Pays pretty good."

"Well, if you're staying, and Hornet is staying, I'll stay, too. But first, I think some rest and recuperation is in order. On the high seas. Don't you agree?"

My blush increased to match my rose suit when I thought of us, alone on a sailboat. "Yes," I smiled. "I agree."